THE
CAFÉ
ON
Amelia Island

SEVEN SISTERS
BOOK TWO

HOPE
HOLLOWAY

Hope Holloway

Seven Sisters Book 2

The Café on Amelia Island

Copyright © 2023 Hope Holloway

Cover designed by Sarah Brown (http://www.sarahdesigns.co/)

❋ Created with Vellum

Introduction to the Seven Sister Series

Meet the Wingate women, seven sisters who are all unique and unforgettable...but they all share inner strength, abiding love, a few quirky traits, and the ability to support each other through every challenge. This family is founded on love and laughter and a sisterhood unlike any other.

The series consists of seven books with recurring characters, continuing stories, heartbreaking and hopeful moments, later-in-life romance, a touch of mystery, and lots of happy tears. All of the books will be available in digital, paperback, and audio formats.

Visit www.hopeholloway.com for release dates, covers, and sneak peeks into the series!

The Seven Daughters of Rex Wingate

Born to Charlotte Wingate

Madeline Wingate, age 49
Tori Wingate, age 45
Rose Wingate D'Angelo, age 43
Raina Wingate, age 43

Born to Susannah Wingate

Sadie Wingate, age 35
Grace Wingate Jenkins, age 33
Chloe Wingate, age 29

Chapter One

Chloe

Chloe Wingate never liked saying goodbye. She preferred to slip out, skip the hugs, and hide any tears that came with farewell. Which was why the dramatic, public, heart-wrenching, and, *whoa*, expensive goodbye she'd delivered at the altar on her wedding day had been the most difficult of her life.

After that, any other goodbye was a piece of cake.

Maybe that was why her move from Jacksonville to Amelia Island felt so easy. Not only was it less than an hour away, but she'd started the transition, mentally and physically, three weeks ago when she became the first runaway bride in her family's long and storied history.

Since then, she'd said so long to her job, her local friends, and her favorite Starbucks. Today, it was goodbye to the two-bedroom apartment that she'd been sharing with Hunter Landry as they'd planned the wedding-that-wasn't and a life she'd never live.

Today, she'd move to her childhood home of Amelia Island to start working as a waitress at the family-owned Riverfront Café, and figure out what she wanted to do with the rest of her life. Yes, she should probably know that by now, considering she was twenty-nine, and had an advanced degree in journalism.

But apparently, Chloe was a slow starter. And a slow finisher.

After all, she'd known deep, deep inside that she shouldn't marry Hunter for months before the wedding. But she kept hoping the relationship would change, or at least go back to what it had once been.

They'd met when they lived in different cities, and long-distance became "normal" for them.

For a few years, he'd been in Minnesota and she was clawing her way through tiny TV markets in and around the mid-Atlantic, trying to get established as a reporter. Then he got a plastic surgery residency at the Mayo Clinic in Jacksonville. Of course, she'd jumped at the chance to move back to Florida, to be closer to family and for Hunter and Chloe to try their hand at being in the same city.

She'd taken a job in public relations, even though it meant giving up her dream of being a reporter. And they'd gotten engaged, which made her feel better about living with him.

For the most part, it worked. But then, so did he—about eighty hours a week. With each passing month, she disregarded the gut instinct that said something wasn't quite right...that Hunter was far more controlling than she realized, and opinionated, and self-involved. She'd foolishly ignored all the red flags until the last possible minute.

"Never again, gut." She poked at a spot below her heart and above her belly, where she imagined that elusive thing called "instinct" resided. "I will never ignore you again."

After breaking up with Hunter while wearing a wedding gown in front of a hundred and fifty people in St. Peter's Church, everything else seemed easy.

"Why do you think that is, Lady Bug?" she asked the doe-eyed Shih Tzu curled up on the back of a sofa cushion. "Do you think it's been easy because we were living a life that was all wrong for us?"

Lady Bug lifted her head, then dropped it with a sigh, as if the packing and change and philosophical questions were all too much for her.

"Because leaving this..." Chloe gestured around the apartment living room that seemed naked even though the main pieces of furniture were still in place. "Is a breeze."

She'd stripped the walls of memories and color, packed her many cozy blankets and pillows, and removed everything that said "an engaged couple who are in love and planning a life together lives here."

Now, it was simply a beige sofa, a cheap wall unit, an eyesore of a massive flat-screen, and a gray area rug. She stared at the hooked pattern, realizing that she hated that rug most of all. She'd only accepted it because Lady Bug had an accident on the pretty blue one, and Hunter had thrown that out in a fit, all the while complaining about the dog she loved more than anything.

Yep, moving was remarkably easy.

"I guess I've been dragging things up to Amelia Island every couple days for the last few weeks, so move-out day isn't quite as elaborate as I'd feared." She plopped onto the sofa, putting her hand on Lady Bug's tiny white and mushroom-colored head. "Plus, we'll be living with your Auntie Rose, Uncle Gabe, and four kids who think you are an actual stuffed animal, so we don't need much. We'll leave everything else for...you know who."

She didn't dare say her former fiancé's first name. Not because it hurt, not at all. But mentioning Hunter, who'd been living somewhere else these past few weeks, always sent Lady Bug flying to the door. She stood there with her tail wagging in expectation, dancing on her little paws, her bark high and excited in anticipation of seeing the man she loved.

"But he didn't love you," she whispered to the dog, taking the sting away from the news by petting her silky fur. "You didn't see it, like I didn't, ya know? We both wagged and ran and obeyed and begged for love that he doled out so infrequently that we got used to the scraps."

Lady Bug cocked a brow at the word "scraps."

"But it wasn't enough, Bugaboo. It wasn't enough for me, and it shouldn't have been enough for you." She leaned in and lifted a floppy ear to whisper, "You'd cry if you knew how many times he referred to you as a 'Hollywood handbag mutt,' not a 'real dog' like the golden he'd grown up with. He also rolled his eyes when I asked him to take you out, or he insisted on closing the bedroom door so you had to sleep alone out here."

Lady Bug seemed unfazed, but Chloe was still

reeling from the impact of having taken her blinders off where Hunter was concerned.

"Never again," she added. "I will never again be fooled by a man. In fact, I may never love again. I think it's time for a man hiatus, Lady B. We'll leave here, start over on Amelia Island surrounded by our big, fat, awesome family, and it'll be the two of us and legions of Wingates. You'll like that."

Her feathery tail flipped from side to side.

"And, no, I won't be the next network news anchor or even a TV reporter at a small-market TV station like I once dreamed." That fantasy was dead. At her age, she'd missed every step on the ladder that would take her to that kind of career anyway.

"It's fine," she said, as though stating it out loud helped. "I'll wait tables at the Riverfront Café, save up some cash living with Rose, and spend my weekends babysitting nieces and nephews. But no man, not one single carrier of the Y chromosome, will turn our heads for a long, long time. Fool me once, shame on you. Fool me twice, and I'm the fool." She could practically hear her father's voice making that pronouncement as she kissed Lady Bug's little head. "And Rex Wingate didn't raise no fool."

Buoyed by the thought, Chloe pushed up and took one last look around.

"Three suitcases are all I have left," she said. "I can make that in two trips. You wait here, Bug. You'll go on the next trip."

Grabbing the handles of the two smaller bags, she

dragged them to the door, then down the hall. She bypassed the stairs she usually took to and from the parking lot and headed around the corner to the elevator. It took a minute to load the suitcases into the hatchback of her crossover, then she bounded up the three flights back to the apartment.

And froze when she stepped into the hallway, gasping at the sight of her open door and the sound of that very high-pitched and excited bark she'd just been thinking about.

That could only mean...Hunter was here. Now? Hours earlier than he'd agreed to in one of their very few, very brief text exchanges? No doubt he'd come up the stairs while she was going down in the elevator. But why?

They'd timed it so they wouldn't have to talk and—

Lady Bug came flying out the door, barking wildly as she raced toward Chloe as if to say, "Guess who's here, Mommy!"

"Hey, mutt face!" Hunter bellowed. "Get back in here."

Just as Chloe gathered up the dog, Hunter bolted into the hall, slamming to a halt at the sight of her.

"Oh. Hey. I...uh, hi."

She swallowed and gave Lady Bug a squeeze for strength. "You're early."

"Yeah, I...I thought you'd be..." He wore crisp green hospital scrubs, which was kind of laughable, since he'd completed his residency a month ago. He claimed he wore them for comfort and ease, but Chloe knew he loved walking around in an outfit that made people think he'd just stepped out of surgery. "I wanted to talk to you."

"Well, here I am. One suitcase away from gone," she said, heading back to the apartment to get that bag and get out of here.

"Hey, Chloe." He tried to snag her arm as she passed but she managed to evade his touch. Lady Bug, on the other hand, attempted to leap from Chloe's grip to get closer to Hunter.

"I'll get that last bag," she said. "And I'll be out of your way."

"You're not..."

She didn't stay for the rest, zipping into the apartment. Could she just—

"I have to talk to you, Chloe."

At the insistence in his voice, she gave up and slowly lowered Lady Bug to the sofa, then turned to him.

"Hunter, honestly, there's not a lot left to say."

His coppery eyes shuttered. "Yeah, except for you to explain why you turned me into a total tool in front of my family, friends, and half my graduating class of Johns Hopkins Med School and the residence staff of the Mayo Clinic."

Could he ever utter a sentence that didn't somehow include his resume?

"You know my reasons, Hunter," she said, shifting from one sneaker to the other, wishing she could use the shoes for their intended purpose—to run. "I realized we were wrong for each other."

She refused to elaborate. He couldn't absorb a litany

of his many flaws anyway. They simply didn't compute to a narcissist. She'd tried. For three years she'd tried, and now, she was done trying to change him into what she hoped he could be.

Hunter Landry might be handsome, brilliant, and fairly entertaining, but he was also incapable of giving the kind of love she'd grown up seeing her father shower on her mother. He was the wrong man for Chloe and, yes, it was unfortunate that she'd let herself get swept up into wedding madness and come to her senses at the very last possible moment.

But she *did* come to her senses, and that's what mattered.

"Was it because I didn't want Rex ruining my wedding?" He spat out the question, loud enough to make Lady Bug raise a brow as she observed the conversation.

All Chloe could do was stifle a soft laugh, and mentally thank Hunter for reminding her *why* she'd made that difficult and painful decision.

"I mean, what did it matter what I wanted, Chloe?" he demanded. "You defied me and put the old man on a walker to—"

"Hunter! He's my father, not an old man. I didn't defy you! I made myself happy on my wedding day by walking down the aisle with my dad. He found strength and courage to get out of a wheelchair and onto a walker for me, six weeks after a stroke. And, for the record, I asked you to postpone the day after he got sick, and you practically had a stroke yourself."

Hunter shook his head and crossed his arms, leveling his gaze. "Well, never mind about that. I came early to talk to you. I need something from you, Chloe."

"What is it?" she asked.

"If someone asks you what happened, I need you to take full responsibility for the way you handled our wedding."

She frowned, parsing each of the phrases in that sentence and coming up with...nothing that made sense.

"Of course I take responsibility for our breakup, Hunter. I hate what happened that day. I hate that I embarrassed you and left that church and failed on every level. I'm so, so sorry for that."

"But you did it."

"Yes, I did, because..." She swallowed as her throat thickened. "I knew our marriage would be a mistake. So, obviously, I take responsibility. Is that what you mean?"

"I mean that I'm in the process of a final interview with that plastic surgery group in L.A."

She nodded, knowing that, but still confused as to what he was asking. He'd been in negotiations with the medical group before the wedding, talking animatedly about their lives in Southern California, an idea she abhorred.

She'd pleaded with him to consider the offers he had closer to her big family, most of whom lived on Amelia Island.

But Hunter didn't care about family. The salary was thirty percent higher in L.A. and—of course, this was most important to him—the group had true cachet. They did "work" on hundreds of famous faces, and celebrities were where the real cosmetic surgery money was, according to Hunter.

Still, his comments didn't make sense.

"Why does where you're going affect what I say about the wedding?" she asked.

"Because the SoCal docs haven't made a final decision. The offer is going to me or some clown from Harvard."

She fought an eyeroll. Hunter took his rivalries seriously and, according to him, Johns Hopkins was truly the best medical school, while Harvard slid by on its name.

"What are you asking me to do, Hunter?"

"It might not happen, but it's possible someone from the practice might contact you," he said.

"Me? Why?"

"Because we were engaged."

"We're not anymore. Why would they contact me?"

He let out an exasperated sigh like he did when he had to explain something medical to a mere mortal.

"Social media, for one thing," he said. "The fact that we were going to get married, then all references to that wedding were removed, has raised some eyebrows. So, thanks *a ton* once again for screwing up my life."

She ignored the sarcasm, waiting for the explanation.

"Anyway, if someone from HR calls you, I hope you'll say the right thing."

In other words, let him completely off the hook and allow him to be the victim.

"They may or may not call," he continued, "but if

they do, I'd really appreciate it if you could swing some of your never-ending blame onto your own shoulders for a change. Our issues went both ways, you know."

Only because he was a controlling jerk and she'd been a compliant doormat...until she wasn't.

"I'll tell them the truth, Hunter," she said. "I'll tell them I realized we were not right for each other. Period. They don't need more than that."

"They might want more details. I honestly don't know, Chloe. I'm covering all my bases."

"Does that mean you're asking other people to color the truth to make you look good?" she challenged.

"This is a seven-figure job, Chloe," he said, adding a smug expression as if *that* justified lying.

She blinked, still stunned when she realized how she'd ignored red flags like that all along.

"Yeah. That's right," he said, misinterpreting her reaction. "Now I bet you're sorry you ran out of that church."

And her jaw dropped. "Honestly, Hunter, I've never been happier. Look, if someone contacts me, I'll simply say I...I fell out of love. Is that taking enough of the blame?"

"And if they ask *why* you fell out of love?" There was the slightest, mildest, almost impossible-to-discern hurt in the question.

She searched his face, wondering if this whole visit was a charade—*no one* was going to contact her—but Hunter needed answers. Not that he'd ever face his own flawed character, but she understood he needed them.

"Well, then, I'll tell them you cared more about the aesthetics of a man on a walker than my feelings about sharing the day with my father. And that was a red-flag, turning point moment for me."

He stared at her, silent, maybe finally realizing that his issue over Dad being in the wedding was symbolic of his whole narcissist personality. Doubtful, but she could hope.

"And who knows, Hunter? That might help you get the job. I bet plastic surgeons to the stars value aesthetics above all."

"I'd really prefer if you said you met someone else," he said softly.

"*Excuse me?*"

"It's just...cleaner."

For *who*? "Tell them...I cheated?" She could barely form the words.

He shrugged as if he were asking her to confess to jaywalking. "It doesn't exactly put me in a good light," he said. "But it's more sympathetic than...than..."

"Than the truth?" she finished.

He blew out a breath, then walked into the kitchen like he wanted something there. "Oh, yeah, I was, uh, wondering about the ring."

They hadn't discussed this, but she certainly wasn't going to keep the expensive engagement ring. Was that the real reason he was here? Did he not trust her to give it back? Or did he simply stop by to talk about a call that he said—*twice*—might not even happen.

She closed her eyes, so over him. "It's in the box next to the bed."

He nodded and walked into the bedroom, disappearing from sight for a moment, then returning with the box in his hand.

"Well, then, Chloe. Guess I'll see you. I'll come back when you're gone."

"'Kay," she said. "I guess this is goodbye."

He gave her a tight smile. "Yeah, bye."

She stood stone still as he walked out, the only sound the door latching behind him.

No, she didn't like saying goodbye. But, wow, that was one for the books.

"C'mere, Lady Bug." She scooped up the little body and pressed her lips to the dog's soft fur, closing her eyes, biting back tears she did not want to shed.

After a moment, she grabbed the handle of the suitcase, picked up her purse, and walked out, punching in the code to lock the door.

"Let's go start our man hiatus, little pupper. May it last for a good many years. Maybe forever."

Chapter Two

Raina

This one was different.

 Raina didn't know how to explain it, but deep in her soul, she knew this pregnancy was different from the three she'd lost in their first trimesters. Fourth time's a charm, right?

One hand on her stomach, which had been wonderfully settled today, she thumbed the *What to Expect* app on her phone and leaned against the bathroom counter to read.

It's Week Seven! Your baby is the size of a cucumber seed.

"Oh." She bit her lip and whimpered softly. "Did you hear that, little seedling?"

The brain is developing into five areas and blood is now pumping through the main vessels to all parts of the body.

She rubbed her tummy and whispered, "Mine sure is pumping just thinking about you."

Have you seen the doctor yet?

"Yes, I have," she confirmed to thin air. "And in about three weeks, I'm going back to hear your little heart—"

"Raina? Do you have a minute?"

At the sound of Susannah's voice, Raina flipped the app off the screen and looked guiltily in the bathroom mirror, staring at herself. Once, during one of her three unsuccessful pregnancies, she'd heard an old wives' tale claiming that you could tell if a woman was pregnant by looking into her eyes.

Would her mother know from a good long look at Raina? She'd hidden the news from everyone but one sister for three weeks now, but she wasn't sure how much longer she could keep this to herself. It had to be a secret, at least until she heard the heartbeat.

And...told her husband.

"In the bathroom, Suze," she called out, staring at her dark blue eyes in the mirror.

Did they look different? Well, yes, there were deep shadows, but those could be explained away by a lot more than a surprise baby for a forty-three-year-old woman.

For one thing—and everyone *did* know this—Raina's husband of sixteen years had set into motion a divorce that under any other circumstances would make Raina feel like a complete and utter failure.

But within the same five minutes that she'd learned of Jack Wallace's emotional infidelity, she'd learned she was pregnant...*again*. And that knowledge hadn't merely kept her from collapsing in grief as she faced the end of her marriage. It had lifted her, infused her with strength and determination, and given her an entirely new purpose in life.

Raina Wingate wanted a baby more than anything, with or without a husband. And this time, it had to be different.

"Can I talk to you for a minute?" Susannah called.

"Sure, hang on." Raina took a deep breath. How much longer could she go on keeping the news from everyone but Tori?

She had to, at least until Jack knew. And she wasn't going to tell him until she heard a heartbeat and passed the "danger zone" of three months.

Even though part of her believed he'd forfeited a husband's rights and privileges when he announced he'd fallen in love with another woman, he was this baby's father, and had to know first.

But if she lost this baby? She wasn't telling him, or anyone, anything.

Taking a steadying breath and giving her stomach one last rub, she stepped out to find Susannah in the guest suite, looking out one of the windows, staring at the waves pounding on the shores of Fernandina Beach.

"What brings you up to my little corner of the world, Suze?" Raina approached her and offered a light kiss, tamping down guilt for not squealing the truth and sharing a true mother-daughter moment.

Susannah had earned that moment, she thought. Although she was technically Raina's stepmother, she'd raised all seven Wingate girls with equal love, as nurturing to the older four as she was to her own biological daughters. But even with that love and nurturing, Raina was scared to whisper her secret, a little terrified to jinx the pregnancy.

"Is Dad okay?" she asked, taking in the worry on Susannah's features.

"He's fine, actually having a very good day. He's had breakfast, and I got him dressed, and we even managed a shave before rehab." The morning sunlight highlighted a few new lines on Susannah's attractive face. But lines were to be expected on a sixty-one-year-old woman who'd spent endless weeks nursing her husband through a stroke.

Yes, Dad was on the road to recovery—using a walker as much as a wheelchair, talking clearly, if slowly—but he still wasn't the powerhouse of a man the world knew as Rex Wingate.

"I need a favor, Raina," Susannah said.

"Anything. What can I do for you?"

"I have to stop by Wingate House and talk to a vendor who's going to do some work on the inn's roof, but Dad's physical therapist is running half an hour late."

"Want me to meet with the roofer?" Raina asked without hesitation.

Managing the family property business while Dad recovered was the reason Raina had made the temporary move from her home, job, and life in Miami to live here, settling quite nicely into this third-floor suite.

With Jack's confession, there was no doubt Raina would stay here at the opposite end of the state on Amelia Island while he remained in Miami. Living here at her parents' beach house, she felt safe, surrounded by family but able to keep her secret—at least for a little while.

"I'd like to meet the roofer," Susannah said. "It could get dicey when it comes to talking money."

"You sure? Dicey money discussions are my specialty."

Susannah frowned, which only deepened a few of the fine lines. "I need to get out of this house," she admitted softly. "I'm going nuts."

"Oh, Suze! Of course!" Raina put an arm around her mother, but her heart dropped knowing this would leave her alone with Dad. Meaning she had to talk to him.

Raina had found every imaginable excuse to avoid that conversation for three solid weeks, but she couldn't avoid it much longer.

Forget the baby she was carrying—she had another pressing situation to discuss with Dad. And this time it had to go better than the last.

Not only had she discovered someone had taken a half-million dollars from one of her father's business accounts, the ensuing discussion had triggered a seizure and sent Rex to the hospital. All she'd learned in those harrowing moments was that he knew the money was missing and he wanted her to...*replace* it.

She'd never gotten an answer to her most basic questions...like who, how, and why.

Unwilling to risk another seizure, Raina had tried to tackle the problem herself, but she'd hit nothing but brick walls. She desperately needed to talk to her father, but the very idea of that freaked her out.

So she'd avoided being alone with him since then, sensing he wouldn't mention the missing money if anyone else was in the room.

But now? Now Susannah was handing her the opportunity to have a private talk with Dad—carefully, delicately, with nothing but love.

She had to know what her father meant when he told her to "replace" the money. Not find it, not report it missing, nor even hunt down who could have made bank transfers from an account in Dad's name while he was in the hospital. No, he wanted her to *replace* it. But how?

Guess it was time to find out.

"Of course you need a break, Suze," she said. "I'll stay with Dad until the physical therapist gets here."

"Oh, good, Raina. Talking business with you always cheers him up."

She swallowed and smiled at her mother, guilt strangling her as she mentally acknowledged yet another secret she was keeping from Susannah. But Raina didn't have the heart to dump this on her mother. The woman had been through the wringer, and all Raina wanted to do was smooth all the bumps in her life and make things easier.

"I'm glad you're getting out," Raina said, and meant it.

"Thank you." Susannah sighed and turned back to the window, staring at the creamy sand, sparkling water, and the distant surfers catching one of the endless waves.

She let out a preoccupied sigh, and Raina stepped closer, suddenly wondering if maybe Dad *had* told her about the money.

Susannah had known there was a "little cash flow problem," and that Raina had been looking for a password book to help her find answers. But Dad had that seizure, then they were swept up in the wedding, and in the aftermath of Chloe's decision...her mother had forgotten the problem. She certainly had no idea how much was missing.

"Is there something else you wanted to talk to me about?" Raina asked gently.

"No, no. It's just..." She swallowed. "He's doing so well, right?"

"Dad? Amazing. The addition of a speech therapist has really improved things, and he's not the least bit afraid of the stairs. He's able to sleep in the master again, and that has to be nice for both of you to not be apart at night."

"It also lets me know how much he *doesn't* sleep."

"Maybe he's, um, worried about something?" Raina suggested gently, knowing in her heart what that something was.

"I don't know. It's more like he's...sad. He's so down. I don't know why, when every day he's better by leaps and bounds."

Maybe he was sad because he lost five hundred thousand dollars.

Raina tried to think of another reason he'd be sad, and it wasn't hard to come up with a few.

"Leaps and bounds to us," Raina said. "But to a man like Rex Wingate? A man who scoffed in the face of seventy-five, and ran one of the most successful real estate businesses in the county? A man who loved being an involved father and active grandfather? It's hard for him."

"True, but I've never known him to be *sad*," Susannah said. "Angry? Oh, yeah. But not...sad. Not quite this preoccupied." She squeezed Raina's hands. "Talk to him and bring him out of his blues, Raina."

Would this conversation do that, or just the opposite? "I'll do my best," she promised.

"Thank you," Susannah whispered with relief. "I'm so grateful for all you've done."

"Oh, please." Raina placed a gentle hand on Susannah's back. "You're not in this alone. You've got seven daughters who would do anything for you and for him. We're doing what families do in a crisis."

Susannah turned, her look one of pure pity. "Honey, *you're* in your own crisis, and don't even try to tell me divorce is anything less."

"I'll get through it," Raina assured her. "Much more easily because I'm here, so thank you for giving me this refuge. Down in Miami, I'd have to witness his infidelity first hand."

Susannah let out a soft grunt. "You know I don't use foul language, but if I did? Oh, I have a few choice names for that man."

"'Cheater' is all that's necessary," Raina said. "Foul enough for me."

"And it's taking a toll." Susannah put a hand on Raina's cheek and scrutinized her face.

Oh, boy, Raina thought. Here was the test of the old wives' tale. Could her mother see something different? Change? Hormones? Joy?

"You look as tired as I feel, Rain," Susannah remarked. "I see circles under your pretty eyes."

"I haven't put my makeup on yet."

"But this is what you do," her mother mused. "You solve everyone's problems but not your own. You've always been that way."

"I'm a fixer," she acknowledged, hating that it was one of the things Jack once said he loved most about her.

"Don't forget to fix yourself, honey. Even if you can't fix your marriage."

Raina gave a soft choke. "No fixing there, Suze. That ship has sailed. Now that it's out in the open, the lawyers are circling, and he and..." She shuddered at how much she hated to say the woman's name. "He and Lisa aren't really doing much to hide their relationship. My assistant told me it's not exactly a secret at our company."

"How shameful of him, ruining your marriage and a business partnership." Susannah bit her lip. "Are you sure there's no chance this is just some weird—"

"No." Raina held up her hand, stopping the suggestion before it came. "He stood in front of me and said he had fallen in love with another woman. I'm done. No second chance."

Susannah conceded that with a tip of her head. "I understand. But I worry how you'll get through it."

"I will," Raina said with bone-deep confidence. If she could hold onto this pregnancy? The world would be right. Joy would be hers and Jack could...make appointments to see their child. She'd let him, of course. But this baby would be *hers* to have and to hold, for better or worse.

She may have lost a husband, but by the hand of God and one night of desperation trying to get their marriage back on track before she knew about Lisa...she'd gained a child.

"Oh, there's that smile I've missed," Susannah said.

Raina laughed, covering for the burst of happiness in her heart every time she really thought about having a baby. "Go and enjoy a morning out of this house, Suze. It's a gorgeous June day and you deserve some time off."

With another hug, Susannah left and Raina stayed right where she was, mentally preparing for a conversation with her father.

He didn't really expect her to "replace" half a million dollars, did he? And not even tell her why?

She was about to find out. It was Go Time.

AFTER SHE SAW Susannah pull out of the driveway, Raina made her way down to the main living area, pausing for a moment to bask in the sunshine that was even brighter and hotter on this middle floor of the sprawling beach house.

Warmed and ready, she went down to the first floor,

where Dad spent the vast majority of his time during the day.

A week ago, he'd mastered the stairs and got the all-clear to sleep in the main bedroom with Susannah again. But after breakfast, he went back down to the game room that had been converted to at-home rehabilitation. There, and on the ground-floor patio that faced the beach, he worked hard with the therapists—physical, occupational, and speech—who all contributed to his amazing progress.

Before going in, she lingered at the bottom of the steps, glancing into her father's darkened home office, reliving that last private conversation.

"You can fix this for me, Raina. Replace the money... make it rain, Raina."

And with that, he'd spiraled into a terrifying seizure. It hadn't been serious or caused another stroke, but she never wanted that to happen again. So this conversation had to be...gentle.

She took a few steps through open double doors to find her father in his wheelchair by the sliding glass doors, looking out at the dunes and the ocean beyond, deep in thought. He hung his head with a sigh, then wiped under his eyes.

Was he crying? Her heart just about shattered.

"Hey, Dad," she said softly from the doorway, so as not to startle him.

"Oh." He cleared his throat and took one more swipe under his eyes. "Hi, Raina."

He could say her name—all of their names, actually—

clearly now, which was a huge step from the early days when he was only capable of grunts and vowel sounds.

He could also, with assistance, push up from that chair and use a walker, too. His left side was still compromised, but he was right-handed and that had made things easier while he strengthened the weaker side.

"I guess the physical therapist is late," she said, coming into the room.

"Physical torture, more like," he said, drawing his words out as he did now, fighting to get each syllable clear. "But I got the woman today. And she's nicer than that other guy."

"That's good," she said, eyeing him as she got closer. If she hadn't seen him wipe his eyes, she'd have never known he was crying. "Suze said you're having a good day, and if that rosy color in your cheeks is any indication, she's right."

"She made me sit in the sun."

"Vitamin D is so good for you," Raina said brightly, putting a hand on his shoulder and dropping a light kiss on his white hair.

He reached up and patted her knuckles, saying nothing, looking into her eyes with a very clear expression despite the slight changes a stroke had caused in his features.

He was ready to talk. She could read Rex Wingate like few others. Raina had studied under him, learned the real estate business at his feet, and prided herself on being the most like him of all seven daughters.

Letting out a breath, she sat down in the club chair across from him.

"So, Dad, we had two closings last week," she said, starting with some easy stuff. "Made a decent profit on both."

He gave a nod, never one to shower with praise. He had high expectations of her and she always met them.

"I've also got a few new listings cooking." She looked down to pluck an imaginary thread on her cotton dress. "And I think I can get an offer on that beach lot since I dropped the price. Only ten thousand," she added with a quick laugh. "I haven't forgotten the cardinal rule. 'The first three letters of reduction are RED...don't end the deal in the red.'"

He gave a faint smile and she noticed that the right muscles of his face were still stronger, but the left was catching up. Was that a sign that his whole body had improved enough to dip her toes into this touchy topic?

She shifted on her seat, so wanting to put that off. "And you know that building right off Lime Street? I heard they might—"

"Have you replaced it yet?"

She drew back an inch, a little surprised, but then why would she be? With or without a stroke, Rex did not beat around the proverbial bush. The man was direct and blunt.

"Um...no." She gave a tight smile. "Are you sure that's what you want me to do?"

She waited breathlessly for him to answer. He shifted

his gaze to the sliding glass doors behind her, staring at the vista for a few long heartbeats.

"Yes," he finally said.

"Okay, well, Dad." She managed a shaky breath. "Does that mean you don't want me to try and find out what happened to it? If you give me power of attorney, I could—"

"I know what happened to it," he said, forcing his eyes to narrow so he could pin her with a dark, determined gaze. "It's gone. Now replace it."

"Gone...like lost or invested or—"

"Gone!" he barked the word, startling her.

She stared at him, silent, considering and rejecting every possible response. If he hadn't had a stroke and wasn't at risk of another or a seizure, she'd demand to know.

But she had to protect him from any dangerous physiological reactions.

"Okay," she said. "Then maybe you can guide me on...how."

He lifted one shoulder. "Make it rain, Raina."

The demand she'd heard a hundred times when learning the real estate business from him kind of irked in this situation.

"I really want to do that," she said very slowly and calmly. "But I can't get into the account, for one thing. As I said, I need the power of attorney or—"

"No." He closed his eyes, looking as frustrated as she felt. "You will not do that. Ever."

Boy, he could make his words crystal clear when he wanted to.

She wasn't going to find out what happened to the money, which was frustrating but fair. It was, after all, his business, not hers. As long as it wasn't stolen, she had no reason to press for an explanation.

"With nothing coming on the market quite that big," she said, "I'm not sure how to proceed."

"Then think of a way," he said, sounding very much like the father and boss who'd shaped her into the problem-solving business owner she was today.

"I could make some changes in the business structure," she said quietly. "It would save money, not make it. I could scale back on salaries or—"

"Don't fire anyone."

He was right. Cutting costs wasn't going to produce that kind of money.

"I'm looking at some bigger properties on the mainland," she said. "If I could get a listing on something commercial, we might recoup twenty percent. It's a start, so—"

Rex held up his hand, stopping her, his eyes misting as he stared at her.

"Dad?" she asked when he didn't say anything. "Are you okay?"

He searched her face, his expression so...sad. Yes, Suze was right. He looked dejected, defeated, and utterly depressed.

"Raina, I need you to do this for me." He reached out with his good hand, taking hers. "Before I die."

Is that why he was sad? He thought he was dying? She slid to her knees in front of his wheelchair, aching to make those words go away. "Dad, you're not going to—"

"Give me peace, Raina," he whispered, putting his hand on her cheek exactly the same way her mother had. "No one else can do this but you."

"Your faith is daunting." But never once had she backed down from a Rex Wingate-issued challenge. She wasn't about to start now. "But I'll try."

As she stood, he looked up at her. "I love you, Raina. I'm glad you got rid of that lug nut."

She let out a soft laugh at the nickname, which was so...Rex. "Oh, Dad. I love you so much. And you can't die, so please don't ever say that again. Please?"

His smile was so dejected, it broke her heart.

She knew exactly what would cheer him and give him a reason for living. It wasn't money—it never was with him. It was family. Telling him about the baby wouldn't jinx anything. It would take the agony out of his eyes.

"Dad, I have to tell you—"

"Hello?" The woman's voice floated into the room from the front door. "Your friendly physical therapist is here! May I come in?"

"Tell me what?" he said.

"That I'm going to..." She heard the PT's heavy footfalls. "Make it rain. I promise."

"That's my girl."

"Good morning, Rex!" A sturdy, middle-aged woman

in a blue sweatsuit came in. "Are we ready for a fun day of PT?"

With a kiss on his head, Raina left him to do his work, knowing she had to do hers. She had to make it rain.

Except she had no idea *how*.

But she'd learned one thing in these months on Amelia Island—a Wingate was never really alone. It was time to enlist some help. One person on this island knew the truth about the baby *and* the money.

Maybe Tori could help.

Chapter Three

Tori

Somehow, the kitchen of the Riverfront Café had become Victoria Wingate's home away from home. Even when Tori had gone back to New England for a week after Chloe's "unwedding," she'd missed this dumpy little windowless kitchen with its sizzling grill, inconsistent ovens, and Miguel, a sweet but not terribly inventive line cook.

How exactly had that happened in a few weeks?

This kitchen—and the sixty-seat restaurant it served—wasn't quite on par with Victoria Wingate Catering, her small business outside of Boston. There, she enjoyed a view of the garden where she grew her own herbs, cooked on high-quality equipment, and shared the workload with two eminently qualified sous chefs. She functioned with the knowledge that she owned her own business, made a sweet profit, and frequently created mouthwatering menus for appreciative clients.

Here, on the other hand, she was working for Wingate Properties, and was limited to one daily special and a menu that hadn't changed since she was a young girl who came in here for breakfast with her sisters.

But there was a comfort level in this kitchen—on all of Amelia Island, in fact. And Tori's decision to spend the summer here with her teenage daughter, Kenzie, while her ex-husband took their son on a six-week baseball tournament tour in an RV, felt so right it was like she was walking on air.

Of course, it didn't hurt that she'd met a man who made her feel...things. She wasn't quite sure exactly what, but she liked the feeling almost as much as she liked Dr. Justin Verona.

Add in the fact that Amelia Island, where she'd been born and raised, was chock full of a family she loved? Everything was lined up for a terrific summer ahead.

Smiling at the thought, she put the finishing touches on her notes for today's special—a chicken and andouille gumbo served over wild rice—and headed out to the hostess stand. She hoped Bambi had mastered the black acrylic sign that Tori had brought back from Boston, one of many items that she and Kenzie had loaded in the family SUV for their summer on the island.

"Hey."

Tori looked up from the notebook in her hand, darn near colliding with her sister.

"Raina! I didn't know you were stopping in." She leaned in to give an air kiss, but barely made it when Raina drew back, her blue eyes clouded with worry. "Are you okay?" Tori asked, reaching for her to whisper, "Chickpea's okay?"

Raina gave a hint of a smile at the nickname Tori had hung on her unborn child. "Not quite a chickpea. Just a cucumber seed. And it's fine."

"Ah, we shall dry roast and cook that cuke seed in ghee," she teased, but Raina's smile faded. "What's wrong, Rain?"

"Can we talk?"

Tori's heart dropped at the tone and the unhappy look in Raina's eyes. "Of course. Any hints? Is it Jack? Please don't tell me he's groveling for a second chance, because—"

Raina shook her head. "No, no. It's...a family thing."

"Dad? Is he okay? Did something—"

"Stop guessing. I was hoping you were between breakfast and lunch rushes and I could steal you for a few minutes."

"Absolutely! Go, sit by the window in that two-top. I'll be right there." She gave a nudge to Raina's shoulder. "I'll bring you coffee."

"Decaf."

"Of course. Anything to eat? Please don't tell me saltines again, because they offend my chef's heart."

"I'm kind of craving something sweet and comforting," Raina said.

"My specialty, baby. Gimme a sec."

Tori watched her walk to the table, her heart heavy when she thought about what Raina was going through. Divorce was the absolute worst experience in the world, as she knew firsthand, especially when the ex was a cheater. Add to that a much-wanted pregnancy after so many miscarriages? *And* she was running Dad's company?

No wonder Raina looked strained to the max.

At the hostess station, Tori waited a second for Bambi, a middle-aged woman with a massive bosom and a beehive hairdo, who was getting off the phone. She had some shortcomings as a hostess, but her heart was definitely in the right place.

"That was a weird call," Bambi said as Tori pulled a page from her notebook.

"What was it?"

"Some woman from..." She wrinkled her nose. "Netflix? Nah, that's impossible, but I could have sworn that's what she said."

"Selling us service?" Tori guessed.

"Oh, no. I don't think so. She talked so fast it was like one of the tourists from New York. She wanted to know if we were open for dinner and I said no, breakfast and lunch only, and then she asked if we'd rent the place for dinner. I said—"

"Yes, indeed, I hope."

Her eyes widened. "Um, no. We close at two-thirty."

Raina laughed softly. "I know that, but renting out for an event? First of all, catering large groups is my specialty, plus that's a great way to add revenue to the bottom line. Did you get her number?"

"Sorry, no. Didn't even catch her name, she whizzed it by me so fast. I told her to try the Salty Pelican." She tipped her head in the direction of the popular waterfront restaurant. "And she said she would. I'm so sorry, Tori."

Tori gave a tight smile. "It's fine, Bambi. Can you put this special on the board before the lunch rush? I need a few minutes to chat with my sister."

"Of course!" Bambi took the paper and glanced at it. "Oh, gumbo! Now that's a meal I understand."

Tori laughed. "Unlike yesterday's goat cheese truffles."

"They must have been good, though," she said. "I got two calls this morning asking if they'd be on the menu, but I said no."

No? Was that her favorite word? "Next time, tell them I can make anything they want. I don't like to turn away business."

"I understand. Now, go sit with Raina and I'll make you a specials board."

"Thanks, Bambi."

Tori filled two coffee cups and grabbed an icing-slathered cinnamon roll from the covered pastry display. On the way to sit with Raina, she glanced at the wharf that ran along the wide and picturesque Amelia River.

Of course, her gaze moved to Slip 7, where a live-aboard sailboat bobbed on the water. She knew it was empty now, since its owner was at work being the world's best-looking neurologist. But last night?

Yes. Justin had been on board and had made the loveliest dinner, which they ate under the moon, laughing, talking, and doing a fair share of kissing.

"Look at that face," Raina cracked wryly. "Like a lovestruck teenager."

"That obvious?" Tori took the other seat and put down the cups and pastry. "Eat this and you can look lovestruck, too."

Raina eyed the roll suspiciously. "Couldn't do, like, a bran muffin with raisins?"

"Cinnamon staves off nausea."

"Really?"

"No, but that baby will thank Aunt Tori and so will you." Tori lifted her cup. "What's going on?"

Her sister took a minute, closing her eyes, visibly grounding herself and giving in to the first sweet bite of the roll, which earned Tori a satisfying moan of appreciation.

"I came to you first for a number of reasons," Raina said after dabbing her lips with a napkin. "For one thing, you don't have a horse in the race."

"What are you talking about? What race?"

Raina stole one more bite, then leaned in. "Remember the money I told you about?"

"One doesn't forget the disappearance of a half-million dollars, Raina. Any news? Have you finally talked to Dad? What did he say happened to it?"

"He won't, except to indicate it didn't disappear," Raina said. "He knows it's gone but will not give me even the vaguest clue where or to whom or why. Closed subject. But he's adamant that I somehow replace it with five hundred thousand *new* dollars."

Tori sank deeper into her chair. "How can you—never mind. If anyone in this family can do it, you can."

"But no pressure, right?"

Tori smiled. "I'll help." Then the smile disappeared. "How are you going to do it?"

"Well, with that help you just offered."

"I don't have that kind of cash, Rain. My catering business is decent, but not *that* good. And this one isn't exactly a money-maker."

"Precisely," Raina said. "I have pored over the portfolio of Wingate-owned businesses, and there are only two that don't support one of our sisters. The florist is Rose's, and the bookstore is Grace's. Madeline owns her dressmaking business, and in all of those cases, Dad owns the buildings. Well, Wingate Properties does."

Tori nodded, starting to see where she was going with this. "He owns this building, too."

"And Wingate House," she said. "Also, the ice cream parlor, but Silas Struthers has run that place for so long, he's practically family. So, of all the properties he owns, Wingate House and the Riverfront Café aren't supporting a Wingate family member, per se."

"And you want to sell one of them?" Tori asked, already a little sick in her heart at the possibility.

"I don't *want* to," Raina said. "I loathe the idea, but it's the answer to how I'd find that kind of money. This place? A commercial listing on prime waterfront? We'd get over a million to sell it outright, and I could do it in no time at all."

Tori looked at her, surprised at how truly unsettling

that idea was. "Yeah, you could sell it, but..." She glanced around at the underwhelming café, a place in need of a renovation but still comforting and authentic. "This café has been in the family for decades."

"Almost seven of them," Raina said. "Trust me, I know what the Riverfront Café means to us."

Tori nodded. "And the inn?" She grunted. "Our great-grandfather built that Victorian, Raina. It's called *Wingate* House for a reason. It's the first place in town with the signature brick and wrought-iron gate and the golden W."

"It's also another easy seven-figure sale."

Tori groaned at the idea, looking out at the avenue that bore the family name. "But that and this café are the two buildings that anchor Wingate Way. We can't sell either of them."

"Tori, do you think I didn't consider all that history?" Raina asked, sounding as pained by the idea as Tori felt. "Didn't think of the meaning of this street? The importance of our family to this town? Yes, I have. Until I can't think of anything else. But the only person whose livelihood would be affected by selling Wingate House is Doreen, and she's in her seventies. She could retire and we would set her up for life."

Tori let out a sad sigh, thinking of the crotchety manager who'd run the inn since...well, forever. Throwing her out and changing the name and letting go of the house that had symbolized the family since the early 1900s? It was unthinkable.

But here was her sister, the problem-solver, thinking it.

"I don't know, Raina. I don't like it."

"Dad is in trouble, Tori," Raina countered. "I don't know how or why. He's unhappy and worried and that's delaying his progress. I bet his neurologist would tell you the same thing." Raina added a look. "Between kisses."

Tori's eyebrows flicked. "So many kisses," she said dreamily, a flash of a memory from last night dancing in her head. "I don't understand why Dad would simply accept losing that kind of money. I mean, was it a bad investment? A loan? A gamble? He doesn't throw away that kind of money. He's too smart."

"I don't know, but this much was clear: he doesn't want to talk about it."

"Susannah has no idea?" Tori asked.

"She's so wrapped up in his recovery," Raina said. "She knows there's a cash flow problem but assumes I'll wave a magic wand and fix it. I didn't want to tell her the details until I figured out what happened, but I've been stymied. The money was in some account in Iowa."

"Iowa." Tori shook her head. "Why there?"

"Beats me. But the credit union won't tell me a thing without power of attorney."

"Won't Dad give you that?"

"Nope. Just the power to...produce money."

"Oh, wow, Raina." Tori reached across the table to take her sister's hand. "What a thing to put on your shoulders in the middle of a divorce. Not to mention...the cucumber seed."

Raina smiled and lifted one of those shoulders as if to say it was narrow but strong. "I was scared just talking about it would upset him."

"I told you Justin thinks he's out of the worst risk period for a second stroke," Tori said. "Good to have his neurologist so close, huh?"

"So good," Raina agreed. "How was your dinner date last night?"

Tori made a whimpering noise as she poured more cream in her coffee.

"That good, huh?"

"Downright delicious," Tori replied. "And I'm not only talking about his bolognaise, which was amazing."

"High praise from a chef."

She sipped and closed her eyes, remembering the food...and the company. "Yeah."

Raina laughed softly. "You're literally gone over him."

"I'm a goner," she agreed. "But I feel bad every time I see him and leave Kenzie alone."

"Don't. She loves Dr. Hottypants."

Tori chuckled at how easily his unintended nickname slid off all of her sisters' lips. "I hauled her down here for the summer and I don't want to make her work at the café and watch TV all night."

"She can always hang with me at the beach house, or at Rose's with all the kids. Don't let your daughter keep you from having fun this summer."

"Thanks, and she's so supportive. She really wants me to have my summer fling. It's sweet."

"So do we all," Raina said. "And I swear I'll be with Kenzie anytime you want to go out with him."

"Thank you. Now, what about this money?"

"I guess just...help me, okay? I'm going to need your support if I drop a bomb like, 'We have to sell property,' on our family."

"I'm on your side, whatever you want to do," Tori assured her. "But no one is going to like this solution. Selling Wingate House or the Riverfront Café is..." She couldn't think of a word for how bad it was. "Not a great solution. Will Dad even let you?"

Raina closed her eyes. "I don't know. I haven't talked to him about it yet because I want to dream up another way out of this, but...what? I'd do anything."

"I know, I know." Tori looked up as she saw the door open with a small crowd of tourists who were probably on the one o'clock ferry to Cumberland Island and wanted lunch quickly. "I better go, Rain. Duty calls."

"Of course. Thank you for running this restaurant, Tori." Raina reached out and took her hand. "I know it's a step down from your catering company in Boston."

Was it? Maybe a step...sideways. "I like it. It's different and fun and..." She glanced around the place, which was filling up fast. "I've never run a restaurant before, only a catering kitchen. I like it."

Raina made a face. "Don't get too connected and make it impossible to sell this jewel. It could solve Dad's problem with one stroke of the listing pen. I'd have multiple offers in no time."

The thought of it made Tori's heart sink. "You know,

Chloe's coming today and she said she can start working here tomorrow." She lifted a brow. "So that will be three Wingates working here."

"Twist the knife, Tori," Raina cracked. "I can focus on the sale of Wingate House."

"Eesh." Tori made a face. "Even saying those words out loud kind of hurts."

Raina angled her head and gave her a narrow-eyed glare. "You're not helping, Tor."

"I know, I know." In some ways, the history of that house made it an even less attractive option than this restaurant, but Tori knew Raina had enough on her heart today. "Listen, let's do a sisters' night soon now that Chloe's going to be here. I feel like you've been avoiding everyone these last few weeks."

Raina lifted her brows. "Hard to be with everyone and not tell them..." She glanced down toward her stomach. "I don't know how much longer I can keep this secret."

"Maybe you should bite the bullet, tell Jack, and then you can share the news with the family."

"I'm not ready yet," Raina admitted. "For one thing, I have no reason to feel confident I can keep this baby. If I do, if I make it to the magic twelve weeks and hear a heartbeat, then, yes. I'll tell Jack and we can share with everyone else. I just..." She sighed. "I have no idea how Jack is going to react."

"And I don't care," Tori shot back.

Tori had overheard Jack's entire confession that day, and no woman deserved to be told by her husband that he'd fallen in love with someone else. That he'd "man-aged" not to sleep with her...yet. No one should endure that, especially Raina, who spent her whole life solving other people's problems.

"Definitely yes on a get-together," Raina said. "How about later this week, when Chloe's settled in? Right here at the café?"

"Perfect." She reached for Raina's hand. "Maybe our sisters can help."

Raina nodded. "We don't have to tell them about the astronomical amount out of deference to Dad, but I can share that Wingate Properties has a cash flow problem. Maybe someone will have an idea I'm not thinking of." Around them, the restaurant started filling and Raina's eyes widened. "Wow. This place is busy!"

"Word's getting out that the last cook, Jimmy, is gone. The food's better, and that brings in people. We're gonna make a million," Tori teased. "And, trust me, I'd give you half."

"Thanks." Raina lifted her cup in a mock toast and smiled. "You're the best, Tori. Go make great food and happy customers. I'll free this table in a second."

Tori took off to the kitchen, but a customer she recognized waved her down.

"Please tell me you have that coconut mahi that was on your menu last week," the woman said as she settled in with four other ladies. "I brought all my friends to taste your food."

"Oh, thank you! No mahi today, but how do we feel about gumbo?"

"Yes, please!" The women seemed delighted as Tori slipped away to check on the large pot she had simmering on the stove.

Maybe it was serving food—no matter where, when, or how—that made Tori feel at home. Or maybe it was connecting with her sisters. Or maybe it was that doctor she'd nicknamed Hottypants.

Whatever had Tori so happy these days, she hoped nothing changed.

But something told her that it was all about to change, no matter how much she didn't want it to.

Chapter Four

Grace

Grace Jenkins could no longer deny the terrifying truth. She had a stalker. And right this minute, in the middle of a busy afternoon, he was standing on Wingate Way outside of her bookstore pretending to be interested in the display of "Summer Reads" she'd arranged in the front window.

It wasn't the first time she'd seen Isaiah Kincaid in and around The Next Chapter. Sometimes he came in, once he bought a book, and always he'd tried to strike up a conversation, but she was cool and aloof.

That didn't seem to deter the man she'd first met when he somehow shifted from guest to maid and cook at Wingate House. No one else in the family seemed the least bit put off by the tall, muscular man who happened to appear at the inn right when Doreen Parrish, the manager, had taken ill and Dad was in the hospital after his stroke.

All of her sisters, especially Raina, seemed to think this wonderful creature who could whip up an eggs Benedict one minute and fix the broken plumbing the next had been dropped down from heaven to help when they needed it most.

No one thought it was strange that he easily took over cleaning and cooking at the inn. No one thought it was remarkable that he managed to get along with a woman so famously nasty that they'd called her Dor-mean since Grace had been a child. And no one thought it was that awful that he'd asked Grace out for coffee.

But Grace did, because she knew that day when Isaiah helped her carry a box of books to the library at Wingate House, he'd seen her wedding ring. She saw him stare at it, then, not five minutes later, he asked her for coffee.

What kind of man did that? He had no idea she was a widow. And he'd been a Marine—or claimed to have been one—like her late husband. Nick would have understood how wrong that was. Nick would have...

She sighed and looked back at the paperwork in front of her, concentrating on the invoice she'd received from Random House.

As she had trained herself to do for four years—and two months, six days, and a few hours—Grace forced herself to focus on something else when thoughts of Nick threatened to bubble up.

She'd gotten rather adept at it. True, she sometimes felt like a woman wading through Jell-O—opening this bookstore, surrounding herself with family, raising the child she'd been carrying when Nick was killed. She wasn't *living*, not really. But she wasn't hurting, either.

Because if she let herself go to a dark place and really

think about Staff Sergeant Nicholas Jenkins, and how he'd been killed in Afghanistan in a car bomb explosion so intense they never even found his wedding ring, she would lose it.

So she thought about her darling daughter and her ailing father and dear mother and wonderful sisters and her precious bookstore. She shoved her mind and heart full of other things so she couldn't think about Nick.

Was that grief? Or was that coping? She didn't know, but the last thing she wanted to think about was—

"Hello, Grace."

The baritone in his voice felt like it reached right down to her toes. It took a split second to swallow, breathe, and finally look up with an expression of complete and utter disinterest.

"Yes? Oh, hello. Are you looking for a book?"

His lips lifted in a half smile, revealing perfect teeth and enough crinkles around his ebony eyes that she guessed him to be well into his thirties, maybe even forty. His features were strong and distinctive, his skin the color of rich espresso, and he smelled unexpectedly of fresh air and rosemary, like he'd stopped in Rose's garden and picked some herbs on his way over.

And the way her family gushed over this man? She wouldn't be surprised if he had.

"I was just hoping to talk to you," he said.

She felt her cheeks warm and dropped her gaze to her left hand, still splayed over the invoice...where her ring was clearly on display.

Okay, maybe he'd been on Amelia Island and

working for her family long enough to know she was widowed. Maybe that's why he seemed to show up more often lately. A man with a purpose, determined to talk to her.

"Well, I'm very busy," she said, not tempering that with a smile that might encourage him. "Did you need something in particular?"

He tipped his head in concession, as if he'd expected that. "Surely you get a break at some point in your day."

Didn't he realize she wasn't interested?

Quiet by nature and not a fan of confrontation, Grace merely lifted her left hand and pressed it to her chest, hoping he couldn't miss the implication. Widowed, yes, but still attached.

"Oh, I'm sorry. I just never leave this place."

"Not even to go get your daughter?"

She felt the blood drain from her face. "I...yes...I..." She narrowed her gaze and took all the sweetness out of her voice. "Not very many people keep track of my schedule that closely. Again, was there something in particular you needed help with?"

He regarded her for a moment, an inexplicable look in his eyes as he nodded. "I understand, ma'am. But I really only want to spend a few minutes with you. Somewhere private, if possible."

She shrank back a millimeter, uncertain how else she could make it clear that she did not want that. She'd have to be honest.

"I don't socialize much. I'm sorry."

He let out a soft sigh, but didn't move.

"So, if you don't need a book or...something, then..." She added a cool smile. "I hope you have a nice day."

He didn't move. "I have something, Grace. Something you want."

Was he serious? "I don't want anything from you, Mr. Kincaid. I don't want to be rude, I don't want to be nasty, and I don't want to be unkind. I just...I'm not interested."

"Please," he said softly. "It's important. Five minutes is all I need."

"Can you tell me what it is?"

"No. Not here. Not like this. You'll want privacy."

She'd want privacy? Or he did?

She thought about crossing her arms and insisting he leave, but there was something in his voice, something in his eyes. Something real that tugged at a heart that so did not want to be tugged at.

And, honestly, wasn't that what scared her most? That this man—this tall, strong, solid, kind man who everyone already loved—wasn't a stalker at all. He was... attractive and interested and, oh, God, *no*.

"I'm very sorry, Mr. Kincaid, but I don't have time or...no. I can't meet you, not for five minutes. Thank you, though."

"I understand," he said, although it sounded like he didn't.

With that, he gave a quick nod and walked out, leaving her staring at his broad back and thinking about...

Nick.

Immediately, she tried to push that thought from her head. The invoice wasn't distracting her enough, so she shelved books for twenty minutes, did her email for a while, ordered some children's books, and helped customer after customer find something wonderful to read on their vacation.

But like it always did on dark days, time moved at a glacial speed, each minute longer than the one before, each day empty because he was gone.

Nick. Nick. *Nicholas Louis Jenkins.* Blue eyes. Corn-silk hair. Square jaw. Tender hands. Hearty laugh. Big heart. Happy calls and long kisses and the utter, inde-scribable joy of learning they had a daughter on the way.

I'll be home a month after she's born, baby. I promise.

But he didn't keep that promise. He didn't—

"You look lost."

Grace gasped and looked up, practically whimpering at the sweet face of her sister, Rose, who stood on the other side of the desk. She held a signature Coming Up Roses bouquet so glorious there was no doubt that Rose, a skilled florist, had arranged it herself. All Grace could do was stare and try to pull herself out of the dark place.

"Are you okay?" Rose asked, concern in her brown eyes. "Grace?"

She managed a nod. "I'm fine, Rose. What...why...are you on your way to make a delivery?"

"Oh, honey, you look so upset." She set the bouquet on the counter and scooted around, arms out. "My sweet little sister, come here."

She melted into Rose's arms, shocked at how much she needed this comfort. But who wouldn't want a hug from Rose Wingate D'Angelo, equal parts angel and half-sister? But like she always did with the four older Wingate girls, Grace mentally dropped the "half" part.

They may have had different mothers, but they had one heart.

"I'm so sorry, Rose. I slipped into...sadness today. I've been so good, then..." Her voice cracked with an unshed sob. "I need a minute."

"Oh, baby." Rose put a hand on her cheek. "Go, go upstairs to your apartment." She nudged Grace to the back stairs that led to the second floor. "Take all the time you need. I'll watch the front desk for you."

"I can't ask you to do that."

"You didn't," Rose assured her. "I'm offering. And I'll get Nikki Lou today, if you like. I'm going to the school to pick up my kids anyway. I'll bring her to my house. It's gonna be wild, because Chloe just got here and you know Nikki Lou loves little Lady Bug, who is currently running around my house barking for joy."

"I...guess. Jennifer will be here soon to spell me for school, but...oh." Grace pressed her hand to her temple. "I don't know what's wrong with me today. Ever since that man came in, I—"

"Isaiah Kincaid?"

Grace blinked at her. "How do you know?"

Her lips lifting in a sly smile, Rose cocked her head to the bouquet. "Yes, I am making a delivery...to you."

"From..." Her heart shifted around in her chest.

"Yes, from the kind and lovely Mr. Kincaid."

Grace's jaw dropped. "He's unbelievable! I told him

no, in no uncertain terms. I basically kicked him out of here and told him not to come back."

"Why?" Rose asked. "He's really nice."

"Rose! He's...he's..."

"A man. I know. They make you run screaming from the room, especially when they show any level of interest at all."

She huffed out a breath. "It's too much," she said. "I'm sure he's nice and as wonderful as everyone says, but the first time he asked me out, he didn't know I was a widow and he saw my ring. Now, maybe he knows, but can't he tell I'm not interested?"

"Maybe. Maybe he knows that your husband was a Marine and thinks you might want to talk to him."

"I don't want to talk to every Marine just because Nick was one. And I don't want..." Her gaze shifted to the bouquet. "Roses."

"Pink ones, too. I gave you the prettiest I had in the shop."

She groaned, closing her eyes. "What does the card say?"

"A lot."

"What do you mean?"

"It's not a flower card," Rose said. "He bought a greeting card, went across the street for fifteen minutes, came back with a sealed envelope, and personally tied it to the stems."

Oh, goodness. "Really?"

Rose shrugged. "The man was on a mission."

"For what?" The very idea that she was the object of that mission made Grace reel backwards a step or two.

"I don't know," Rose said. "But Gabe's the best judge of character I know, and he's off from the fire station today and working with me at the flower shop. He talked to Isaiah and thinks he's...good. Genuinely good."

"I can't accept his flowers or his interest, Rose. I don't know what to say to him."

"You don't have to say anything," Rose told her. "He mentioned to Gabe that he was taking a few days off and won't be back until next week."

"But he will be back, and I'll have to say something to him."

"By then, you'll have figured it out. Now go, take the flowers upstairs, read the card, and take a moment to regroup. I'll handle your customers."

Grace let herself be guided from behind the counter, wrapping both hands around the vase and getting a sweet whiff of the flowers' heady fragrance.

"Thank you," she whispered to Rose.

"Just keep an open mind."

Grace smiled, but her mind was closed as far as Isaiah Kincaid was concerned.

She carried the bouquet up the stairs to her apartment, the floral scent filling the hall outside her front door. She slipped inside and went straight to the kitchen to put the flowers on the table. They were beautiful and he was nice, but she was *not* interested.

Very slowly, she reached in between the stems and

baby's breath, finding a ribbon that had been poked through the envelope, securing the message to the flowers. She'd give him this: he didn't want that card to get lost.

She dropped into a chair and stared at the white envelope with "Grace Jenkins" printed on the front in square, neat lettering.

But it wasn't only a card, she thought as her fingers grazed the envelope. There was something in here. Something small created a bump in the paper.

And it was heavy, like there was a coin or a metal clip or something inside. A gift? Another thing to tell him she didn't want?

She tore at the back seal, opening it gingerly and peeking in to see something gold and round and...

"Oh my God." All the blood drained from her head, making her dizzy and weak. What *was* this?

But even as her fingers closed around the circular band, she knew. She didn't even have to read the inscription inside, because she knew she was holding Nick's wedding ring.

His ring!

On a painful sob, she brought it to her lips, kissing it over and over again. Finally, she wiped her eyes and turned the ring, reading the inscription she remembered so well.

NJ & GW 11/30/16

Nicholas Jenkins and Grace Wingate, November 30, 2016.

With trembling hands, she pulled out the card. Tears

blurred the words that she skimmed, but she read enough to understand.

Sgt. Jenkins came into my mess before his patrol, ate two grilled cheese sandwiches, drank a half gallon of milk, and shot the breeze with a few of us cooks. He talked about his wife, Grace, who was pregnant, and then looked down at his hand and realized he'd forgotten to take off his ring.

She didn't bother with the rest. She would, later. Now, all she wanted to do was hold this ring and weep.

Chapter Five

Chloe

After two days on the job, Chloe realized that the best part about being a waitress was that she didn't have one minute to think about what she was going to do with the rest of her life. The worst part about being a waitress?

Being a waitress.

It wasn't that she hated the work—it was kind of fun and worked wonders to take her mind off all she'd been through. The parting conversation with Hunter had taken a toll, sending her reeling for a few days of remorse and regret and sorrow that she'd put herself and him through such a devastating and public breakup.

So the work distracted her, mostly because of the customers. There were tourists from all over the country, and they all had interesting tales of what brought them here. And there were lots of locals, too, some she'd known since childhood.

The people were far more fascinating than the food, so Chloe tried to make a game of it.

For every order she took, she learned something

about the person who gave it. But sometimes...that got her off track.

"Table five is from Minnesota," Chloe said as she put the order on the grill, still thinking about the conversation she'd had with the lovely couple. "They come here every year in June for a week."

Miguel took the slip and looked at it, adding an exasperated sigh that the line cook seemed to give her a lot since she started working there. "But how do they want their eggs, Chloe? Just 'eggs' doesn't work for me."

"Oh, yeah. Whoops. Scrambled, I think? No, wait, she wanted Benedict." With a grunt, she looked skyward. "I'll go back and confirm. Oh, and get this. The two people on table nine? From Los Angeles, and I heard them mention Netflix. Hollywood types, you know?"

"But what do they want to—"

"Whoa, wait a second." Tori came sailing into the kitchen from the walk-in fridge, egg cartons in her arms. "Did you say someone from Netflix?"

"Yep, a guy and a woman. I heard her call him Marcus, and mention something about production values. And they haven't ordered yet," she added as an aside to Miguel. "But I'll get it right, I promise. And those are definitely Benedict. And I'm so sorry I am the triple W—World's Worst Waitress."

"Don't worry," Tori said. "You're doing fine. At least you didn't make a TikTok video of customers...like *some people*."

Kenzie inched out from the condiment station, making a face. "I didn't post it, Mom, but that lady with the dancing dog on the patio was social media gold. What can I say? I'm a little bored hanging out here with nothing to do."

"I'm sorry, honey. I had no idea that this county had a law that you had to be sixteen to serve food," Tori said. "Three more days and you can do more than hang out back here."

"Three more days and you'll officially be a better waitress than I am," Chloe joked.

"It's fine. I can stock condiments." Kenzie rolled her eyes. "And *not* make content."

Tori turned to Chloe. "Did you say table nine was the Netflix guy? And there's a woman? Find out if she's the one who called looking to rent out the restaurant for an event. Bambi told her we don't do that—"

"We don't," Miguel said.

"We *could*," Tori insisted. "I don't want to pounce on the guy, but, Chloe, if you could use your powers for good and find out if they still want to rent the place, then I'll pounce. I'd love to start doing events here. It's a perfect space for it, with the water view and the location."

"Will do!" Chloe said, excited for the assignment.

"And find out if that's a Benedict or not," Miguel called as she walked out.

"And, um, Chloe."

She turned to see Tori holding out a plate. "This order of pancakes is up. Table four?"

"Yikes. Sorry." She took the plate and gave an apologetic smile. "Like I said, world's worst waitress."

"World's best sister," Tori countered. "And if you bring in an event, you'll get a small commission."

"Really? Watch this!" Grabbing the plate, she headed back into the dining room, delivering the order to...no, not *that* lady. The one with the gray poof.

"Sorry, this took a little longer than I expected," she said as she put the plate down, then pulled the order pad from her apron and headed to the Netflix table, wondering how to approach the topic of their event.

The couple was deep in conversation, with the woman furiously writing notes.

"And you have a budget for every location?" she asked. "Because you are getting into scary numbers, Marcus."

"So sorry to interrupt," Chloe said.

"We're not eating," the man told her. "Just coffee."

"Gotcha," she replied, making a quick decision to fill their cups before asking anything. She scooted over to the coffee warming station, grabbed the fullest pot, then headed back to the table.

As she turned over the cups, she glanced from one to the other and settled on the friendlier face of the man, who was mid-forties, shaggy hair, clean-shaven, with sharp hazel eyes that appeared to miss nothing.

Time to put some of that journalism school training to work.

"So, I hate to intrude, but can I ask you a question? Are you with Netflix, by any chance?"

"Not exactly," the man answered, a frown tugging. "How did you know?"

"I, um, thought I heard you say that."

"It's probably around town already," the woman said to the man. "Once we talked to a single person, the fact that we were scouting for a location will fly through this place like wildfire."

"You're filming here?" Chloe's asked with interest. "A series?"

"A movie," the man said. "And we're not technically with Netflix, but the production company making the film."

"Oh, I see. That's so cool," she cooed. "What a fun thing for this town. Great news."

"Except we're off to a place called St. Simons Island," the woman told her in a thick New York accent. "Where we got a much better reception and the locations we need for *Christmas on Main Street*."

"Is that the name of the movie?" Chloe asked as she poured the coffee. "That's so cute and Hallmarkish."

"Except it's for Netflix," the man told her. "So characters will actually kiss."

She laughed. "Gotcha. I guess you're catching that small-town vibe, huh?"

"Brick," the woman replied. "Our director wants as much brick, views of water, and as many painfully quaint shops as possible."

"Well, you've come to the right place," she said cheerily. "There's the river, quaint is our middle name, and—here's a fun fact—we have more brick than any other beach town in Florida."

The man gave her a skeptical, but slightly interested, look.

"It's true," she said. "There was a huge fire in the early 1900s, and it burned downtown Fernandina Beach. The city made a law that everything had to be brick or stone after that, so that's why it's so pretty."

"A law?" he scoffed. "Not surprised. This place has more regulations than the Pentagon and is about as easy to work with."

"Oh, that's a shame," Chloe said.

"Yeah, apparently Centre Street is so important, it can never be blocked off." The woman gave an exaggerated eyeroll. "I mean, really. For a movie that could have put this unknown island on the map?"

Unknown? Chloe had grown up on Amelia Island, and it wasn't exactly *unknown*.

Remembering her mission, Chloe crouched down at the table to get eye-level. "You know, my sister—er, my boss—thought someone had called about renting the restaurant for an event. Was that you guys?"

"It was me," the woman said.

"You want to film here in the café?" Chloe's brows shot up at how fun that would be.

"Actually, we needed a centrally located place to meet with cast and crew, and eat dinner. I tried a few restaurants—"

"We could do it," Chloe said without hesitation. "I mean, you could talk to Tori, who is currently the manager, and she's also a catering chef, so we could provide the food and space."

"Too late, isn't it, Marcus?"

He shrugged. "I need a cooperative location, and this town isn't."

"I'm so sorry to hear that," Chloe said, and meant it.

The woman sighed. "The look of this place is ideal, but we can't be constrained by local governments. We couldn't get anyone to even meet with us."

"What were you asking to do?" Chloe asked, looking from one to the other.

"Film in stores and on the street," the man said. "So people basically have to give up control of their business or home for several weeks, but trust me, the location fees are fantastic. Likely more than any business would make in that time. But no one liked that idea. Or having that main street decorated for Christmas for most of the summer."

Chloe nodded. "I can see why the shop owners wouldn't want to do that. There are so many street fairs and festivals here, and tons of tourists. But, wow, a movie being filmed here would be cool. Especially if you're looking for extras."

"Hundreds of them," the woman said.

"And thousands of dollars to the shop owners." The man picked up his coffee cup and offered a toast to his friend. "Here's to that other island. Not quite as much brick, but maybe those business owners will take a hundred grand for being closed for a month."

Chloe whistled. "I am surprised people turned that down."

"Nobody even got to the point of finding out what we

pay, just that it is a major disruption, which is true," the woman conceded. "We need one of those big Victorian houses and at least three different stores, maybe four. Granted, we take over and redecorate and traipse through a store with a crew and equipment, but most people love that big payday, plus the fun of seeing your home or store in a movie."

"And no one wanted to do that?"

"Maybe they did," the man said. "But we were blocked by the town council more than the shop owners. We never even got to store owners."

"Very sad." And there was the real story, Chloe thought, already seeing a headline under her field report.

Local Politicians Shun Hollywood.

"Excuse me, miss?"

She rose and turned toward the customer who'd called her and nodded goodbye to the movie people, bummed that something as exciting as a movie being filmed here couldn't happen. On the way to the kitchen, she gave someone a check, refilled a coffee, and promised to take an order for a new table.

"Well?" Tori asked, waiting for her in the kitchen.

"No dice," Chloe said. "They were actually here to film a movie but the local government wouldn't let them redecorate Centre Street for Christmas in the summer."

"Aww." Tori crossed her arms. "That's a shame."

"Yeah, they would have turned this place upside down, though."

"Did they call about an event?" Tori asked.

"Yeah, but not an event. They wanted to use the café

as a central gathering place after we close, for the cast and crew for dinner and meetings for the entire time they filmed. Cha-ching, right?"

"Seriously, that would have been nice."

"And the locations?" Chloe said, raising her brows. "They're paying *a hundred grand* to each shop or home-owner. But the town council—"

"What?" Tori's voice went up an octave. "For how many locations?"

"I don't know, a bunch. They need a house and some shops and the whole street."

Tori's jaw practically hit the floor. "Are you serious?"

"Yeah, but apparently we have 'more laws than the Pentagon.' So they're off to St. Simons, which is pretty but, oh..." Chloe turned to the grill. "Is that my order?"

Tori grabbed her arm. "Raina."

"No, I'm Chloe, the youngest, best known for becoming the runaway—"

"You have to get Raina," Tori insisted. "She has to get down here right this minute."

"Now? I have an order up. And new customers waiting for coffee. And a check due. Do you *want* me to be the world's worst waitress?"

"I want Raina here as soon as humanly possible." She whipped out her phone, stabbing the screen, then grunting in frustration when she put it to her ear. "Voice-mail. This cannot wait!"

"What can't?" Chloe asked.

"Just...can you run to Wingate Properties, fill her in

on every detail they told you? I'll hold them here. I'll tie them down if I have to."

"Mom?" Kenzie came closer. "Why are you crazed?"

"Because this is it! This is the answer!" She gave Chloe a shove. "Go text her on the way and brief her."

"I can go," Kenzie said. "But you'll have to brief me."

"No time for that!" Tori gestured for Chloe to leave. "Give Kenzie your tables."

"But I'm not allowed to serve for three more days," Kenzie said. "The law—"

"We're breaking the law," Tori said. "And if the city council tries to get in our way, we'll break them, too."

"Tori!" Chloe barked a laugh. "What is—"

"Go! I'm going to talk to the Netflix people."

Chloe grabbed her phone and took off, watching Tori thread her way to the table with purpose and speed.

"You aren't leaving Amelia Island," Tori announced. "We have everything you need, all under the Wingate umbrella. Give me five minutes and let me introduce you to my sister."

Without waiting to hear more, Chloe tore out the front door, ran across the railroad tracks and hustled to Wingate Properties as she sent Raina a text to meet her outside ASAP.

As she hit Send, she slammed into something, or *someone*, letting out a shriek as her phone flipped out of her hands, into the air, and right into the street as a car about twenty feet away headed toward it.

"Oh my—"

"I got it!" A man—the one she'd just walked into—

leaped past her into the street, holding up one hand and fearlessly jumping in front of a car that careened to a stop with a furious honk. "Thank you, sorry, thank you!"

He bent over and snagged the phone, giving the driver one more wave, then popping back to the sidewalk to hand it to Chloe.

"Oh...wow." She shook her head, glancing at the phone, which miraculously hadn't broken. "That was... wow, thank you." She looked up at him, vaguely aware of light brown hair, green eyes, and shoulders. So much... shoulders. "It was also entirely my fault," she added, as she realized what happened. "I was—"

"Texting and walking. There should be a law against that." He smiled and his eyes crinkled and her heart did a little dance.

He was thirty-something in a navy blue T-shirt with a logo that she couldn't read, because that would mean taking her eyes off his face and she physically could not do that. Plus, hero bonus! He'd saved her phone!

"I'm sorry," she said. Sorry she was on a man hiatus.

"'Sokay. I got the phone."

"And risked your life." She added a smile and got a blinding one in return. "Thank you."

He shrugged as if phone-saving and heart-stopping were no big deal. "The car wasn't coming that fast. I'm Travis." He reached out his hand. "What's your name?"

He closed his hand over hers and she...forgot her name. Or at least her man hiatus. And she really forgot her urgent errand. Briefly. Dang it!

"I have to go!" she said quickly, not wanting to let Tori down. "I'm sorry, but I'm...I gotta go. Bye!"

But he wouldn't let her hand go. "Just tell me—tourist or local?"

"Local," she said.

Finally, he let go. "So there's hope I'll see you again."

She let out a sigh. "No hope. But I might see you again."

"No hope?"

"None." She laughed. "I'm on a break from all men."

He lifted one of those impressive shoulders again. "'Kay. Let me know when that break ends."

In her hand, her phone hummed, pulling her attention.

Tori: *Where are you two? Hurry, they're going to leave!*

"I have to go," she said. "Bye!"

She darted past him, tearing up to the Wingate Properties building, not daring to turn around and look to see if he was watching her. Because if he was, she and her hiatus were in trouble.

Chapter Six

Raina

C hloe's story about "the Netflix people" came in breathless bits and pieces but it was detailed enough for Raina to put two and two together and come up with...half a million.

With each piece of information Chloe handed her, Raina sped up, but when her youngest sister said a hundred thousand a setting, she almost forgot she was pregnant and ran full speed to the restaurant.

"Tori's a genius," she proclaimed as they bounded toward the café. She stopped at the front door and caught her breath. "And you're the best for going along and not asking too many questions."

"What's to ask? Tori smells an opportunity and she thinks you can get it."

Raina gave her little sister an impulsive kiss and focused on the job at hand. Sell the idea, sell the location, sell the Wingate family name. No one did that better than Raina. Well, except for Dad, who would approve of this wholeheartedly.

Based on what Chloe said, she'd have to persuade

these two Hollywood folks to stay, use Wingate-only locations, and give Wingates all the money. She just hoped it added up to what she needed. At least they'd be a lot closer than they were right now...and nothing had to be sold.

As she swung open the door, she nearly collided with her sister and the two people who looked like they wanted to leave, but Tori was chatting them up hard and keeping them in place.

"You're here!" Tori exclaimed when she saw Raina. "Thank goodness! This is Bridget Hawking, location scout, and Marcus Ferrari, the executive producer. Meet my sister, Raina Wingate, currently in charge of Wingate Properties, which would include all of the businesses and homes you could need."

Raina reached out her hand to the woman first. "Bridget? Nice to meet you. And Marcus, is it? Great. I know you're about to leave, but this sounds like an incredible opportunity and I would love to show you the locations."

"How?" Marcus asked.

"I'll walk you there right now."

"No, how can you get around the laws that say we can't shut down the main street?"

"Because this street?" She pointed out the door and toward the avenue that paralleled the water. "Is Wingate Way. Not Centre Street, true. Not quite as adorable or chock full of as many stores. But the Wingate family owns almost every building on it and we can bypass those laws and do whatever we want. Christmas in July? Let it snow!"

A slow smile pulled at Marcus's lips as he adjusted frameless glasses and regarded her with true interest. "Well, I have to admit that the town left an unpleasant taste in our mouths with all the rules and regs, and we've lined up another place—"

"And we'll work out a deal. A better deal than you can make with anyone else. Give me one hour."

He glanced at Bridget, who shrugged.

"All right," he said. "But before we talk numbers, you need to show me the following and they need to be perfect."

"Tell me," she said, smiling up at him, because when a client told her what he wanted, Raina delivered. Jack had called it her super power and she was about to flex.

"First, we do need a central headquarters that can be our 'office' during late afternoons and evenings."

Tori stepped in. "You can have the Riverfront Café for that. We close at two-thirty. After that, the place is yours and we'll cook for your cast and crew."

Marcus and Bridget exchanged a look, visibly impressed, and Raina reached down and squeezed her sister's hand, so incredibly grateful for the love and support.

"What else?" Raina asked. "Chloe said you mentioned a Victorian mansion?"

"One of those really pretty houses with the turrets and the curved windows and the wraparound porch," Bridget said. "It will be the main character's house."

"Have you seen the blue and white one at the other

end of Wingate Way? Three stories with a swing under a massive tree —"

"I love that one!" Bridget exclaimed. "But it's an inn. I'm sure they can't boot out people who have reservations."

"I'm sure they can," Raina said. "'Cause *they* is *we*... it's Wingate House."

Bridget blinked and Marcus looked even more interested.

"Please tell me you have a nice bakery in your portfolio," he said. "Since that's where we need to film the first scene, our meet cute."

"No bakery, but would a bookstore work? Or a florist? Maybe a dress shop, or—"

"Yes to all," Marcus said, gesturing to the door. "Lead the way, and don't make a promise you can't keep. That's all I ask."

Tori beamed at them. "I'll be waiting here for you when you're done and we can work out how we'll turn this place into a mini movie studio."

Raina leaned in to give her a hug. "You're a queen, Tori. Text Rose, Grace, and Madeline to let them know what's going on. Tell them they *cannot* say no."

"Done and done, sister," Tori whispered. "Go make it rain."

With that, Raina took off with Marcus on one side and Bridget on the other, sliding into her extremely happy place of showing property and making a sale. And no sale ever felt as important as this—the answer to her missing money prayers.

"I have to say," Marcus mused as they walked. "You and your sister are by far the most enthusiastic people we've met since we've been in this town. No one else seemed quite as excited to turn their business into Christmas for the summer."

No one else needed the money so desperately, she thought.

"We're an entrepreneurial family. My father, grandfather, and great-grandfather were all part of making Fernandina Beach what it is today. Everywhere you see this?" She paused at the gate outside of the café and pointed to the wrought-iron with a gold-toned W in the middle. "You'll find a building owned by Wingate Properties, and quite often that means a business run by someone in my family."

"Oh, thank heavens," Bridget exclaimed, dropping her head back. "This is what we needed, Marcus. Someone with power, access, and brains."

Marcus gave a dubious tip of his head. "And good family connections, it seems."

Raina smiled. "Coming from a man named Ferrari, you must understand. Any relation to the car company?"

He laughed, giving his head a shake. "But I do appreciate the power of family, since most of mine is in some aspect of show business."

"Well, I think you're about to appreciate the power of *my* family, and you'll be impressed."

"Have you lived here your whole life, Raina?" Bridget asked.

"Actually, I live in Miami now," she said. "But I've

been staying up here for a while and running the family business."

"Would you be our point of contact for everything?" Marcus asked. "I don't want to deal with sixteen different opinionated shop owners. Just one person to liaise for me. Would you do that?"

"Absolutely," she said confidently.

"Oh, look at that place," Bridget cooed, looking at the Wingate Properties building, pulling the others toward the brick and stone edifice and the glorious mahogany and glass doors. "Now that screams small town with a deep history.'"

"Because it is," Raina told them. "That is a hundred-year-old bank building designed and constructed by my great-grandfather. You're more than welcome to add it to your list of locations. Come on, I'll show you inside."

She gave them a quick tour, and immediately they buzzed with excitement about "filming the montage on the steps" and "a perfect setting for the dark moment." She didn't quite understand the movie talk, but she understood...*one hundred thousand per setting*.

They only needed five.

Outside again, Bridget stopped as they crossed a side street and looked up at the brick storefront and the hand-painted sign on the door. "The Next Chapter!" she exclaimed. "What an adorable name for a bookstore."

"Which happens to be owned by my sister, Grace," Raina said, looking at the brick home that had, for as long as Raina knew, been retail on the first floor with private living quarters above.

"I'm in love with that turret-like thing." Bridget stared up at the rounded second-floor balcony trimmed in white.

"The view from there is lovely, too. It's my sister's apartment. Would you like to talk to her?" Raina asked.

"Yes, but let me get some outside shots." Bridget madly snapped pictures of the bookstore, the street, and the beautiful display window, featuring a beach umbrella and chair with brightly colored books pouring out of a canvas bag.

"If the owner is willing to decorate for Christmas in July, this *is* perfect for the meet cute," Marcus said, peering inside.

"Then let's go in and meet cute my sister." Raina opened the door and gestured them in before her.

Grace was ready and waiting behind the long sales counter, with a warm smile that reached her golden eyes, her long brown hair pulled back for her workday. Raina hadn't seen her for a few days and she seemed happier than she'd looked in a while.

"Hello." She came around the counter and welcomed them into the sunny store. "Welcome to The Next Chapter."

Raina made the introductions and immediately Bridget went off to snap pictures of the homey bookstore. Behind the front window, there was a fireplace with wingback chairs that customers loved, and the entire back wall was built-in shelves with exposed brick between them. The brightly colored children's book section had a play area and sofas to encourage reading with parents.

"How do you feel about Christmas?" Marcus asked Grace.

"Well, we love Christmas on Amelia Island," she said. "You should see this place when half the town dresses as characters from Charles Dickens' *A Christmas Carol*."

"I want to see it...in June and July. Maybe not the costumes," he added. "But you'd need to be willing to let us deck these walls and close this shop for a few weeks, up to a month. We'll compensate for lost business."

She glanced at Raina, who shot her a secret look that any of the seven sisters could read. It said: Go along with everything and it would be explained later.

"Of course," Grace exclaimed, turning to the fireplace. "Hang the stockings and put the tree right there. I always do."

He gave a satisfied nod and stepped away, following Bridget.

"What exactly is going on, Raina?" Grace asked under her breath. "Tori only said 'cooperate or else.'"

Of course she did, Raina thought with a burst of affection.

"Wingate Properties stands to not only gain a ton from this, but this will address a fat cash flow problem that...that really has Dad upset. I think it might have been what brought on the stroke."

"Seriously? Of course I'll help."

"It might mean a soft summer for you, but you know the landlord." Raina put an arm around her. "We'll waive rent and take care of you. But this could be an answered prayer, so—"

"Count me in," Grace said quickly. "Anything for Dad."

"Let's all get together tonight and I'll fill you in."

"At the beach house?"

"Let's meet at the café. Suze has enough going on and Dad goes to sleep so early."

Grace agreed and then gave Marcus and Bridget a full tour, including her spacious upstairs apartment, leaving them gushing about the balcony and the sweet baby grand in her living room.

After that, Raina took them to Coming Up Roses, the one "pink" house on the street that Rose had completely transformed into a charming, fragrant, colorful florist shop. There, Raina introduced them to her twin sister and Rose's husband, Gabe.

When they learned he was a local firefighter, Bridget actually gasped.

"Please, please tell me we could film at the fire station," she said, pressing her hands together in a plea. "We'll limit it to one day, but it is the site of our big Santa scene and we don't want to build a set."

Gabe smiled. "Assuming you'll give away a few cameos to the team and be willing to wait through any calls, I think I could convince the chief to do that."

From the look on Marcus's face, Raina sensed that might have sealed the deal.

Still, they continued the tour at Madeline's dress-making showroom, blown away by the gorgeous light in the upstairs studio. They sat by the fountain outside taking pictures, like many brides did, taking advantage of the sun on the white studio and the array of gowns in the first-floor window.

Lastly, they were flat-out floored by Wingate House, where they stood outside for ten minutes, staring at the Victorian architecture and pronouncing it a dream location.

Until Doreen Parrish opened the door and scowled at them. Then Raina realized Tori hadn't briefed their ornery inn manager. Isaiah Kincaid, who now worked there, sometimes met guests now, but Raina remembered that he'd gone out of town for a while.

"Oh, just a second," Raina said to Marcus while Bridget took more pictures. "I want to chat with our inn manager and see if it's a good time to tour the inn."

She darted up the stairs to the wraparound porch, taking a breath and praying *Dor-mean* was in a good mood. Well, a less-than-awful mood.

"Hello there, Doreen," she said, blocking her view of the two guests and gesturing for her to go back through the vestibule entryway. "Can I talk to you for a moment?"

"I don't have vacancies this week," she said sharply. "I hate when you Wingates throw a last-minute problem at me and—"

"Doreen, I don't have a last-minute problem. I have a tremendous, exciting, and once-in-a-lifetime opportunity."

Doreen sniffed, but stepped into the entryway, crossing her arms over her bony chest and looking up at

Raina with eyes that seemed more creased and sad than the last time they'd talked. She had to remember that Doreen led a fairly lonely existence and had worked one job—running this inn—since she was a young woman.

Raina needed her buy-in to the project. Yes, technically the woman worked for the Wingate family, but she'd been around fifty or more years and most of the time she called the shots at Wingate House.

"What is it?" Doreen asked.

With all the enthusiasm she could muster, Raina explained what the producers wanted. With each sentence, she could practically see Doreen digging in her heels.

By the time Raina finished, Doreen looked like she didn't know whether to laugh or cry.

"What are you suggesting?" she asked with a scoffing cough. "That I throw out our guests to make *a movie?* Are you kidding me, Raina?"

"The guests could be told that the inn would be decorated for Christmas and we could comp their stay if that's a problem. We could offer another week later in the year for a discount, or they could be offered roles as extras in the movie. Or we could cancel them and take the hit, because this company is paying us *way* more than ten rooms would make in that time frame."

"I won't allow it," she said simply. "I won't participate and I won't assist you."

"Doreen, please. You are the employee," she said gently. "And I want this."

"Does your father want it? Because I work for him."

He would when he found out she was doing this to "make it rain" and save him. But Dad had no patience for this woman, and preferred to keep his dealings with Doreen to a minimum. They all did, to be honest. But she was a fact of their lives.

"I represent my father while he is recovering, and we are going to do this." Raina tempered the order with a smile. "And you, too, can have a part in the movie."

"As if I care." She shuttered her eyes with resignation. "Fine, but you can't come in now. I have guests in the living room and library, and they're preparing for a bridal shower in an hour. Come back another time."

"Okay," she said, nodding in understanding. "That's fine. But we will be back. How's tomorrow?"

"Not good."

"Doreen."

She huffed a breath. "Fine."

Raina turned to look through the front door to see Bridget and Marcus deep in conversation, both of them nodding as they talked and listened, pointing to the house.

"I'll give you more notice next time, I promise," she told Doreen. "And thank you."

With that, Raina walked back to the two people out front. "There's a guest event scheduled in the next hour," she said. "We can't go in until tomorrow."

"Oh." Marcus sighed, looking unhappy for the first time since they started the tour. "This will be the main setting in the movie. I have to see the inside."

"Tomorrow, I promise." And sometime between now

and then, she'd get Doreen's full cooperation. "So do you want to go back to the café and pound out a deal?"

Bridget and Marcus looked at each other, a mix of uncertainty and hope in their expressions.

"We're still in negotiations with another location," Marcus said. "Once we talk to them and see the inside of this inn? We'll make a decision."

Bridget was flipping through her phone. "I don't need to see the inside," she said. "This is the website, and if it photographs this well, then it will film gorgeously."

Marcus considered that. "Okay, let's talk numbers, then I'll weigh what you're willing to do against the St. Simons location and let you know."

After a lifetime of selling real estate, Raina had heard this a hundred times, so she knew that once they left, there was a very good chance they'd find something easier or better or cheaper at another location. The best close was a real close, not a "maybe after we look at more property" close.

And the way to do that was money.

"I can set the price for every one of these locations," she said. "And I can get you a 'Wingate' special that will save you a lot of money, and I do mean a lot."

Marcus raised a brow in interest. "How much?"

"Five hundred thousand will get you every single location you need, no limit," she said. "We own seven properties and control the entire street. You can have full access to any Wingate business and can redecorate every inch of the street if you like, and bring in snow."

Marcus and Bridget shared a look, but said nothing. Raina moved in for the close.

"The café will be available as a central meeting place, open exclusively for you from afternoon to midnight, and we'll cook for the cast and crew for nothing but the cost of the food. We'll throw in the firefighters for at least one day of shooting at the station and I will personally manage any issues with the city, any business, or any local individual."

Marcus stared hard at her. "You really want this, don't you?"

"Very much."

He narrowed his eyes. "I want no issues, is that clear?"

"I can't guarantee there won't be an issue," Raina said with the same tone she'd use with a buyer before a final inspection. "But I can guarantee you that whatever arises, I will fix. No matter what it is, as long as you exclusively use Wingate properties on Wingate Way. It will be easy and convenient and less expensive, because you have carte blanche use of any location anywhere on the street in addition to the entire street for outdoor shots."

He looked hard at her, and she could tell he was teetering on the edge of a big decision, then nodded. "Okay, then. Let's sign a deal."

"Yes!" She almost threw her arms around both of them, but thought better of it and settled for a high-five with each. "Excellent decision!"

Hallelujah, she'd made it rain.

Chapter Seven

Tori

At night, the café had a whole different vibe that Tori absolutely loved. Outside, instead of sunshine on the river, all she could see was the soft lights of the wharf shining on an array of boats bobbing in their slips.

Without the noise of a full house echoing up to the vaulted ceiling, the restaurant felt hushed and homey, especially with her sisters around two tables they'd pulled together in the back.

While Tori served them wine, cheese, and some pastries, Raina filled them all in on the entire project—without detailing why they needed the money, just that business was tight while Dad was out and this would really make him happy.

That was enough for the Wingate women.

"Cheers to making movies on Amelia Island," Tori said as she sat down between Raina and Chloe, lifting her glass.

"To all of you who are helping so much," Raina

added to the toast, leaning into Tori. "And to you for the genius idea."

Tori pointed to her. "But you made it happen."

"We all did," Raina said, never one to bask in her own glory. "Madeline, Rose, and Grace not only made the production team feel welcome and comfortable, they are about to turn their lives—and livelihoods—upside down for the better part of the summer."

Rose flicked her hand. "So they fill the front of the store with poinsettias. I can still stock, store, and sell floral arrangements from the back. Plus, I love Christmas decorations. They put me in a good mood no matter what the calendar says."

Raina beamed at her. "You were born in a good mood, Rosebud, and that will never change."

"I can schedule fittings around the production issues," Madeline assured them. "And Bridget said there's a wedding scene in the movie and they'll use a Madeline Wingate dress. Win for me."

"And Nikki Lou will love having a Christmas tree in the store in the middle of July," Grace said. "Might not love the strangers traipsing around, but we'll make the best of it."

They all nodded, understanding their little niece's profoundly shy personality.

"Well, you all are wonderful," Raina said, turning to Chloe. "Starting with you sniffing out the story like the good reporter you are."

Chloe smiled. "It was fun. Especially the part where

I ran into a cute guy—literally, like a head-on collision—who then risked his life to save my phone."

"What?" Tori asked, inching back. "When did that happen?"

"When I broke records to run up Wingate Way and get Raina." She held up her hand to stave off questions before they came. "Don't even think about it, my dear sisters. I'm fresh out of a front-of-church breakup, figuring out what I want to do with the rest of my life, and officially on a man hiatus. No one, not even some hottie named Travis, could change—"

"Travis McCall?" Rose sat up straight.

"I didn't get his last name. Why?"

"That's Gabe's probie at the fire station. Very cute and very single."

"As am I." Chloe narrowed her eyes at Rose. "And I intend to stay that way. Not to mention that I already cost Dad way too much with the wedding-that-wasn't, so whatever you need, Raina, count me in."

"Thank you, hon." Raina put a hand on the youngest Wingate's arm. "Dad's so happy you didn't make a mistake and that you've come back here. We all are."

"Especially me," Tori said.

"Please." Chloe choked out a laugh. "We all know I'm not doing this place any real service as a waitress, but I'm happy to work nights and get the movie people anything and everything. Make me the night manager if we get the deal."

"Don't say if," Raina warned her. "They said yes and

all we need to do is ink a contract. Pray there are not weird clauses."

As they toasted and praised each other, Madeline's dark gaze was intent on Raina. "You seem different, Rain."

Tori felt Raina's body stiffen as she lifted her glass— which only Tori knew held apple juice, not chardonnay— to her lips.

"Just relieved," she said. "This is going to be a great windfall for Wingate Properties and I think it'll go a long way to giving Dad the boost he needs."

"Could the deal still go south?" Madeline asked, brushing back the thick dark bangs she'd worn forever like a signature style.

"Well, sadly, things do happen between verbal and final, but they seemed very happy and positive. We don't get all the money up front, though. It will come in installments, after certain locations are used. There's a clause that says they can back out for some really flimsy reasons, but I know how to get around a contingency. Oh, they also haven't seen the inside of Wingate House yet, because Dor-mean was in rare form. They have to like that, but they loved the pictures online."

"But not her," Chloe quipped. "'Cause...who does?"

"Isaiah Kincaid does," Grace said softly, and they all turned to the quietest sister, whose cheeks deepened with the attention.

"Have you told them yet, Grace?" Rose asked.

"Told us what?" at least three asked in unison.

A slow smile lifted Grace's lips along with a soft flush

of color. Like her daughter, Grace was more than a little shy, never hungry for attention. And when she got too much of it, it usually made her uncomfortable.

But that wasn't an expression of discomfort on her face as she slowly lifted a chain around her neck and slid it out from under her high-collared blouse, her golden-brown eyes misty.

"Isaiah knew Nick and somehow, through the grace of God, was holding his wedding ring the day Nick died. He returned it to me."

For a moment, no one said a word. They sat in stunned silence, the only sound a few soft gasps of disbelief before the explosion of emotion and joy erupted. Then Grace looked uncomfortable, laughing as she hugged Madeline and Chloe, who were sitting on either side of her.

"Talk about burying the lede, as they say in the news biz," Chloe exclaimed. "Grace! That's...I can't believe it."

"I couldn't either," Grace told them, holding the ring between her fingers like it was nothing less than the Hope Diamond. "It's like he gave me back a piece of my heart."

"That's why he wanted to take you for coffee!" Raina said.

"You know about that?"

"Susannah told me, and that you thought he was all kinds of wrong for hitting on a woman wearing a wedding ring."

Grace's delicate features fell. "I feel terrible about that. I was downright rude to him."

"Well, now that you know, I'm sure you've apologized," Madeline said.

She shook her head. "I never got a chance. Because I was so dismissive, he ended up getting a bouquet of flowers from Rose and putting the ring, and an explanation, with them."

That caused another flutter of oohing and awwing around the table.

"He told me in the letter that he'd seen Nick the morning he went out on patrol, and he'd forgotten to take off his ring..." Her voice cracked as she squeezed the ring. "I'm so grateful to him."

"He's such a nice guy," Raina said. "And now I understand why he's here." Then her eyes widened. "Do you think he's going to leave now? Because I'd love him to stay and run interference between the production company and Doreen."

"He should," Madeline added. "Suze told me he's working out well with her and that Doreen actually likes him."

"Holy cow, who is this guy?" Tori asked on a laugh. "Has he cast a spell? Sprinkled fairy dust? Did you say Dor-mean *likes* him?"

Grace smiled at that. "I haven't talked to him since the flowers, because he's out of town for a few days. But he's back tomorrow, I think, so I'll stop by Wingate House. I want to thank him properly and maybe I could ask him to work his magic with Doreen."

"That would be amazing," Raina said. "Can you fill him in on everything?"

"I'd love to," Grace said, a smile pulling with a spark in her eyes Tori rarely saw. "I owe him a proper thank you and an apology."

Tori put a light hand on Raina's arm. "So what else do you need? I've got Chloe for the night manager, Grace is going to talk to Isaiah to get Doreen on board."

"Well, I guess we'd better get the official approval from Dad and Suze," Raina said. "They won't have to do anything special, but I'm really hoping it lifts Dad's spirits."

"Which are low," Madeline said glumly. "I spent a little time with him yesterday and he seems so down in the dumps."

While they all agreed and discussed that, Tori's phone vibrated with a text from Justin. Chloe looked over her shoulder at the screen.

"Hottypants alert," Chloe teased.

"I'm not on any man hiatus, so cool your jets, little sister." Tori picked up the phone, angling it from prying eyes and reading the text with a smile. "Oh, he wants to know if I want to come over for a nightcap."

"AKA booty call!" Chloe reached her hand up and Raina high-fived her.

"Not a chance!" Tori denied hotly. "We've kissed and that's it."

"You should go," Raina said over their laughter. "Life's short and he's cute and we'll close this place for you."

"Thanks," Tori said. "You think Kenzie will mind if I come home later tonight?"

"She's at my place watching Nikki Lou," Grace said.

"And she just texted to ask me if they could go to Rose's and take Lady Bug for a walk," Chloe added.

Madeline stood, making them all look up.

"Are you leaving?" Tori asked.

"Do you have a booty call, too?" Chloe quipped.

Madeline snorted at the very idea. "I have an early fitting and want to finish the hem tonight. But I want to say..." She sighed a little, her eyes misting as she looked from one to the other. "It sure is nice having Tori, Raina, and Chloe here. Now all we have to do is lure Sadie away from her glam European life and we could be the Seven Sisters of Amelia Island again."

For a moment, they all looked up at her, their de facto leader and beloved oldest sister.

"I don't know how long this interlude will last," she added with a smile. "But I love this season and each one of you more than I can say."

It was enough to get them all on their feet for group hugs and kisses. As Madeline inched back from them and the group quieted, she looked hard at Raina.

"I have to ask the question that no one seems to want to ask."

Was Tori the only one who noticed Raina pale a bit at Madeline's question?

"What's that?" Raina asked.

"Are you sure you can do this? Be point person for something this big when you...you're..."

"I'm what?" Raina asked in a reed-thin voice.

"Well, honey, you're in the middle of a very difficult situation."

And did anyone else notice Raina unconsciously slide her hand to her stomach? *Come on, Rain! Tell your sisters!*

Tori bit her lip to keep the exclamation from coming out, because this was *the* perfect time to share her pregnancy.

"I'm fine," Raina said. "I'm just...happy for the distraction."

Madeline—all of them, really—looked dubious about that.

"And, yes," Raina added. "I can handle this and whatever gets thrown at me. You know why?" She draped her arms around Tori and Grace, pulling them closer. "I have you guys."

It took a few more minutes of hugs, kisses, and sisterly affection, but then Raina ushered Tori to the door.

"Thanks for the cover," Raina whispered when they were away from the others.

"What are you waiting for?" Tori demanded under her breath.

"Twelve weeks, a healthy heartbeat, and the conversation with Jack," Raina reminded her. "Now go forth and enjoy Hottypants with the knowledge that we are all talking about you while you're gone."

She laughed at that, then hugged Raina and slipped out the door toward the wharf.

TORI HAD ALREADY BEGUN ASSOCIATING the sound of waves lapping against boat hulls and the soft clang of metal against a mast with the sheer pleasure of folding herself into Justin Verona's strong arms.

They'd only been "dating"—was that what she should call this?—for a few weeks, but being with him was a roller coaster of comfort, thrills, laughter, and discovery.

And Tori couldn't get enough.

As she approached Slip 7, she spied him leaning against the rail of his forty-foot "staysail ketch," as she now knew his live-aboard sailboat was called.

In their long conversations, many of them right here on the boat, he shared that his divorce—after his wife left him for a woman—had been difficult but amicable. It left him uncertain about the future, so when he moved from Pittsburgh to accept a position with a neurology group on Amelia Island, he didn't even want to rent or buy a house.

He chose to live on a boat he'd yet to name, looking out over the wide Amelia River to the west for breathtaking sunsets, or toward the town of Fernandina Beach for rosy sunrises.

She loved the boat, but it was a constant reminder that he was temporary and so was she. As much as she enjoyed every minute with him, this relationship was the quintessential summer fling—and when it was over, it would be completely over.

"Ahoy there, matey," he called as she got closer.

That made her laugh—or maybe it was the sound of his voice that made her happy—but she was still smiling when she reached the slip.

"Hey, Captain."

He reached out for her hand and guided her onto the deck, easing closer. "That's Captain Hottypants to you, Vicky."

She gave a hearty laugh that he quieted with a kiss.

"Our two most hated nicknames," she joked, wrapping her arms around his waist.

"I don't hate mine." He looked down at her and brushed a strand of hair from her face. "But I know how you feel about 'Vicky.'"

"Not my choice, but when you say it?" She gave an easy shrug. "You make it sound good."

He guided her to the small seating area behind the cockpit covered in pillows.

"Would you like some wine? Something to eat?" he asked. "Anything at all?"

"Water for me. I had some drinks and food with my sisters."

"You left a bunch of Wingate women for me? I'm honored."

"You wouldn't be if you heard the teasing I took."

He handed her a bottle of water and settled closer. "What else did you and your sisters talk about?" he asked.

"Mostly the movie stuff." She'd already texted him the news, but filled him in on the details while the boat rocked gently on the water.

He listened, occasionally peppering her with questions.

Justin was a great listener, maybe from being a doctor and having to pay attention when people described their symptoms. He maintained eye contact—which could be disconcerting, since his eyes were that dreamy dark blue that now reminded her of moonlight on the water—and held her hand, thumbing her knuckles while she talked.

In fact, she was so lulled by the air and the man that she slipped and mentioned the missing money, making him sit up a little and frown.

"Excuse me?"

"Oh, I shouldn't have—"

"Yes, speaking as his neurologist, you should have." He thought for a minute, then nodded. "I suspected there was a catalyst with Rex's stroke," he finally said.

"You think money stress caused it?"

"Not a one-for-one causation, but it played a role. Can you give me a short version with no confidential details?"

She nodded and briefly described what Raina had discovered, and her father's reaction.

"Bottom line," she finished, "he won't say what happened to this money, but wants Raina to recoup the loss."

"Is it a lot?"

She grimaced. "Half a million."

He whistled noisily, looking suitably surprised at the amount which, she had to admit, would stress anyone out.

"According to Raina, it didn't get withdrawn from the account until after the stroke," she added. "He doesn't seem to be fazed by that, which is weird, because he certainly didn't do it. Still, he won't say who did or why."

"But maybe he knew what was happening, with a bad investment or loan. Whatever it was, that's enough anxiety to initiate the kind of incident he had. Not," he added quickly, putting his hand over her hers, "that I'm reducing your father's ischemic stroke to an 'incident.'"

"Oh, I know."

"Nor, like I said, can we place blame on this specific financial situation."

"Can't it be something built up over time?" she asked.

"Absolutely," he agreed. "With the exception of his weakness for cigars, your father's health is top-notch, even at seventy-five.'"

"Was," she corrected. "He's certainly not top-notch now."

"He will be again," he assured her. "It just takes time and no more stress."

She eyed him, remembering the discussion at the café. "Do you think we should try to keep all this Christmas movie stuff from him?"

"Why would you?"

"I don't know. Stress reduction and avoidance? He might worry about our businesses suffering because of him, or what if it falls through?"

He took a pull on his water bottle, shaking his head. "It's an extremely positive thing, Tori, that you're doing for him. If you want my professional opinion? Involve him. Bring him into the whole thing."

"Really?" She sat up. "Don't you think that's too much for him?"

"Nothing is really too much for him now, except a huge shock. The fact that his girls are pulling together, opening up their businesses, and saving him from the consequences of a mistake—no matter what caused it—is not *stress*. In fact, it's the opposite."

"Are you sure?"

He nodded. "Very much, especially now, and I'll tell you why, since I had an appointment with your father this morning."

She wasn't sure she liked the ominous tone of his voice. "And?"

"The gift you're giving him is a reason for living. That, in my professional opinion, is far more important for his long-term health."

"Do you think he needs a reason for living?" she asked, hearing the fear in her voice. "I mean, he has seven daughters, six grandchildren, a beautiful, loving wife, and a thriving business."

Justin angled his head as though he saw things differently. "He also can't walk without assistance or a walker and is struggling with half his body not functioning properly. His brain is frequently foggy, even if he denies it, and he isn't able to go into his office, close deals, take a stroll down the beach with one of those grandchildren, or —excuse me for getting graphic—make love to his beautiful wife."

She stared at him and he tempered the words by taking her hand.

"My point, as his doctor, is this: He's already under low-grade stress. During the window of danger, I didn't want his blood pressure or cortisol levels—and a whole host of other brain chemicals and hormones—to spike. Now, the site of the stroke is healed, but he's facing another medical challenge and that, I'm sorry to say, is the very most common side-effect of a stroke in a geriatric person."

"Depression?" she guessed, and nodded before he answered. "We danced around that tonight, using words like 'down in the dumps' and 'not himself.' Justin, do you think he's suffering from depression?"

"I think it is a far greater threat right now than another stroke. He's distant and removed. Susannah did all the talking today, and he only answered my direct questions and seemed a little lost."

Tori's heart cracked at his words. "I know. He's miserable that he can't walk like he used to or think with his tremendous brain. He's frustrated by his progress, which, however good, isn't good enough for a man like him."

"You don't want him withdrawing from life," he said. "So, I'd use this movie to get him excited and involved. That's every bit as important as the money."

Tori eyed him, exhaling softly. "You're right. Any idea how we can do that? I mean, he's not exactly able to stroll down Wingate Way for the cameras. And Susannah would be your next patient if I suggested using the beach house for a movie location."

He chuckled at that, taking a sip of wine as he considered her question. Then a slow smile pulled, which made him even more attractive, if she could believe that. "Why don't you let him do what he does best right now?"

"All he does well right now is sit," she said glumly.

"Exactly." He grinned. "Just like a certain man with a big white beard and jolly laugh does."

Her jaw loosened as she looked at him. "That is brilliant! What's a Christmas movie without Santa?"

He smiled and snuggled closer. "You're welcome."

She looked around, reaching for her purse. "I have to send a group text to—"

He put his hand over hers as she withdrew her phone. "They can wait."

She laughed and dropped the phone, taking his hand in hers. "You're right, Dr. Hottypants. You need to be properly thanked for that incredible idea." She smiled slyly. "You want a part in the movie?"

He snorted. "Nope."

"A free lunch at the Riverfront Café?"

"Nope."

"Well, then...what could I possibly give you?" She chuckled as she leaned into him and kissed him lightly.

"Yep."

As they cuddled and kissed in the moonlight, Tori tried to remind herself that this was a summer fling and nothing more. Except sometimes, when he sighed against her lips or whispered her name, it felt like a whole lot more.

Chapter Eight

Grace

Grace awakened a little unsettled but excited to see Isaiah Kincaid. She couldn't wait to thank him for the ring and find out every detail of his last conversation with Nick, so none of that should make her nervous. Was it asking him about the movie and Doreen?

No, but Grace was used to feeling tension when she had to do anything out of her ordinary routine.

In some ways, she was just as shy as her little girl, who, right this minute, was squeezing the life out of Grace's hand as they walked toward her preschool classroom.

Please let this be an easy day, Grace thought. No meltdown, no tears, no heartbreaking goodbyes, no rolling into a ball to hide from the world.

She didn't want to spend the hour she'd carved out for Isaiah here at the preschool calming down a miserable Nikki Lou.

"Oh, I see Miss Betsy," Grace said brightly as they came around the corner and looked through the double doors that opened to a play area. "I know you love her."

Nikki held back, her eyes widening. "Stay, Mommy."

Oh, boy, here we go.

"Nikki Lou!" Miss Betsy hustled over with open arms. "There's my number one girl."

Instantly, Nikki spun around and jammed her little face into Grace's legs.

"Honey, it's your favorite teacher," Grace reminded her.

But her little girl looked up with giant eyes that screamed shyness. Yes, speaking as an introvert herself, Grace totally got it.

But she wanted Nikki Lou to have a better social life than she had. She hoped her little girl could conquer her fear of people—not strangers, but *all* people—which was the reason she'd made sure to enroll her in a short summer preschool program for two- and three-year-olds.

It wasn't school, per se, more of a "play-care" situation, but Grace hoped it would help eliminate some of Nikki's troubles before she started in a "big girl" classroom for Pre-K.

"Why don't you tell Miss Betsy what you did last night, honey?" Grace crouched down, knowing her daughter hated being loomed over.

Nikki's eyes grew wide at the idea of talking. Even to her teacher.

"What did you do, sweet Nikki Lou?" Miss Betsy asked, then gave a soft hoot. "Well, I do believe I'm speaking in poems today."

Grace laughed lightly, but Nikki cowered.

"She had a fun night with her cousin, Kenzie, who

babysat her for a few hours. And she walked her Aunt Chloe's dog."

"A dog!" Miss Betsy leaned over, hands on her thighs. "What is the doggie's name, Nikki?"

"Tell her, honey."

Nikki Lou shook her head and popped out her lower lip.

"Is it...Fido? Rover?" Miss Betsy guessed. "Scooby-Doo? Then you could be Scooby-Doo and Nikki Lou!"

Grace sucked in a breath, because she could see it all happening in slow motion. The lip quivered. The eyes filled. The face paled. And Nikki folded to the ground, pressed her head in her hands, and started to silently sob.

No matter how many times she'd seen this, it tore Grace's poor heart to shreds.

"Oh, dear," Miss Betsy said in her high-pitched, preschool teacher voice. "I guess I'm a scary poet today."

"Come on, Nik." Grace put her arm around her, but that made her roll up into a tighter ball. "I see your friend Hannah over there. Do you want to say hi?"

Nikki shook her head and buried her face in her hands again, believing, like any three-year-old might, that if she couldn't see them, they couldn't see her.

"She'll be fine, Grace," Miss Betsy assured her, reaching to guide Grace to her feet.

But would she? Why did Nikki Lou fall back into this behavior, even in a classroom she'd been coming to for a few weeks?

"Let her go," the teacher said in a calm, steady voice.

"And you should leave rather than try to pull her out of it. She'll have a moment, but—"

"No, no." Grace shook her head and looked down at little Nikki on the floor. "I can't let her have anxiety."

The other woman exhaled slowly and her whole expression changed. "Grace." She ushered her a few steps away, no doubt about to deliver the "you have to let her go" speech Grace had heard a dozen times.

"Have you considered having her tested?" Miss Betsy asked in a whisper.

Grace blinked at her, not expecting that question. "For...shyness?"

"For autism."

There it was. *There it was.* The fear, the word, the dark thing she didn't want to face.

"She's not autistic," she said, repeating the words she'd said in her head more than a few times.

"The neurodivergent spectrum is wide," Miss Betsy said. "But the sooner you know that she's suffering from a learning disability, the sooner we can make accommodations—"

"No," Grace said, hating this conversation. "She's not autistic or neuro...anything. She knows her alphabet and can write her name, and have you heard her make up stories with her dolls? She's just deeply introverted."

Betsy lifted a shoulder, unconvinced. "I can give you the name of—"

"Mommy!"

Grace looked down, surprised to see Nikki Lou next to her, looking up through a tear-streaked face.

"Yes, honey?" She bent down, wiping her cheek. "Are you better now?"

"I want to go home."

"Oh, but—"

"But it's a school day," Miss Betsy interjected. "And we are going to make paper flowers today! You can't leave."

Nikki Lou's lip quaked. "I'm sick," she whined softly.

"What hurts you, Nik—"

"You'll feel better after morning circle time," Miss Betsy said, reaching for her hand. "Let me take you—"

"Mommy!" She whipped away and started to crumble again. "No!"

Grace stood, frozen, knowing that what she should do was have the same bright strength as the teacher, give Nikki Lou a kiss on the head, and walk out.

Her mother had done that once, when Grace was in kindergarten. And to this day, Grace could remember the hole in her heart when her mother had left. Abandonment. It was awful at any age.

And did she really *have* to leave Nikki Lou here? She played all day in the children's book section while Grace worked and the only other thing she had to do today was...see Isaiah.

She could bring Nikki Lou with her. What a joy for him to see the baby Nick had told him Grace was carrying.

"I'm going to take her home today," she said, bracing for a fight from Miss Betsy.

The other woman, deep into her fifties and probably

highly experienced with wishy- washy moms of preschoolers, just smiled and nodded.

"I understand, Grace," she said softly. "And we will see you..." She bopped Nikki's nose. "In a day or two."

Nikki put her head down and turned to the safety of Grace's legs.

"Thank you," Grace said. "I appreciate your genuine caring."

"She's a great little girl," the other woman replied. "Do let me know if you want the name for testing."

Grace gave her a tight smile, swallowing the lump in her throat. She did not want the name, but she did want help.

She simply had no idea where that would come from.

Nikki Lou practically skipped up Wingate Way after they left the preschool, tears dried, joy back in place, cobblestones and butterflies doing their job to fascinate her.

"You've bounced back pretty nicely," Grace mused, clinging to her daughter's tiny hand as she looked to the other end of the street, eyeing the inn and hoping Isaiah wasn't too busy with breakfast to chat with her.

Nikki Lou didn't answer, so Grace slowed her step, the teacher's warning echoing in her head.

"Why were you so scared in the classroom, Nik?" she asked.

Again, no answer, all her attention on a crack in the ground.

"Is it because you don't want to me to leave or you feel...awkward?" She had no idea how to delve into this child's young mind. "Why did you cry?"

"'Cause I love you, Mommy."

"I love you, too, but we can be apart sometimes. You have fun in preschool."

"I love you more than school."

Normally, that would touch Grace, but now it worried her. Shouldn't Nikki Lou want to go play with friends? Was she too sheltered by an overprotective helicopter single parent?

She puffed out a breath of frustration. What should she do with Miss Betsy's suggestion?

Grace was truly the only person who knew this little girl had a perfect mind, a dear heart, and a sweet soul. All that was hidden to the world who thought she...should be tested.

They walked for a few blocks, passing Wingate Properties and Coming Up Roses, then glancing up at the latest bridal creations in Madeline's shop window.

"Are you scared that I'm going to leave and not come back?" Grace ventured after a moment.

"No," she said, so softly that Grace had to bend over to hear the word.

"Of Miss Betsy?" Grace asked. "'Cause she seems harmless to me."

Nikki Lou shook her head. "Where we going, Mommy?"

"To Wingate House to see..." How would she describe Isaiah? And, good heavens, would *he* scare Nikki? He was a big man with a booming voice and a bald head. "A man who has been very nice to me," she finished. "He works there."

"'Kay. Will Miss Doreen give me a lollipop?"

"Maybe." She looked down, suddenly curious. "You like Miss Doreen, don't you?"

Nikki nodded, and Grace had to fight a smile. Funny —the only person in Nikki's whole world who could be considered "scary" and Nikki liked the woman. What did that say? Anything?

They reached the gate at the edge of the property and Nikki lifted her hand and touched the golden letter in the circle.

"W is for window," she announced.

"Very good! Also for Wingate."

"And wonderful worms who wiggle!" she exclaimed with a giggle, quoting the book they'd read last night.

"Oh, Nikki." Grace bent over and scooped her up, hugging her while little arms and legs circled her and kicked with joy. "You are wonderful and wiggly, too." And not, she added mentally, in need of any testing. "Let's go meet our new friend."

Nikki stilled in her arms, a frown forming. "Who?"

Without explanation, Grace lowered her to the ground and opened the gate. "You'll see."

They weren't halfway up the walk when the front vestibule door opened and Isaiah Kincaid stepped out, looking large and in charge and quite intimidating.

"Hello, Grace," he called. "And mini-Grace."

For a moment, Nikki Lou froze and the whole thing played out in Grace's head before it happened. The lip. The tears. The rolling into a ball. And the inevitable explanation...she's very shy and blah blah *blah*.

Maybe she should listen to Miss Betsy and—

"Hi." Nikki's whispered greeting pulled Grace's attention and made her look down at her child.

She was staring at Isaiah, not cowering, not running, not rolling into her shy ball. Just staring, wide eyed and interested.

"You must be Nikki Lou," Isaiah said, coming down the two steps from the porch very slowly. "I've heard a lot about you."

She remained mesmerized. Was it his size? His voice? His looks? Something had Nikki Lou fascinated, which was fine. At least she wasn't bawling in fear.

"Nik, this is Mr. Isaiah." Grace put a hand on her shoulder, very easily guiding her toward the house and the stranger.

"Zay...uh," she whispered.

"That'll work." He chuckled and dropped down to sit on the bottom step, instantly putting himself at her height. "Hello, Nikki Lou. Welcome to Wingate House."

Clinging to Grace, she approached him, her eyes wide and unable to look away.

"W is for Wingate," she said softly, stunning Grace, who gave a light laugh.

"It sure is," he said, and finally looked up at Grace. "Hello, Miz Jenkins."

For a long moment, she looked down at him, lost in his dark eyes, sinking into a sweet spark in them that she hadn't noticed last time. Sighing, she lifted the chain around her neck. "I came to thank you."

He smiled, which crinkled his eyes and touched her heart. "I bet you have some questions, too."

"A few."

He lightly patted his thighs and looked back at Nikki Lou. "How do you feel about chocolate chip waffles?"

She looked up at Grace, a question in her eyes.

"I'm pretty sure you love chocolate chip waffles," she said with an encouraging nod, a zing of joy and relief that Nikki Lou seemed perfectly normal.

Stop, Grace, she chided herself. *She* is *normal. And perfect.*

"I thought so," Isaiah said. "Why don't you come in and I'll make you the best chocolate chip waffle you can dream of, and while you gobble that down, I'll talk to your mommy."

She nodded very slowly, unable to take her eyes from him.

Nikki Lou stayed silent as they walked through the front rooms of the inn and turned into the dining room, which was just about empty now. Only two tables were occupied by lingering guests, enjoying the morning sunlight that poured from a garden window and the aroma of coffee that hung in the air. From the living room and library, soft chatter and laughter could be heard, adding to the comfort of the place.

Isaiah led them to one of the tables that was already

set, and suggested Grace get some coffee at the station on the side of the room.

"Do you like chocolate milk?" he asked Nikki Lou.

She nodded, more mystified than terrified.

"There's some of that, too. You two get all settled with your drinks and I'll be right back."

After he left, Grace took his advice and headed to the coffee bar, getting a hot cup for herself and a juice glass of chocolate milk for Nikki Lou. She wasn't sure how much she could talk to Isaiah privately, but his calming presence already gave her a sense that all would be okay.

They sipped their drinks and, a few minutes later, he came out with two plates of waffles, chocolate chips on one, strawberries on the other, and whipped cream on both.

"Can you talk for a moment?" she asked when he served them.

"I have a little bit more to do in the back. Why don't you eat and then we'll talk." He gave a wink to Nikki Lou, which would normally send her diving for cover under the closest table.

She gave him a baby-toothed grin and stuck her finger in the whipped cream, then licked it with a sly smile.

"Nice move," he joked, making her giggle. Then, he smiled at Grace. "Enjoy your breakfast. I'll be out in a little bit."

It was a strange turn of events, and not at all what she expected, but there was something about the man that made her not want to question anything right then.

When he left, Grace leaned closer. "He's a nice man, isn't he?"

Nikki looked up. "I like him."

Wow. High praise. Not wanting to push it, she dropped the subject and they ate a second, insanely delicious breakfast. True to his word, Isaiah came back out into the now empty dining room about half an hour later.

He had a coloring book and crayons that he put on one of the tables a few feet away.

"How were the waffles?" he asked.

Before Grace could answer, Nikki Lou looked up. "Yummy," she whispered.

"Well, praise the Lord for that," he said on a hearty laugh.

Grace looked from one to the other. This big, muscular man and teeny-tiny Nikki Lou smiling at each other. It was...unbelievable.

"Can I color?" she asked.

"Till the cows come home." He leaned in and let out a chest-rumbling "Moooo."

That made her giggle again and she slipped out of her chair and went straight to the other table, and Isaiah took her seat.

"Please tell me your secret," Grace said softly.

Both brows lifted. "I did. You're wearing it around your neck."

She touched the ring again. "I meant with Nikki Lou. She's terribly shy and most strangers—heck, most *people* —send her retreating into her little shell."

He lifted one mighty shoulder. "Guess I'm not most people."

For a long time, she looked at him, vaguely aware that her own butterflies of nervousness had settled down. He certainly had a gift.

For a beat, neither said a word.

Finally, Grace reached over the table and put her hand on his much larger one. "I only have two things that must be said. Thank you and I'm sorry."

He smiled. "No need to apologize, Miz—"

"Grace. Please call me Grace."

For a few heartbeats, he stared her, holding her with a powerful gaze. "Amazing Grace," he said. "How sweet the sound. That's my all-time favorite song, and my all-time favorite gift."

She wasn't sure how to respond to that. "Well, speaking of gifts, this one was...unexpected. And I'm afraid there is every need to apologize, Mr. —" At his look, she laughed. "Isaiah. I truly misinterpreted your intentions and I am obviously sorry I did."

"Not necessary," he said. "I could have told you I had it the day we met, but I..." He let out a breath. "Would you believe me if I said I was scared?"

She searched his face, taking in the gentleness of his gaze, the authenticity of his smile. "I think you've convinced me to believe anything you say. And if you were scared that I would burst into tears and embarrass you, then you were right."

"I was scared I would," he admitted. "That ring has

burned a hole in me for years, and I wanted to give it to you in the right way."

"And I wouldn't let you do that. I'm so sorry."

"No, no, please, Grace. I didn't mean to be, you know, creepy. I just..." His voice faded out. "Anyway, you have it now."

"I do." She grasped the ring, warm and round and precious. "This means the world to me. Every time I thought of it..." She shook her head. "It was symbolic of losing him. And now?" She closed her eyes on a sigh. "It's so comforting, I can't even begin to explain it."

He smiled, true kindness in his eyes. "I'm glad."

"Did you know him well?" she asked after a beat.

"I met him one time, and that was the day he died."

"Really?" She drew back in surprise. "Then how did you get his ring?"

"It was an afterthought, honestly. I was a cook at Bagram, and he came in my mess hall that morning, like I mentioned in my note." He swallowed and closed his eyes for the briefest second. "It was an off-hour for food service, but I always fed the soldiers, no matter if it was chow time or not. I knew his team had a difficult day ahead, and he'd missed the meal for some reason."

"I know the reason," Grace said. "He called me. I remember the call, of course, since it was the last time we talked. He said he had a choice to eat or call and he chose to call. So, thank you for feeding him on off-hours."

"I'm not surprised he called you," Isaiah said. "He mentioned you multiple times in our brief conversation."

"Oh." She let out a soft whimper as heat crawled up her chest, imagining Nick talking about her as one of the last things he'd said. "What did he, um...what did he say?"

It was embarrassing to ask, but she *had* to know.

"He said he was married to the prettiest girl in Florida, when the conversation between a few guys turned to family."

She smiled. "That's sweet."

"I remember, because one of the other Marines was also from Florida, and he asked if this pretty girl had any sisters. Jenkins got all excited and said, 'Six of them!' And we all laughed."

She closed her eyes, sucker-punched by the idea of Nick bragging about his six sisters-in-law and calling her pretty. It was so like him. He adored the Wingates and couldn't wait to get out of the service so they could move from the base in North Carolina back to Amelia Island, where they hoped to start a small business.

And now she was doing all that without him, and it wasn't nearly as wonderful as it had been in their dreams.

"Then he realized he was late and that's when he looked at his ring and swore, because lots of people choose not to wear them when carrying certain weapons. He didn't have time to get back to his bunk, so I offered to hold on to it for him. He said he'd be back that night or the next morning and thanked me. We exchanged names and he left."

She stared at him, waiting for the rest—the hard part.

"I prayed over the ring for his safety," he whispered, so softly, she almost didn't hear him.

"You...prayed?"

"I don't know why I'd been moved to do that, but I remember I did. Then, when the news hit that one of the patrols had lost...a man..." He struggled, shifting in his seat. "I took it kind of bad. Some of the losses hit you harder than others."

Grace nodded slowly, her throat swelling at the sight of this big man fighting tears over Nick after one brief conversation.

"I'm not gonna lie, Grace, that ring...it affected me," he admitted gruffly. "And to be honest, I put it out of my mind for a long time. I got out of the Marines, and went home to be with my momma, who was well and truly sick."

"Oh, I'm sorry. Is she..."

He shook his head. "She's with Jesus," he assured her with a smile. "But I miss her every day."

"I bet you do."

"Anyway," he continued, "before she passed, she told me I had to give the ring to you in person."

He'd talked to his dying mother about it? "That was thoughtful of her," she said.

"She believed God gave it to me for a reason, and I couldn't really argue that, because I believe in His plan. After she'd passed and I..." He shook his head. "I mourned for some time, then tried to figure out where to go and what to do with my life. I didn't belong there anymore, and didn't want to stay. Anyway, I contacted the Marines and finally got your full name and location. And here I am."

"That was so kind," she said.

"I'm sorry you had to wait so long. Trust me, plenty of times I thought about mailing it, but I couldn't risk it. And I couldn't..." He shook his head, his voice thick. "I felt like that was the easy way out. I never take that."

She smiled and angled her head, studying him, seeing him so differently than she first had. "I'm so grateful."

He nodded, glancing to the side at Nikki Lou, who was coloring furiously, then around the dining room as he corralled his thoughts.

"When I looked up a place to stay in Fernandina Beach, I saw Wingate House and recognized it as your maiden name. I figured it was the best place to start."

"And stay," she added with a laugh. "Did you mean to get a job here, too?"

He exhaled slowly, as if considering how much or what to say next. "It felt like home to me."

"Oh, wow. That's quite a compliment to Wingate House. It feels like a B&B to most people."

"Well, I was raised in a mansion on acres of land."

"Sounds lovely." She frowned. "How is that like this?"

"We didn't own the house," he explained. "It was owned by the Schneider family, an extremely wealthy clan with deep Louisiana roots." He pronounced it "Loo-siana" exactly like a native would. "My parents worked for them since, well, long before I was born. My daddy died young in a tractor accident, and I was a little one, not much older than your girl." He grinned at her and, as if

Grace hadn't had enough surprises, Nikki Lou looked over and grinned right back.

He turned that magnetic smile on Grace and she felt the impact of it right down to her toes.

"Anyway, I lived in that house—going to school and helping out—my whole life. We had a small apartment off the kitchen, and my chores included cleaning, cooking, laundry, and gardening."

"Oh." She nodded. "That's why you feel at home in this job."

"I've had my hands on a vacuum cleaner or a cast-iron pan since I was able to hold one," he said. "And I lived there with my momma right up until I joined the service and did my twenty years. Momma never left the Schneiders, though she retired from housekeeping a few years back. They treated us both as family, and took care of her to the very end."

"I'm happy to hear that."

"Fine people," he said. "And they offered me work but..." He shook his head. "I decided to take off and come here first, with that ring. Then I knew the good Lord would help me figure out my next move."

"And it was to work for Wingate House?"

"For now. I feel called to stay."

"I'm so glad," she said. "Because not only have you worked your magic on my shy daughter, I understand you are the only person for miles who can manage..." She tipped her head in the general direction of the back stairs. "Your boss."

"Doreen? She's a pussycat."

Her eyes popped. "Has anyone told you that my sisters and I grew up calling her Dor-mean?"

He shook his head. "She reminds me of my mother, so it's easy to deal with her moods."

"That's fantastic to hear, Isaiah. Because not only do you have job security for as long as you want it, I—well, we Wingates—have a huge favor to ask."

"Anything," he said without hesitation.

"There's a company coming to town to film a Christmas movie that will be on Netflix."

"Cool, cool."

"It is, and it's very important to my family that they use all Wingate properties."

"I imagine that's fantastic PR," he said.

She hadn't really considered that aspect of the movie project, but couldn't argue it. "It's also a disruption. You see, they want to use Wingate House as a main location with many days of filming, and they need to entirely redecorate for Christmas."

"That should be...interesting," he mused. "I do like Christmas."

She laughed, not surprised by that from this God-fearing man.

"We aren't sure what it will be, other than a hassle. We are going to change reservations, offer comped rooms to some or new dates to other guests, but the fact is, Doreen is not cooperating."

That made him laugh. "I'm not the least surprised."

"You know, she's been with our family for a long, long time. Close to fifty years."

He nodded. "She's told me many times."

"So, she has a tremendous amount of clout and respect from all of us."

"Like my mother did, which I truly appreciate."

"The fact is," she continued, "she could make this very difficult, if not impossible, for us. She's wildly opposed to the whole idea."

"You want me to sell her on it?" he guessed.

Grace smiled at how he knew where she was going. "Basically, yes."

"Look!" Nikki Lou held up the book with a colored unicorn. Not exactly a masterpiece, but as careful a coloring job as any three-year-old could manage.

"Oh, Nik!" Grace cooed. "That's beautiful. That's perfect. That's not..." She let her voice fade out and finished the rest in her head.

That's not the work of a child who needs to be tested.

"I don't think angels could color any better," Isaiah said. "Can I hang that in the kitchen?"

Her whole face lit up as she nodded ecstatically.

"Can you sign it?" he asked. At her confused expression, he pointed to the bottom of the page. "Write your name, Nikki?"

"Nikki *Loooou*," she corrected, dragging out the second word in a sing-song voice, the way she only did for Grace and maybe Auntie Rose or Grannie Suze. But this stranger? He got the Nikki Lou song?

"Nikki Loooou!" he repeated the same way, beaming at her and making her giggle.

He turned back to Grace, the smile wavering. "I suppose she's named after Nicholas Louis Jenkins."

She nodded. "She is. Nicolette Louise Jenkins. I spell Nikki with two K's because I wanted her nickname to be different from his. Of course, he...never met her."

His whole expression softened. "He sees her," he said softly. "He's up in a great cloud of witnesses, looking down on her, and you, right now."

She wasn't sure if she believed that, even though that's what she told Nikki Lou almost every day. It comforted her daughter, and right now, the words comforted her.

"Thank you," she said softly, toying with the ring again. "For everything."

"I think I'll be staying here for a while," he said, shifting again in the chair. "So, I'll talk to Doreen, yes. I'll be happy to help." His gaze was so warm, it felt like he could see right into her soul. "And anytime you want to chat with a Marine, talk about Nick, or just have a friend, I'm here for you."

"I'd like that," she said, and meant it. "I won't throw you out the door for stalking me."

He dropped his head back, letting out a little moan. "I'm so sorry. I didn't know how to, you know, drop that ring on you."

She gave it another squeeze. "The flowers were perfect."

Nikki bounded over with the coloring book. "Mommy, can you"—she held the book out to her—"make it a picture for..." She glanced at Isaiah. "The man?"

"I can, but you should remember this man has a name. Mr. Isaiah."

She looked up through her lashes, smiling just enough to give Grace's heart a little boost. Nikki Lou was fine. She simply needed to spend time with people who were good with her.

And Isaiah was...good. Somehow, she already knew that was the very best way to describe him.

"I'll take that into the kitchen and put it on the fridge," he said after Grace gently pulled the page from the book's spine. "Give me a few minutes and I'll have a chat with Doe, too."

"Doe?" She lifted both brows.

"She likes to be called that. Didn't you know?"

A little embarrassed that a woman who'd been on the outskirts of her family for fifty years had a nickname no one ever used, Grace shook her head. "I don't think I have heard that."

"Well, now you know. Be right back."

As he walked out, Nikki sidled up closer. "I like him, Mommy."

"So do I, sweetheart." She touched the ring again, tempted to share her joy with Nikki Lou, but knowing she was far too young for anything but "Daddy is in heaven" as an explanation.

Not five minutes later, Isaiah returned, this time with Doreen a few steps behind him. Okay, there'd be a debate, but he was on her side, so—

"I'd appreciate if someone could help me adjust all

the reservations," Doreen said without preamble, her features set in their usual dour expression.

Grace stood slowly, probably not doing a very good job of hiding her shock.

"Oh...okay. We can certainly do that when there's a schedule for shooting. Are you..." She looked from Doreen to Isaiah and back again, still stunned. "Are you okay with all this?"

She shrugged. "Doesn't sound like I have a choice, but Isaiah thinks it will be fun."

Fun? Since when did this woman care about fun? "Oh, great. Thanks. I'll tell...yeah, thanks."

"And I have a little something for you, Miss Nikki Lou." Doreen reached into her pocket and pulled out a Tootsie-Roll lollipop.

Nikki beamed at her, then scrambled around a table to get her treat.

"What do you say, Nik?" Grace urged.

"'ank you," she whispered.

"Yes, thank you...Doe."

The other woman looked sharply at her, then closed her eyes and gave the closest thing to a smile Grace could remember. "Please get me the help I'll need."

"Of course."

As Doreen walked out, Nikki looked up at Isaiah, not at all intimidated by his height or size. "Can I color 'nother picture?" she asked.

"We better go," Grace said. "We've taken up a lot of Isaiah's time."

"But you can take the book and make me another," he

said, handing it to her. "I'll hang it in the kitchen with your unicorn."

As he walked them out, Nikki scampered ahead, and Isaiah slowed his step. "I see Nick in her," he said. "I know I only met him once, but I remember his eyes."

"She definitely has his eyes." Looking up at him, she reached out her hand. "Thank you so much, Isaiah."

As his much larger hand closed around hers, she felt nothing but warmth and comfort and...hope. That must be his gift, simply oozing all the things that made a person feel good.

"God bless you, Amazing Grace."

She smiled. "Today? He already has."

Chapter Nine

Chloe

"They're here!" Kenzie came flying into the kitchen where Chloe and Tori were finishing the last of the dinner prep for the production company. "It's happening! A giant truck the size of Kansas just pulled into the lot and Raina is out there showing them the parking spaces she secured."

"Oh, boy," Tori said. "They said a few days from when the contract was signed, and they weren't kidding."

"Based on what I've read, TV movies get made on a wild and fast schedule, but the production crew arrives first," Chloe told them. "They create the sets, plan the shots, set a shooting schedule, and, get this, they're still editing the script, which is done by a script supervisor. Oh, and the director is a woman named India—how cool is that?—and she's made a jagillion Christmas movies for Hallmark," Chloe said. At their surprised looks, she shrugged. "What? I did some background research. The wanna-be reporter in me, you know?"

"Well, the chef in me is more worried about how fast they'll eat." Tori chewed on her lip and eyed the cold food prep table. "I promised we'd feed the crew as they arrived. Kenzie, can you go out and get a headcount?"

She held up her phone. "Can I get content for my TikTok page, too?"

"Sure," Tori said. "But you know I prefer you keep your face off that app."

Kenzie rolled her eyes. "Mom, teenagers are all over TikTok. I don't like to be on camera anyway. I'll stick it in their faces and ask questions."

Chloe laughed. "Another wanna-be reporter in the family?"

"I'm trying to build a following on TikTok," Kenzie said. "And this? A movie being made in the town where I'm spending the summer? This has to be my best opportunity."

"You think the crew is going to stare into your phone and give you content?" Tori shook her head. "Just don't make anyone mad. Including your Aunt Raina. The contract she signed was full of stipulations and they could pull out, move locations, and not pay us. Do not be a stipulation-breaker, Kenz."

"I won't be, but..." Kenzie inched closer to Chloe, tapping her phone screen. "You want to do it?"

"Do what? Make TikTok videos?" Chloe curled her lip. "I'd rather have a root canal and six orders up at once."

"I thought you wanted to be on TV," Kenzie said.

"First of all, I wanted to be a TV reporter, not an influencer. And TikTok makes me crazy. I don't even have the app."

Kenzie looked at her like she'd admitted to murder. "Well, fine. I do have it, and I would love you to be the face and voice of...these stories."

Chloe rolled her eyes. "No thanks."

"You are a darn good reporter," Tori chimed in. "I remember when you interned for that one show and you shared your reports. You were good, Chloe."

"Well, that was several years ago, but..." She *had* been good, Chloe thought wistfully. Until Hunter convinced her that TV news was a tacky job unless you were network level, and anything else was being a hack. He'd roll over and cry if he saw her on TikTok.

"Okay," Kenzie said, clearly defeated. "If you don't want to do *Christmas in June, a TikTokumentary on the making of a Netflix movie* hosted by Chloe Wingate, then I guess..."

Chloe looked at her. "A TikTokumentary?"

"I just made that up." Kenzie grinned. "Clever, huh?"

Actually, it was.

"It's fine," Kenzie added. "I know you think you have to be on some big TV station, but the fact is, when a TikTok goes viral, you get seen by millions of people. And scoff if you like, but those influencers make a ton."

Tori leaned in. "You did say you were trying to figure out what to do with your life, Chloe. Why not do something in front of the camera?"

"Whose side are you on?" Chloe asked her with a laugh.

"The side that makes you happy," Tori said, "and

makes sure my overenthusiastic daughter doesn't go off the rails and lose the whole project for us."

She thought for a minute, absolutely hating that the idea was starting to make sense. Maybe she hadn't given this medium enough credit. Maybe it was a way for her to fine-tune her skills. And maybe it would be fun. She sure could use a little of that in her life.

"You know what? Let's do it. Let's document the whole shebang and throw it on the internet for fun."

"Yes!" Kenzie did a little victory dance. "Except don't say words like 'shebang' unironically. It'll make you sound fifty."

Chloe snorted. "Just so long as I don't look fifty."

Laughing, Kenzie high-fived her mother. "Thanks for the assist, Vicky."

"Call me that again and you die. And go get me a headcount or you're both fired."

"On it like a bonnet!" Kenzie grabbed Chloe's arm. "Let's go film the new arrivals."

"Wait, wait. Now?" Chloe put her hand on her chest. "I don't have any questions ready or a story outline and not a drop of makeup or—"

"Don't overthink it!" Kenzie exclaimed. "Makeup and a story outline are so millennial, Aunt Chloe. This project? Total Gen Z. TikTok is about being natural and spontaneous."

"Also, you'd be gorgeous if that truck full of crew ran over you," Tori chimed in. "You know, the crew that will give you the headcount I need?"

They both laughed as Kenzie dragged Chloe toward the door.

"Are you sure you're okay with the food prep, Tori?" Chloe asked.

"I'm fine. Food service is going to run differently for this movie and we don't need waitresses. Go, make...content."

It wasn't the news, but it had been a long time since anyone wanted Chloe Wingate in front of a camera.

"I can't believe you made up a 'TikTokumentary,' Kenzie," she said as they hustled out and headed toward the lot. "Has anyone ever used that before?"

"Who knows, who cares," Kenzie sang with the freedom of a teenager who didn't fold under the weight of her own expectations. "Look, they've opened that big trailer. Let's go ask them what's in it and what happens next."

Well, those were two questions, and as they walked closer, Chloe thought of ten more. Yep, she could do this.

"Excuse me," she called to a middle-aged man dragging a ramp from the back of the truck. "Mind if I ask you a few questions?"

"We got a permit, lady," he shot back. "If you're with the city, talk to somebody named..." He squinted into the back of the truck, which looked dark and packed to the nines with metal crates and lights and equipment.

"Somebody named Rain?" a man's voice rang out.

"No, not with the city," Chloe told. "I'm with, uh, KENZ."

She glanced at Kenzie, who snorted a laugh, but then nodded for her to continue.

"We're a small social media-based news company," Kenzie added quickly. "And we'd like to talk to some of the crew about this exciting movie."

The man turned and eyed her, his expression softening a bit as he got a good look at Chloe. "What do you want to know?"

She cleared her throat and hoped Kenzie wasn't actually "rolling" with her cellphone. But that's what editing was for, right? Although, knowing Kenzie, editing might be too...millennial.

"What is your role in this movie?" she asked.

"Crew manager. That's Seamus, prop dude."

She smiled at another man, this one much younger, who emerged from the back of the truck. "Official title, prop dude?"

He nodded and tugged at a baseball cap brim. "At your service."

"Can you show us some props?" Kenzie asked, then leaned into Chloe. "You will have to have no shame and put on a Santa hat or something to get people to watch your video."

Chloe choked a laugh. "I'm going to be your reporter, not a clown, Kenzie. We're looking for a story that would interest people."

"From the prop dude and crew manager?" Kenzie asked with a shrug. "Good luck. You talk, I'll record."

Seamus came clunking down the ramp carrying a large container, glancing at Kenzie, then zeroing in on

Chloe. She'd decided in grad school not to depend on her God-given looks to get a job, a story, or an interview but... what had that gotten her?

She flashed him a smile. "Hi, Seamus."

"Hey."

"Mind if I ask you a few questions about life on a movie set?"

He gave her a quizzical look. "If you're hunting down a walk-on part, you better talk to Marcus Ferrari, the executive producer."

"No, no. We're looking for...news. Something that would interest the locals and maybe beyond."

"Totally beyond," Kenzie muttered from behind her phone.

"Can you tell us something about the leads?" Chloe asked. "Are they famous? Nice? Maybe horrifyingly awful and only want blue M&Ms in their trailer? Something juicy but not off the record."

He shot her a look of sheer incredulity. "I gotta go."

With that, he walked off with the crew manager, leaving Chloe feeling foolish and way out of her league.

"Off the record?" Kenzie said with a choking laugh. "This ain't journalism school, Aunt Chloe."

Chloe sighed, feeling frustrated that her about-to-be sixteen-year-old niece knew more about this new medium than she did. Hunter had kept her in a bubble and it cost her. She should know how to make a stupid TikTok video!

Spurred by that thought, Chloe scrambled up the ramp, reaching into an open box and pulling out an oversized stuffed elf and a sprig of what she hoped was mistletoe.

"And I," she announced, "am willing to do what's gotta be done to get the story. Ready? Roll tape!"

Kenzie rolled her eyes. "There's no tape, Aunt Chloe. Are you sure you're twenty-nine and not fifty-nine?"

"Just turn on your darn phone, kid. And get my good side."

"As if you have a bad one." Kenzie stepped back and held up her phone. "Three, two, one. Go!"

"Merry Christmas, y'all," Chloe said, holding up the elf. "Yeah, I know it's June. But we're here in Fernandina Beach, the beautiful downtown area on Amelia Island, where Christmas is in the air. The crew of the Netflix holiday movie *Christmas on Main Street* just arrived, and this guy?" She wiggled the elf and made a face at him.

"Now we're talkin'," Kenzie whispered.

"This guy is taking me into the prop truck. For the next few weeks, I'll be giving you an insider's look at the filming of a Christmas movie. Ever want to know how they set up the holidays in the middle of summer? What the stars really think of their scenes? Who makes all the decisions? And what life is like on a movie set? Who knows—maybe some big-time celebs will show up, so stay tuned! I'm Chloe Wingate, your host for *Christmas in June, The Making of a Holiday Movie*. Come on, let's go sneak into the prop truck!"

She waved Kenzie in and they recorded a few more minutes, pointing at the boxes, making the elf talk, and building up the movie. She ended the short video by holding the mistletoe over her head.

"Until next time, this is Chloe Wingate. Kisses to all!" She made a noisy kissing sound as the crew manager came marching over.

As they ran laughing across the lot, Kenzie grabbed Chloe's arm. "Dang, girl. Why are you not all over the internet influencing people to buy stuff?"

"Because that's not what I want to do with my life." Chloe smiled and let out a sigh, the high of what they'd just done making her body vibrate with the old feeling of exuberance that washed over her every time she got to be on-air.

Why had she ever given up that dream?

Maybe it wasn't too late. Yes, she was staring down the barrel of thirty and believed that to be too old to launch a TV news career, but maybe that was Hunter's voice in her head, trying to keep her down so he could be the important one...the doctor.

"You want to do more tomorrow?" Kenzie asked.

"Yes," Chloe said simply. "I want to more than I want my next breath."

The bug had bitten again, and if a little TikTokumentary was the way to scratch it, then she'd TikTok away.

She was so high on the idea that they totally forgot about that headcount.

∼

CHLOE WAS STILL on a cloud late that night after she left the café. More of the production crew had poured in, and she'd chatted with them at the restaurant, establishing rapport and digging for little stories that she and Kenzie could record.

And, boy, they got a few tidbits. The wardrobe mistress whispered that the leading man was so short, they had him in heels in every scene and he'd never be shot below the ankles. The camera operators explained how they used light to make the actors look younger—that could be a good segment—and shared the fact that they intended to wrap this movie in a month.

The script consultant, a chatty woman named Kristen, was a fountain of information. She explained how she was rewriting the bakery meet cute to be a bookstore meet cute. That would be the first scene filming, after outside shots the minute the street was decorated for Christmas, which was happening this week.

Kenzie and Chloe, both officially consumed with their project, used all this information to plan and schedule. After the last of the twenty-five-person crew was fed and left the café, Chloe walked back to Rose's house with a smile on her face.

"Sorry I missed dinner!" she called as she came in the kitchen door, getting a whiff of something amazing her sister had made. She'd been so busy at the café, she'd never eaten.

No one answered, but she heard her nephews' voices in the dining room, and laughter, of course. Love and laughter was the staple of the D'Angelo household. It started at the top, with sweet Rose, the world's most upbeat person, and her awesome husband, Gabe, a firefighter and EMT. Their four kids, ranging in age from six to fifteen, were just as perfect, all of them living their best life in the same sprawling Victorian where two generations of Wingates, and now this family, had lived for decades.

From the minute Chloe had decided to leave Jacksonville and start over again as a waitress at the Riverfront Café, Rose and Gabe had insisted she live with them until she could get her own place. And living there meant eating around the table in the dining room every night, because Rose was old school and wonderful like that.

"My excuse is that I had the best day in front of the camera," she called, stopping at the island sink to wash her hands and hopefully dive into whatever they were eating. "Which is probably not what you expect to hear from your sister and aunt, the runaway bride!" she added on a laugh.

"Oh, *you're* the runaway bride?"

She looked up from the sink, gasping softly at the sight of a man in a navy Fernandina Beach Fire Department T-shirt. And not any man, but...*that* man.

"Travis," she said, shaking off her hands as she stared at him. "What are you doing at my sister's house?"

"Oh, hey, Chloe." Gabe came into the kitchen a second after Travis. "There's still some food left, but Zach is already eyeing the last of the potatoes." He looked from one to the other, maybe just noticing that Chloe and

Travis were staring at each other. "Have you two met? Travis McCall, this is Chloe Wingate, my sister-in-law who's staying with us for a while. Chloe, meet my probie."

"We met once," Travis said, a slow smile pulling as he looked at her. "In the street."

"You saved my phone," she said. "And I ran away from you."

"Which makes sense now," he said on a laugh.

She studied him as she dried her hands on a dishtowel.

Whoa, he was a nice-looking guy. If she wasn't on a man break, if she hadn't sworn off half the human race, if she didn't still hurt from her last self-inflicted kick in the teeth, she might be...very happy to find out that the probie Gabe talked about so much was none other than green-eyed Travis, her phone-saving hero.

Those very green eyes sparked with interest as his smile stayed firmly in place.

"Travis works at my station," Gabe said, stating the obvious when the beat of silence lasted too long.

"I'm just a probationary firefighter," Travis added. "Not the full-fledged real deal that this guy is."

Wow, and humble, too. It had been a long time since she'd hung out with a man who wasn't arrogant and prideful.

But then, she was on a man hiatus, so it would be an even longer time.

"Come on in and eat, Chloe," Gabe said, grabbing milk from the fridge. "Tell us all about the movie. And hurry up if you want a snowball's chance of getting some food. There's chicken now that you've let go of that pesky vegetarianism. But, fair warning, there are teenage boys and..." He grinned at Travis. "Others at the table."

He disappeared back into the dining room, leaving her alone with Travis.

"In front of the camera, did you say?" he asked. "Don't tell me, they already recruited you to replace the star in that movie."

"Me?" She gave a light laugh at the compliment. "Nah. But I'm doing a little...video thing, so that was fun."

He looked at her again, searching her face. "I didn't know you were Gabe's sister-in-law, the famous runaway bride."

She made a face. "Am I famous?"

"I think infamous is the right word." He leaned on the island across from her. The pose gave her a chance to see how muscular he was and how long his eyelashes were and that little bit of gold in his chestnut brown hair.

Hello. *Man hiatus, remember?*

"They say you tore out of the church in your veil and dress. Talk about a movie."

"It wasn't...like a movie," she said softly. "It was..."

"Probably the worst moment of your life."

She felt her shoulders sink in a sigh. "Yeah. The very worst." She tipped her head and added, "And not many people acknowledge that, so thank you."

"His loss, that's for sure."

"Well, I don't know," she said, suddenly feeling a

little dizzy from looking into his eyes. "But it did...change me."

"And that's why the man break you mentioned?" he asked.

"You, uh, really listened that day, didn't you?"

"To every word."

She looked up at him, aware of an undercurrent buzzing through her like she'd accidentally touched a live wire.

Oh, no. No, no, *no.*

"Yeah," she whispered. "Well, I mean, I joke about it, but..." She swallowed and lifted her chin. "It made me realize that this time in my life is for me, and me alone."

"Really smart, Chloe."

But was it? Just looking at him made her wonder.

"I'm doing the same thing," he said.

"On a man hiatus, are you?"

They both laughed, the joke breaking the tension, but his smile wavered.

"It's a long story and..." He dipped his head and lowered his voice, "If you weren't on a man break, I'd take you to dinner and tell you. But..." He shrugged and pivoted. "Better hurry. The mashed potatoes are worth arm-wrestling Zach for."

She watched him leave, a little stunned at how much she wanted to go to dinner with him and hear his long story.

Chapter Ten

Raina

The exhaustion was epic. From the minute Raina opened her eyes and greeted her little Cucumber Seed to the moment she went to bed, she was tired. Today was no different as she blinked into the morning sun pouring through the third-floor windows and ached for more sleep.

Sleep had always been the lowest priority in Raina's life, but now, she longed for it. That would go away soon, right? At three months, they said.

Today was the start of week nine.

She rolled over and snagged her phone, tapping the app she spent more time in than any other.

Your baby now has arms and legs and facial features are forming!

"Oh, I bet you are a pretty little thing."

Your baby can move, and is currently about the size of a watermelon seed.

"You've grown, my darling child! Now you're a watermelon seed. I hope you don't feel like an actual watermelon on your way out."

Not that Raina would care. This little seedling had to make it that far.

She startled as the phone hummed in her hand and a notification flashed.

Call from Jack.

She grunted and pushed up. Why would he call? They'd texted—rarely—and any actual communication had come from Dani, her assistant, who had provided all kinds of tidbits like...Jack and Lisa came in together every morning.

Raina didn't care. All she cared about was Watermelon Wingate, the baby her husband didn't know about yet. Surely she could wait three more weeks to drop the bomb. She hadn't even told her attorney, let alone her parents and sisters.

After three miscarriages, it was too soon.

She let the call go to voicemail and dropped the phone with a thud. She'd been so focused on keeping this baby growing inside her and the Christmas movie project, that she'd effectively ignored how complicated life could be if this baby made it all the way to the end.

"No *if*, Raina," she whispered, pushing up. "No *if* this time."

The phone dinged with a voicemail and she touched the notification, bracing for the sound of Jack's voice.

"Hey, Rain. We need to talk. Call me when you get a chance."

She groaned and managed to get out of bed, scowling at the phone. "How about 'no,' Jack? How about I don't call you ever for the rest of my li—"

A text came in and for a split second, she assumed it was Jack bugging her, but it was from Marcus Ferrari asking for a meeting in forty-five minutes at the café.

Now, that man? The keeper of the money she needed to make her father happy and whole? She'd respond to Marcus. She texted back that she'd be there, then showered, dressed, and dried her hair. As she was dabbing on her lipstick, her phone rang with a call from Jack again.

"Eh, I don't think so," she muttered, tossing the cell in her bag. With one last check in the mirror, she headed downstairs, glanced around for Suze, but not seeing her, went down one more level to the driveway.

She looked into Dad's rehab area, but the shades hadn't been opened on the sliders yet, so Susannah was probably in his room helping him dress. Rather than interrupt that and risk being late for Marcus, she headed out to her car, and then her phone rang again.

"Seriously?" She pulled out the phone to read Jack's name and grunted as a text came in.

Jack: *I have to talk to you, Raina. Now.*

"Always on your terms, Jack Wallace." Pulling out of the gate, she weaved through some traffic, feeling her whole body tense. What could be so important that he couldn't tell a lawyer or Dani? Or his stupid, precious Lisa?

She swallowed the bitter taste in her mouth at the thought of the other woman, refusing to let her take up one inch of real estate in her mind.

But then the cell rang again, and this time her dashboard flashed with Jack's name.

With a soft curse, she tapped the button on the steering wheel to answer the call.

"I have less than five minutes," she said in greeting. "My client is waiting for me."

"Boy, you wasted no time diving into Wingate Properties, huh?"

And he'd wasted no time spending the night with his mistress and going to work with her. "Yep. What's up?"

"Are you okay, Raina?"

"I'm fine." Not that he cared.

"I mean...are you sick?"

Her heart skipped a beat. "No. Why?"

"Because this morning I got a weird call from your insurance company saying that they couldn't cover your appointment with a doctor...Stephanie Milwood? She's out of network."

Oh, *no*. "Why would they notify you?"

"That's how insurance works. You signed a thing that said they can contact your spouse. Evidently when the next appointment got scheduled, it triggered an alert in your file, so you realize—"

"Well, ignore it. It's not your concern."

"Really? The prenatal appointment and ultrasound is *not my concern*?"

The blood rushed from her head so fast, she felt dizzy. With a glance in her rearview mirror, she pulled to the side of the road, stopping near the large central park between the beach house and downtown.

"Raina?"

She swallowed, furious and frustrated and, honestly,

ashamed. He *was* the father. A cheating, lying, soon-to-be-ex, but he still shared DNA with her watermelon seed. She should have told him, but...she closed her eyes.

"I wanted to wait," she whispered. "Until...well, you know."

"What I know is that you're pregnant." He ground out the words. "And you didn't see fit to tell me?"

"Just like you didn't see fit to tell me you'd fallen in love with Lisa Godfrey," she fired back. "I planned on telling you once...once I make it through the danger period."

He was silent for a few beats, then said, "And then what?"

"Then...*what*?" she asked.

"This baby is *mine*," he said softly. "And that, well, that changes everything."

She bit her lip as the words punched. "What do you mean, Jack?"

"What do you think I mean? I will not be separated from my child."

She could actually feel the blood in her veins growing cold. He was the one who chose this. He was the one who decided to have an affair. He was the one who showed his true colors.

But he *was* the father.

"I won't separate you from your child," she said slowly.

"You didn't even tell me you were pregnant!"

"Because it's too soon," she insisted. "I haven't told

anyone. Not my parents, not my sisters." Well, Tori, but she left that out.

"Not your husband," he added.

"My *soon-to-be-ex*-husband who is sleeping with another woman, speaking of things that change everything."

She heard him puff out a breath as her phone dinged with a "Where are you?" text from Marcus.

"I have to go," she said. "I have a client waiting for me."

"We're not done."

"Really?" she scoffed. "We were done when you entertained Lisa in my bedroom and let her wear my robe. We were done when you admitted you loved her. As a matter of fact, we were already done when we made love in my act of desperation to win back my very own husband."

"That's my baby, Raina."

"You will have parental rights that will be worked out as part of the divorce settlement," she said, sounding much, much calmer than she felt.

"Well, maybe we were...hasty."

She actually laughed. No, he wasn't going to do this. He wasn't going to try and win her back because there was a baby. *No.*

"I'm late. I have to go." She didn't wait for his response but pressed her finger on the steering wheel's "end call" button so hard, she imprinted the oval shape of it on her thumb.

With a deep and steadying breath, she drove to the

meeting with Marcus and hoped her day didn't go further south than this. But it was only nine in the morning and anything could happen.

HUSTLING INTO THE RESTAURANT, she spotted the producer at his favorite table by the window, phone in hand, his frameless glasses low on his nose as he thumbed the screen.

Planting a smile in place, she breezed over to the table and slid into the chair. "Good morning, Mr. Executive Producer."

He instantly lowered the phone and pushed his glasses up to study her through the lenses. "What's wrong?"

Good heavens, was she that transparent?

"You called me, boss," she volleyed back, dropping her elbows on the table to get fully in the game. "The only thing wrong is that my client needs me."

"You look upset and that could mean I should be upset." He frowned at her. "Tell me I'm wrong."

"You're wrong," she said without a second's hesitation.

"I'm never wrong," he said, a tease in his voice. "Just ask my ex-wife."

That made her smile. "It's personal." *Just ask my ex-husband*, she thought silently.

"Personal?" He eyed her closely. "Spouse? Kids? Parents? Those are the Big Three personal problems."

She gave a soft laugh. "Well, all three, to be perfectly honest." She gave a tight smile, deciding to try out her new truth and see how it felt to say it. "I'm actually in the early stages of a divorce, I'm sorry to say."

"Oooh." He drew out the word and leaned back, his sharp gaze softening ever so slightly. "Been there, done that, have the scars to prove it."

She winced at the word *scars*. "I was, uh, hoping to get through the whole thing without any."

"Then you'd be the first divorced person in history. How many years down the drain?"

Is that where her life with Jack was headed? Down the drain? She felt her eyes shutter as she answered. "Sixteen."

"Kids?"

She stared at him, silent as her pulse spiked. "Uh, no. No kids," she finally said.

"Oh, well, that's good, because divorce stinks from every angle but, man, is it hard on the little ones." He frowned and tipped his head. "Didn't you say your problems were all three? Spouse, kids, and parents?"

"Well, I have a lot of nieces and nephews," she said quickly.

"Ah, yes, the young TikToker, Kenzie. I've heard her throw around 'Aunt Raina' when she wanted access."

"Is she a problem?" Raina asked quickly. "She and Chloe, my sister, promised they'd—"

"No, no," he assured her. "She's been very respectful. I wouldn't mind a little PR for the movie."

"Oh, good. Just let me know if there's a problem. And did you have something specific today? Any issues?"

He regarded her for a minute, quiet as he thought. "I'm sorry you're going through this," he said. "I'm divorced a year now and I have to tell you, Raina, it is..."

She waited as he rooted for his description. Not so bad? Horrible? What?

"The saddest thing two people can go through," he finished, and her heart fell to the floor.

"Oh, I'm so sorry to hear that." Sorry for him, and sorry for herself.

"Yeah." He stared out the window, lost in his thoughts. "It made me believe that the worst thing people can do is get married. It's so easy to get married, you know? Such a high, and so much hope at the beginning. Then, slowly, insidiously...it breaks. Little, hairline, nearly invisible cracks like...like in this cup." He lifted the thick white café mug, which was, indeed, veined with tiny fissures. "It functions, that family, but it is so far from perfect."

She stared at him, hating every word he said.

"And breaking it?" he continued, unaware of the cuts he was causing on her heart. "Actually taking and tearing and smashing it apart? That is the ugliest, darkest, most painful thing I personally have ever been through."

All she could do was nod, silent.

"But it won't be so bad without kids," he added. "Because they become property, literally and figuratively. And you and your former beloved are clawing each other's eyes out over human beings. I don't care how old they are, it affects the kids. Puts them straight into therapy."

"Always?" she asked. "I mean, Kenzie's okay. The TikToker? She's been through one and survived. More than that, actually. She's a great kid."

"I'm sure there are exceptions but..." He shrugged. "It's a really hard thing, so I'm glad you don't have kids."

"We have a jointly-owned business, though."

He grimaced. "That's almost as bad. I mean, the only thing uglier than custody is the money fight. A business? Eesh. I don't envy you."

She had to laugh. "You are full of such good news, Marcus."

"I'm full of cynicism," he countered. "And so will you be in a year. Just wait until you start discussing the house —who gets it, who sells it, who profits from it. Ugly, ugly."

Bile rose in Raina's throat, joining the worry and regret that had taken up residence for most of the morning. "I bet. Are you...sorry you got a divorce, Marcus?"

He took another sip of coffee and thought about that. "If I could have figured out any way humanly possible to make it work, I would have. Only for my kids, really. But...she was dead set on calling it quits and I didn't realize how wretched the whole process was going to be."

"Wow, that's...something."

He gave an uncomfortable laugh. "I'm sorry, Raina. I guess I'm not saying anything to make you feel better."

"Not a thing," she agreed with a mirthless laugh.

"Really sorry," he said again. "How can I make it up to you?"

"Get the meeting on track and tell me why you needed me here," she said simply, tempering the request with humor that she didn't feel.

"Have you seen Wingate Way?" he asked.

She'd just driven down it and...yes! Snowflakes and garlands. She'd been so preoccupied, it hadn't registered.

"You've decked the halls," she said quickly. "It's festive and...fun."

"And no doubt offensive to the townsfolk."

She groaned. "Please tell me you're not getting push-back. I've met with the city council, chamber of commerce, historical society, and every other organization that has an opinion, and I am happy to say the Wingate name still carries weight around here."

"No, but we want to use that little train station welcome center in a scene. Can you make that happen?"

"Can you shoot at night?" she asked.

"Yes, actually, we could."

"And break the set by the next business day?"

"By nine in the morning."

She brought out her phone and typed a note. "I can make that happen."

"Thank you," he said. "Are you sure I can't repay my horrific bad attitude about your divorce by doing something nice for you? Jeez, I didn't even offer coffee."

Just then, she glanced toward the kitchen and caught sight of Tori and Chloe stealthily trying to get her attention without Marcus seeing them.

"No, no, I'm good."

Suddenly, Tori pulled on a Santa hat that Chloe always seemed to have in case Kenzie's camera rolled.

What was she doing?

They both mouthed "Dad!" and she instantly understood.

"Oh, yes!" Raina snapped her fingers as she remembered. "There actually is something I need."

"Name it."

She made a face. "It's kind of a major request."

"Hey, I dumped my divorce issues on you and that wasn't fair. What do you need?"

"I seem to recall you and Bridget mentioning a Santa in the script?" she asked.

"Is it a Christmas movie? Of course there is. Only one scene, though. Why? One of those nieces or nephews wants to sit on his lap in the middle of summer? That's no prob—"

"I'd like my father to play the part."

He looked startled, then laughed. "That's funny and cute and impossible. Next favor?"

She leaned in, undaunted. "Why is it impossible?"

"Because Santa's cast—"

"Uncast him."

"The actor has two lines—"

"My dad can deliver two lines." She hoped.

"He has to be SAG—er, Screen Actors Guild. We can't—"

"Why?" she pressed.

"Because my production company only uses SAG talent."

"Okay." She nodded. "How do you get SAG-ed?"

That made him smile. "You obtain a card by...getting a part without the card, then delivering a line that doesn't get cut, then you're in the Guild."

"Wow, talk about Catch-22," she said on a laugh. "You can't get the card to deliver a line until you deliver the line to get the card. There has to be a workaround."

His eyes glimmered as he regarded her. "You're probably very good at your job, aren't you?"

"Insanely so."

He leaned back. "Why is it so important?"

Because Rex had a stroke and was sliding into depression? No. Marcus didn't need to know that. "Because," she said slowly. "It's his dream."

"To act?"

"To be Santa in a movie." A stretch, but Rex did love to dress up as Santa for the grandkids. He even had the outfit packed somewhere with the holiday decorations.

"That's your father's dream?" He sounded skeptical.

She lifted a shoulder. "Who's to judge?"

"Well, the director, for one thing. Dad'll have to audition for India. The director has the final say."

She made a face. "Really? The 'talent' in question is named Rex Wingate, owner of every building where you are shooting, and the street that has been shut down, redecorated, and brought to a halt for this movie. Can we skip the audition and you trust me?"

"Uh, the same Wingate Properties we're writing checks to?"

She conceded with a tilt of her head. "Touché,

Marcus. But listen—this is important to my family. You've met enough of us to know we're good people."

He regarded her for a moment, then nodded. "I'll talk to India."

"Great. Then can you text me his lines?"

Now he laughed. "I feel bad for your husband."

"Excuse me?" she almost choked.

"It's gonna get rough around that negotiation and arbitration table, because you, my dear, don't take no for an answer."

"I guess that will serve me well in the months ahead." She let out a sad sigh.

"Or you could kiss and make up and save yourself headaches beyond compare."

Or...*that*. "He cheated on me," she said softly. "So it's not an option."

"Everything's an option." He finished his coffee and pushed back. "You'll learn that soon enough."

With that, he stood and walked away.

No, getting back with Jack was *not* an option.

Chapter Eleven

Tori

"His lifelong dream?" Tori choked on a laugh. "Raina, are you serious?"

Raina held up both hands, leaning against the walk-in fridge door in the café kitchen.

"Hey, it worked," she said. "He might have to audition, though."

"Audition?" Kenzie called from the other side of the kitchen. "Can Chloe and I record that? Fun content!"

"Maybe. Marcus also said he liked the PR, so go viral."

"We're trying!"

Tori inched closer, her eyes narrowing. "Are you okay, Rain?"'

Raina swallowed and shook her head. "I have to talk to you. Privately. It's urgent."

Tori looked left and right but her kitchen was buzzing with the breakfast rush. "C'mere," she said, yanking the big fridge door and pulling Raina in. "Nice and cold."

It didn't surprise her that Raina came right along, stepping into the chilly cooler.

"What's going on?" Tori asked as she closed the door.

"Can you get locked in here?" Raina asked, looking around, her expression slightly panicked.

"Not unless you don't know where the safety is." She pointed to a red handle on the floor by the door. "What is going on?"

"Jack knows."

Tori gasped. "That you're pregnant?"

"Yep. The insurance company called him."

"They told him you were pregnant?" Her voice rose in disbelief. "Isn't that a breach of HIPAA compliance or some such thing?"

"I signed a form that doctors could leave messages with him, because back in the old days, when I loved him, I didn't care. It was a routine call, but someone used the word 'prenatal' so..." She shrugged. "Dead giveaway."

"Oh, gosh, Rain. How'd he take it?"

"He's...upset. Went straight to, 'It's my child.'"

"Well, it is."

Raina groaned and rubbed her arms against the chill. "Of course, I know that, but...this is going to be hard, Tori. So hard. Divorce is wretched and the kids are hit hardest."

"You're telling *me*?"

"But you still think I'm doing the right thing?"

Tori drew back, suddenly understanding all too well why Raina would start to think about forgiving and forgetting and avoiding the hell ahead.

"Only you know that," Tori said.

"Jack said a baby changes everything."

She lifted a brow. "Does it change...Lisa?"

Raina just sighed. "I don't know, but...it's out. At least to Jack."

"Will you tell everyone else?"

"Soon. I still want to be sure it's not another...false alarm. Also, get me out of here before I freeze to death."

Together, they stepped outside, where Kenzie and Chloe were waiting so close, Tori half expected them to hold up a phone and start asking questions.

"Secrets, you two?" Chloe asked with raised brows of curiosity.

"So many of them," Tori deadpanned.

"Oh, Marcus texted Dad's lines," Raina tapped her phone, looking grateful for the distraction. "Want to hear them?"

They all nodded and stepped closer to hear.

"'And what do you want for Christmas, young lady?'" Raina read in a deep Santa voice. "'I want my mommy to get married!'" she continued in a high child's pitch, making them laugh. "Then it says, 'Santa looks out to the crowd at Ivy and Ben.'"

"That's the name of the lead couple in the movie," Chloe informed them. "And this scene is kind of at the end. I've already read the whole script."

"After that, he's supposed to smile kindly at the couple, who are embracing." Raina flipped through the text. "He has to say, 'I think I can pull that one out of my bag. Ho ho ho.'"

Tori sucked in a noisy breath. "That's a lot of words for a man who had a stroke two and a half months ago. How are you going to sell this to Dad? Since, you know, he *hasn't* had a dream of being Santa his whole life."

"I'm not. You are. You and Justin."

Tori's brows rose, but instantly she saw the sense of that. "It will carry a lot more weight coming from his neurologist."

"I think so, too. And tell him that since he's the owner of all the set locations and the street, they wanted to honor him with this part," Raina said.

Tori rolled her eyes, uncertain about how Dad would take this. But, deep inside, she loved the idea, and it had come directly from his doctor.

"Thanks for running with this, Raina," she said, giving her sister a hug.

"Thank your man Hottypants for the idea."

Tori smiled at the name and the thought that he was her man. She liked that. She liked that a lot.

"I'm as nervous as if I was bringing a man home to meet my father," Tori admitted as she and Justin drove along the beach road to see Dad. "Which is crazy, since he might not be alive if not for you."

From the driver's seat, he slid her that half smile that curled her toes. "He'd be alive. I'm not God, Tori. Just a doctor."

And if that smile didn't slay her, his sweet humility

did. "As long as you're sure this is a good idea and it won't stress him."

"A little stress, but the good kind. The 'I'm living again' kind. He needs this, Tori. I think it's a great way to get him out, around people, and give him a purpose." He reached over and took her hand. "And, by the way, you *are* bringing a man home to your father. I might have met him before, but not in this capacity."

She let her fingers slide through his strong, lean ones, marveling at...well, everything. Every single thing about him was perfection.

"What are you smiling about?" he asked.

"I'm smiling because..." Oh, heck. Why lie? "I've got a crush on you like Kenzie on a boy in high school. It's unsettling."

He laughed. "I think it's very settling. Like, settling is all I want to do with you. Preferably somewhere very comfortable and private and intimate..." He winked. "You get the picture."

Her heart danced around. "And it's a pretty one," she agreed. "But not too comfortable or...intimate." Not yet.

He laughed. "No pressure, Victoria. I'm fantasizing like that high school boy you just mentioned."

"Oh, please. Women must throw themselves at you, Dr. HP."

"If they have, I don't notice much." He gave her another look. "I have kind of a crush myself, you know. Always had a weakness for strawberry blondes with a smattering of freckle perfection."

For a moment, she thought of all the hours in her life

she'd envied Rose's wheat-colored hair, or Raina's dark, dark locks. All the times she put makeup on to cover those freckles.

"And she can cook. Should I continue?" he asked.

"By all means." She leaned her head back and sighed contentedly. "Especially if you want to get me to that comfortable, private, and intimate place real soon."

"Not with mere compliments." He lifted their joined hands and placed a light kiss on her knuckles. "You gotta really like me."

"More than I already do?" she asked.

"No schoolgirl crush," he said. "Because I don't want you to leave."

Leave? Like the morning after...or leave Amelia Island? The question lodged in her throat and before she could swallow and clarify what he meant, they pulled into the beach house driveway and had to get on with their mission.

But she had to know what he meant.

Before she could ask, Susannah opened the door, ready and waiting since Tori had texted her a heads-up.

"Perfect timing," she said after greeting them both with a hug. "He's all done with PT, and it went well. I wheeled him out to the downstairs patio and he's having some tea. I'll bring you two some while you talk to him."

"What do you think he'll say, Suze?" Tori asked.

"I guess it depends on how you present it." Susannah smiled up at Justin, her fondness for him always clear. "He'll listen to anything you say, Doctor."

Tori and Justin walked through the rehab room and

stepped toward the open sliding glass doors. Just as Tori was about to call out a greeting, Justin stopped her, a frown on his face.

"Listen," he mouthed.

She froze in place and cocked her head in the direction of the patio, and then she heard...a sniffle. Was Dad crying? Her whole body tensed as she wanted to fly out to comfort him, but Justin held her back. Raina told her the same thing happened when she caught him alone.

Dad was truly depressed and that hurt to even think about.

"Don't surprise him," Justin whispered. "Don't embarrass him. Call out and give him a chance to regroup."

Grateful for the advice, she nodded. "Hey, Dad," she called, forcing light and brightness into her voice. "You out there?"

Neither of them moved while they heard one more sniffle, then, after a beat, he said. "Tori?"

"Yeah...hang on, Dad. I'll be there in a second. I have to, um, grab something upstairs. Oh, I have a surprise. Justin—er, Dr. Verona is with me."

They stayed where they were, holding each other's gaze, giving her father time to gather himself. As they did, she looked up at Justin, lost in his blue eyes and sweet smile and good, good heart.

"Okay," her father said, and she could picture him wiping his eyes and pulling it together.

"Thank you," she mouthed.

Justin nodded, still holding her gaze.

And that question about the last thing he'd said in the car echoed in her head again. "What did you mean?" she asked.

"About..."

"About how...you don't want me to leave."

His eyes flickered. "I don't."

"Like...if we spent the night together or...what?"

He searched her eyes, placing his gentle but so competent fingertips on her chin, lightly caressing her skin and sending an avalanche of chills down her back. "I mean I don't want you to leave."

"Ever?"

He smiled and lowered his head, tilting her chin up so their lips met in the softest, sweetest, most confusing kiss she—

"So the rumors are true."

They flew apart at the sound of her father's gruff voice, which, for a man ten weeks from a stroke, was pretty darn forceful.

"Hello, Rex," Justin said.

But Dad stared at him, his dark eyes full of an emotion Tori couldn't read. Was he mad? Did he have an issue? Was there a problem with her dating his neurologist?

"Are they true?" Dad pressed.

Tori swallowed and remembered that before the stroke, before the moment that wrecked his blood flow and changed his brain, Rex Wingate was an imposing, powerful, opinionated man who never let anyone near one of his daughters without putting them through an inquisition.

"It depends on the rumor," Justin said slowly. "If you're referring to me falling rather hard for your daughter, then it's true."

Dad managed a deep breath, looking from one to the other. For the time it took Tori's heart to slam her ribs four, five, no *six* times, he said nothing. Then Justin took a few steps closer to reach his hand out to shake Dad's, somehow deflecting the moment.

"You look good, Rex. How are you feeling?"

"Better now that PT is over," he admitted, easily maneuvering his wheelchair closer and lifting his right hand. "What brings you two to see me?"

Relief washed through Tori as she joined them, bending over to kiss her father's cheek. "Hi, Dad," she whispered. "How'd you like to be in a movie?"

"What?"

"You heard her," Justin said. "Seems like Hollywood has come knocking at your door and I'm here in a professional capacity to tell you I think a walk-on—or roll-on, as the case may be—playing Santa in the Christmas flick could be the best thing you ever did."

Tori and Justin shared a look and settled onto two chairs in the small sitting area just as Susannah came in with iced teas. Dad knew about the movie, of course, and Raina had told him why they were doing it before she signed the deal. He'd loved the solution, but Tori had to be careful—she wasn't supposed to know about the missing money.

"You hear that, Suze?" Dad asked.

"I know all about it. Sadly, there's no Mrs. Claus or I'd be joining you."

He managed a good old pre-stroke scowl. "Really? It sounds like a bunch of hooey to me."

Tori fought a smile, happy that Dad was back in full force. That also meant he could be very intimidating, but it felt like Justin could easily handle that challenge.

"You'll have the time of your life, Dad," Tori said. "I think you should do it."

"Plus we'll have a fantastic Christmas viewing party with the whole family," Susannah added.

They all, including Rex, looked at Justin for the final word.

"And because your doctor says you have to." Justin leaned in and held Rex's gaze. "Consider it your final test. You do this, and I will reduce your PT, let you go completely to the walker, and give you permission to..." He closed the space between them and whispered something in Dad's ear.

Whatever it was, Rex pulled back and gave the biggest smile Tori could remember since he got sick. "I like the way you think, Doc. But I want one more thing."

"Name it," Justin replied.

He lifted his hand and pointed from Justin to Tori and back again. "Stay together. That could actually give me a reason to live."

Tori blinked in surprise. Did he say—

"I'm working on it, sir." Justin leaned back, utterly

casual, and crossed his ankles. "Now let's practice your ho-ho-hoing."

Then she turned to Dad and took in the way he relaxed, too, looking...well, not depressed. Not at all.

What would happen when this summer fling ended? It certainly looked like Dad's heart would be broken more than Tori's. Jeez. No pressure or anything.

Chapter Twelve

Grace

It hadn't been easy. It took three outfits—one too itchy, one too pink, one just right— two Hershey's Kisses, and one major temper tantrum, but somehow Grace got Nikki Lou dressed for a little night out on the town.

Feeling the effects of the last few hours and a long day of hunkering in the upstairs apartment while the set designers worked on the bookstore, Nikki Lou clung to Grace's hand like a lifeline as they came down the stairs.

She only let go when they got into the store, both of them wide-eyed with wonder at the festive decorations.

"Is Santa coming?" she asked in a breathless whisper.

Grace laughed. "No, this is for pretend, honey. But, wow, too bad we don't have all these decorations for the real Christmas."

"No Santa?"

She laughed at Nikki's determination. "Not here. This is what they call 'a set,'" Grace explained, always looking for ways to teach her daughter. "And you know the play of Cinderella that Aunt Madeline is taking you and your cousins to see tonight at the community theater?

They will have sets, too. Those sets will look like a palace and a ballroom and probably a nasty fireplace that Cinderella cleans."

But the lure of the evening's festivities with her two cousins paled in comparison to the transformation of The Next Chapter. The set designers had taken the cozy shop from an ordinary bookstore to a winter wonderland, with garlands and lights, a sparkling tree near the front door, and a giant wreath behind the checkout counter.

"Elfie!" Nikki squealed, running toward the children's alcove, which was like a second home to her. She danced on her tiny toes, trying to reach for the beloved Elf on a Shelf. "Down, Elfie!"

With a happy sigh, Grace crossed her arms and watched Nikki dance around. Why didn't the rest of the world see this version of Nikki Lou? The animated, bouncing little girl who...didn't need to be tested for anything except shyness. And a few meltdowns because her dress itched and it was the wrong color.

Grace so understood her shyness...but not the other aspects of her complicated daughter.

With five older sisters who did the talking for her, Grace had always found it easier to stay in the background. Maybe it wasn't being part of a big family that made Grace quiet. Maybe she, too, was naturally introverted and Nikki Lou had inherited that. Nick certainly had been a big, outgoing personality, and that had been part of what had attracted her in the first place.

"Mommy, get Elfie!" Nikki demanded.

"I'm sorry, honey, we can't move him. I promised the

decorating people we wouldn't touch a thing. And we won't have any customers for a long time, either." Which had been very strange on a Saturday in June, when they'd usually be slammed. "Plus, you're going to see a play with Avery and Alyson."

"Who are at Aunt Madeline's studio waiting for you."

At the sound of Rose's voice, Nikki Lou turned from the elf to look at her aunt, uncertain even though she knew her almost as well as she knew her own mother.

"Hi," she whispered.

"Hi to you, gorgeous!" Rose exclaimed, coming closer but always letting Nikki Lou call the shots. Sometimes she hugged, sometimes she walked off.

"Look at you in your pretty blue dress," Rose said brightly.

Grace gave the softest grunt. "Not what we had planned for *Cinderella*," Grace said. "I had something a little fancier picked out but it sent her into itching fits." Probably something Rose, mother of four perfect children, hadn't dealt with too much.

But Rose nodded with understanding. "Ah, the itchy dress problem. Avery hates anything lace." She came a little closer, crouching down to Nikki Lou's height. "Well, now you're beautiful *and* comfortable, Nicolette Louise." She reached her hand out, offering it to Nikki Lou. "And Alyson and Avery are in comfy cotton dresses, too. So you'll all be perfect at the play."

Grace could see her little face processing what Rose had said, and then her gaze shifted between them, taking in the fact that they were both in shorts and T-shirts.

"You go with us, Mommy?"

Oh, boy. She'd explained this, but Nikki had been preoccupied. "Remember, I told you that one of the brides at Auntie Madeline's dress studio gave her four tickets to this play. She wanted to take you and Avery and Alyson. A girls' night of *Cinderella*."

But no matter how cheerful she made her voice, Nikki's expression grew darker and more distrustful. "You're a girl," she said.

"And I'm having my own girls' night with Auntie Rose while you're with the others."

"I go see Elfie," she said, slipping around a tall bookshelf to the children's alcove to gaze up at the stuffed toy. No temper, no tears, but she wasn't happy.

"Think she'll be okay?" Rose whispered.

Grace lifted a shoulder. "Madeline can text me if she has a problem like she did the time they went to the movies, but we had a long talk and Cinderella live and in person—with an actual fairy godmother—is a big draw. Music always settles her down. Today, when she was upset about the dress, she sat at that piano in my living room and pounded the keys. I could have sworn she accidentally played some music, but it was more like noise that got her through the problem."

"And you didn't want to keep that piano when you moved in here," Rose reminded her.

"It takes up a lot of space, but someone got it to the second floor of this building, so who am I to try and take it back down? I'm used to it now. And Nikki frequently messes around on it."

Rose smiled at that. "There was a lot you didn't like about this place when you first got here. Look how far you've come, Grace."

She nodded, remembering those dark days when she'd come to Amelia Island, pregnant and widowed. The space had been a used book and antique store, but the couple who'd lived upstairs and run the retail wanted to move to the West Coast to be with their daughter. The timing had been perfect for Grace to take over and elevate the space to something very special.

With the help of her sisters and parents, Grace had moved in, revamped the interior, and by the time Nikki Lou was three months old, she'd opened the doors of The Next Chapter, a very successful bookstore.

"You were the one who came up with the name," Grace reminded Rose.

"It was Gabe," Rose said, putting an arm around her. "But he lets me take credit for the idea because he's wonderful like that. Come on, Nikki Lou! Your Auntie Madeline will not tolerate lateness."

"That's an understatement," Grace murmured.

A few minutes later, the three of them walked toward Madeline's dress shop to find Rose's little girls in front of the wedding dress show room window, oohing and ahhing over a ball gown style she'd just completed.

"In honor of *Cinderella*," Madeline told them as they arrived.

Immediately, Grace noticed that Avery and Alyson were much more dressed up than Nikki Lou, but oh, well. She was three. No one cared what she wore and there were no tears, which was all that mattered.

After a few moments of chatter, the little girls each took one of Nikki's hands. They never failed to calm and surround her, and the loving gesture always touched Grace's heart.

At six and eight, Rose's daughters were old enough to take their roles as Nikki's big cousin protectors very seriously, and they rarely grew impatient with her shyness or tantrums—or at least they were too well-behaved to show it.

And not one person in the entire Wingate clan had ever suggested she be tested for anything.

With hugs and kisses and not a single tear, they took off to walk to the small theater a few blocks away.

A few minutes later, Rose and Grace were tucked into a booth at the local Mexican restaurant, munching on chips and sipping margaritas.

"No one else wanted to join us?" Grace asked.

"Tori has a date," Rose said.

"Ah, yes, Hottypants. Raina? Chloe? Kenzie?"

"Chloe said she wanted to chill at home and is alone now, but..." Her lips lifted in a sly smile. "She might not be for long."

"What do you mean?" Grace asked, biting off the end of a chip.

"Travis McCall is going to swing by and pick up some gear that Gabe doesn't need anymore and..." Rose's eyes twinkled mischievously. "Chloe will have to answer the door."

"Rose! Are you matchmaking our just-broken-up little sister?"

She gave a guilty laugh. "It isn't much of an effort. Travis was over for dinner the other night, and Gabe and I agreed we were singed by the sparks flying between those two."

"Not too soon for her?" Grace asked.

"Have you seen Travis?" When Grace shook her head, Rose leaned in and whispered, "Travis is, as they say, a dime."

"A dime?" Grace laughed. "Well, that should be interesting. But where's Raina? Movie stuff?"

"No, thank goodness. Raina was sound asleep when I called and woke her up at four o'clock in the afternoon. She said it was her first day off and all she wanted to do was sleep. That Marcus guy keeps her hopping, plus the other regular business with Wingate Properties."

"She's not tired," Grace said. "She's sad about Jack. I slept a lot after Nick died. It was my only escape."

"Well, you were pregnant, but she is struggling with this. That's why I wanted her to come out tonight, but she begged off. Oh, and Gabe took the boys to see a movie and they asked Kenzie, so I guess she likes action heroes more than Mexican food."

"She likes everything," Grace said wistfully, still a little blue from her battle over the dress with Nikki. "What is it like to have such a cooperative daughter?"

"None of them are cooperative at three years old," Rose said, inching closer. "Is that what's bothering you? I can tell something is eating away at you, Gracie. Talk to me."

She blew out a sigh, knowing that if anyone was going to make her feel better, see the positive, and probably talk her out of worrying about Nikki, it would be Rose.

"I felt like you've been so happy lately," Rose said gently, her gaze slipping to the wedding ring around Grace's neck. "Did something happen?"

She lifted the ring, letting her finger slide over the now familiar metal. "Getting this back helped a lot. This has nothing to do with Nick, but..." She grimaced and leaned in. "Do you think there might be, I don't know, something not quite right with Nikki Lou?"

"She's too perfect?" Rose scoffed. "Too beautiful and smart? What are you talking about, Grace?"

Grace closed her eyes. "Rose, please. You have four kids. You know how they're supposed to act."

"Supposed to? Nikki Lou is supposed to act exactly as she does. But..." Rose put her hand on Grace's arm. "I know she can be frustrating, even for a three-year-old. You were shy, too, you know."

"I still am, if I'm being honest. But was I terrified of everyone?"

"Not of me." Rose sighed and smiled. "You were so cute, my little Gracie. I was ten when you were born and I thought you—and Sadie and Chloe—were miracle baby dolls dropped on my little girl lap from heaven. I still do." She squeezed Grace's hand. "What brought this on, honey?"

"A teacher at school suggested I get her tested."

"Tested? For autism?"

Grace nodded. "She thinks Nikki might be on the spectrum, which I know is wide and can encompass a lot of different character traits, from social skills to language problems."

"There is nothing wrong with her language," Rose insisted. "She barely uses baby talk and she's three. If anything, she's on the genius side of that spectrum."

Grace smiled at her ever-optimistic sister. "It's the social stuff I worry about. Although some people—often the ones you least expect—can really draw her out."

"That makes her a good judge of character," Rose said.

"She's a little young to judge characters."

"I don't know about that." Rose pulled back her platinum hair to lean closer and make a point without getting a strand in the salsa. "Children have a sixth sense about a person who is good or bad. They instinctively know when they can trust someone. I'll look up the studies for you."

"You don't have to," Grace replied. "I see it myself with her. She met Isaiah Kincaid a while back, when I went to thank him for the ring. She adored him. Didn't flinch, and he's a big man with a deep voice, but such a sweet smile."

"He's an angel," Rose agreed. "And I don't bestow that compliment lightly. Gabe is the only other one I know."

"But do you think I should get her tested, Rose?"

"I think you should do what feels right. If you're worried about it, maybe you should."

Grace sighed, cracking a chip in half. "It's so hard to do this alone."

"A Wingate woman is never alone, Grace."

"I know, I know, but Nick would know what to do. Maybe Nikki wouldn't even be that shy if he were alive. He'd carry her on his shoulders and make her laugh and tell her bedtime stories and make her believe she was..." Her voice cracked. "Safe."

"Gracie!" Rose practically crawled over the booth to offer comfort.

"It's okay," Grace assured her. "I know I have the most amazing, supportive family right here. I was thinking that when darling Alyson and Avery took their bodyguard positions around Nikki. I know I'm not alone, per se, but—"

"You are a wonderful mother, strong, capable, loving and wise."

"Rose, please don't wash this in optimism. I need real advice."

Rose nodded. "Okay, here it is. You'll know in your heart what's right for Nikki Lou, and you'll know if and when you need to do something. Trust your instincts."

Grace felt her lids close on a sigh. "I guess."

"Would testing hurt her?" Rose asked.

"I doubt it."

"Would it terrify you?"

"Probably."

"Would it change anything if they tell you she *is* on the spectrum?"

Grace considered that. "Maybe the way they teach her or...I don't know. Maybe an expert could give me some guidance for helping her. I really don't know."

"Then, if only for peace of mind, maybe you should, Grace."

"Peace of mind. Do you ever have that as a mother?" she mused.

"No, but..." Rose pointed toward a server coming toward them with sizzling platters. "You can drown your worries in fajitas."

Grace smiled at her, grateful that Rose not only knew the right thing to say, she knew when to let go and let Grace figure things out on her own.

"Amen, sister," Grace whispered, inhaling the spicy scent of beef and cilantro, sneaking a peek at her phone and saying a silent prayer of gratitude that Madeline hadn't texted with a problem.

Rose was right. She'd know if and when to get Nikki Lou tested. She had to be ready to deal with the results, which was what was really stopping her.

Chapter Thirteen

Chloe

"All right, Lady Bug, let the games begin." Chloe patted the massive recliner where she sat, feeling a little like she'd usurped Gabe's throne that he only shared with a daughter or two when they watched movies in this den. "Sit with me."

There was plenty of space for a tiny little ball of fur. But Lady Bug gave her a wary look from the floor, and for good reason.

"What?" Chloe demanded of the dog. "It's a clay face mask. Yes, I look like I'm slathered in Crisco and have my hair in fat curlers, but deal. It's self-care. So get up here, Bugaboo."

Finally, Lady Bug leaped onto the chair, turned, and wedged between Chloe's leg and the armrest with a sigh.

"Now, we have cheap sweet rosé." She lifted the hefty glass of wine she'd poured. "Buttery popcorn that you act like you don't want, but sneak eat when I'm not looking." She slid the bowl closer. "PJs, fuzzy slippers, and a blanket covered in..." She lifted up the throw that Avery had left on the chair last night. "Unicorns. All we have to do now is pick a heartwarming rom-com with a predictable ending—that Hunter refused to watch with me, but I'm not bitter—and we're officially having what is known as a girls' night in. You like?"

Lady Bug tucked in closer, squirreling her tiny body as close as she possibly could without actually climbing into the Wonder Woman sleep pants that Chloe's co-workers had given her as a gag gift last Christmas.

"Okay, maybe it isn't the most fantastic Saturday night ever," she muttered as she picked up the remote and hit the button for a streaming service. "But the fam is out for the night and I'm exhausted after a crazy long week of work at the café and making TikTok videos."

Which reminded her... Had Kenzie posted the last one?

She snagged her phone and tapped the app, thumbing the search bar.

Immediately, her latest video came up with the fun music Kenzie added in post-production.

"The stars have arrived and aligned!" TV Chloe announced on the small screen. "And that right there is the dressing trailer for Georgia Caravello—who is playing Ivy, the main character in *Christmas on Main Street*. Georgia—or Gigi, as she's known to her friends—is in hair and makeup and she said we can interview her. Come with me!"

Of course, Kenzie had given it a perfect edit with some stars flashing, then Chloe was standing in front of the actress in her chair.

"Oh, my gosh, what is that highlighter?" The camera zoomed to the actress's face.

"Wait, what?" Chloe bolted forward, her heart jumping. "Kenzie! You didn't use this part, did you?"

She watched another thirty seconds, which was the start of a two-minute tutorial by the makeup artist completely transforming Gigi's face, while Chloe peppered her with comments and jokes, and then...only then did she get to the legit interview.

But not on this video.

"Kenzie!" she shouted to the air. "That wasn't what we agreed on! Why did you—"

Lady Bug shot off the sofa with an earsplitting bark, bounding toward the front of the house with purpose before the doorbell even rang.

Chloe sat frozen for a moment, seriously considering ignoring that bell. Whoever it was didn't need to see her like this. But then the visitor knocked and she pushed up with a groan.

It was probably one of the kids' friends and she'd scare them off with one look.

She walked to the front door, peering through the leaded glass to see a shadowy figure on the other side, male and tall, so probably a friend of Zach's.

"Zach's out for the evening," she called through the door.

"Uh, not here for Zach. Is that you, Chloe?"

Oh, *no*. Not Travis McCall. Anyone but Travis McCall.

She swallowed and refused to steal a glance in the

entryway mirror, because she didn't want to know how she looked.

"Yes," she answered, her voice strained.

He waited a second, no doubt for her to open the door, as anyone would...if they didn't have a clay mask on their face, four-inch-wide rollers in their hair, and Wonder Woman pajama pants under a baggy T-shirt.

"Um...I need to get some gear from Gabe," he said. "In the garage."

"I'll open the garage door," she said quickly, pivoting to head there.

She could open it and stay inside and he could get what he needed and be gone. Dashing to the kitchen and into the mudroom with Lady Bug hot on her heels, she opened the door to the garage and touched the button. But before she could back away and disappear, Lady Bug shot out and darted through the garage, whisking under the rising door.

"Hey!" she called, taking a few steps out but the garage door froze when Lady Bug crossed the sensor, just high enough to reveal Travis McCall on the other side.

"Oh..." She backed up, but it was too late.

"Whoa." His jaw dropped in disbelief just as Lady Bug shot down the driveway.

"Can you get her?" Chloe called.

He spun around and snagged the little dog with the same ease he'd saved her phone that day, grabbing her with strong, capable hands, moving so gracefully all she could do was watch.

Then he turned and lifted both eyebrows, walking back to the garage. "Interesting look."

Under the thick layer of white clay—which was starting to harden—she felt her cheeks flame with a blush.

"We're having a girls' night," she said.

"Oh. Sorry to interrupt." He was clearly doing his best not to stare and laugh, and failing as he offered her the squirming dog. "Here you go. One...Lady Bird? Bed Bug? I forget her name."

"Lady Bug." She took the dog, managing not to react when their fingers brushed, suddenly remembering how Rose and Gabe didn't exactly insist that she join either of them tonight. "Funny Gabe told you to come now."

But was it? Or was this a calculated setup on Gabe and Rose's part? She wouldn't put it past them the way they waxed on about how fabulous Travis was, having given up some cushy corporate job to be a firefighter.

"He left some equipment in here for me." He glanced from side to side in the garage, but then back at her as if he simply couldn't look anywhere else. "I'll get it and be out of your, um...hair. In beer can things."

She had to laugh. What else could she do?

"They're rollers," she said. "And you can stop laughing."

He bit his lip. "It's taking all I got, Chloe."

"I'm sure." She nodded toward the side of the garage, crowded with bikes and tools, a generator, and a pile of firefighter things. "That's probably what you're looking for."

He smiled and looked down at Lady Bug in her arms, a wine glass in her free hand. "Rosé?" he guessed.

"It pairs well with cheese...cheesy rom-coms, which I'm about to watch."

He nodded knowingly and finally stopped staring, turning toward the gear. "Which one?" he asked.

She frowned at the jacket and helmet, not seeing another. "All of it, I guess."

"No, I meant, which rom-com?"

She blinked, processing the question. "Oh, I'm not sure. I was about to look for something."

He turned from the gear back to her. "I say go old school Eighties, like *Working Girl* or *Romancing the Stone*. Oh, *Pretty Woman*." As she stared in shock, he lifted up both hands like he was holding something. "'Big mistake. Huge.'" His grin widened. "Love that scene."

"Wow," she said on a laugh. "Wouldn't take you for someone who could quote chick flicks."

He lifted a shoulder. "Blame my mom, the original chick who loved a good flick. She made me watch them all many times."

"And you did?" She tried to imagine any boy—like the two that lived in this house, for example—watching movies like that with their mom. Rose could never rope Zach or Ethan into being in the same room as a rom-com, let alone remember the lines.

"I did," he said, quiet as he walked closer to the generator and the gear on top of it.

Curious and mesmerized, she took a step deeper into the garage, her ridiculous getup forgotten as he suddenly looked a little lost. Tall, handsome, built like he could be on a firefighter calendar...but his expression had grown distant.

"You must be a very good son to do that," she said softly, sensing on some level that his change had to do with the mention of his mother.

He looked down. "It was all I could do for her when she was...sick." He swallowed. "But I think it helped her get through to the end."

"Oh." A small whimper escaped her lips. "I'm sorry, Travis."

"'Sokay," he said quickly, obviously pulling it together as he zeroed in on the jacket, picking it up. "And thank you, Gabe D'Angelo. Boots, a bunker coat, a couple of helmets, and a gear bag."

He lifted the boots high enough to examine them. Or pretend to.

"How long ago did she pass?" she asked.

"Coming on a year soon," he said, turning to her with a tight smile. "She'd have been right with you on that..." He gave a general wave toward his face. "Mask thing. She loved that. Now, I never went *that* far." He laughed, but the smile faded. "But then, she never asked or I probably would have."

She crossed her arms and studied him for a moment, imagining a grown man watching thirty-year-old movies with his dying mother. And her heart slipped around her chest.

"Well, if you ever need a fix of, you know, Julia Roberts or Meg Ryan, I'm your girl."

He lowered the boot and regarded her, and she knew what was coming. *Are you anyone's girl? I thought you were on a man hiatus.*

But he smiled. "I do love *Pretty Woman*. I hated that they made her a prostitute, though. It could have been the same movie without that."

"What?" she choked the question. "It wouldn't have been the same story if she hadn't been a hooker."

"She could have just been down on her luck," he said. "She didn't have to walk the streets."

"But that's how he found her."

"She could have been, you know, shoplifting or something. Because she was hungry and broke."

"But he paid for the week. Remember? That's the whole story? He bought her services but didn't want sex."

"He could still have bought her services."

She put her hands on her hips, shaking her head. "No. No. A thousand times no."

That made him laugh. "Well, you watch it again and see it my way."

"*You* watch it again and see it *my* way."

For a few heartbeats, he looked at her, his smile returning, which made her feel better than it should have. "Pretty hard to take you seriously like that, but, okay. Let's watch it now and decide."

She sucked in a soft breath. "Now?"

"Sure. I'm not doing anything and you..." He lifted a brow. "Well, I'm going out on a limb and guessing you're alone. You expecting someone else to watch with you?"

"Just Lady Bug." She tried to smile but the clay cracked.

"Well?"

"Okay, but..."

"But you're on a break from men. I know, Chloe. I'm not here as a 'man,'" he said on a chuckle. "Do I have to mask up to prove that?"

She laughed. "You're fine exactly as you are." Which was the understatement of the century. "Get your stuff and meet me in the den." She tried to lift her brows but her mask was solid. "And prepare to be proven wrong in your ridiculous movie logic."

She stepped back inside, aware that her whole body felt lighter at the possibility of watching a classic movie with him, then darted straight into the powder room, washed her face, and took her hair out of the curlers.

She almost ran upstairs to her own bathroom to throw on some makeup, but shook her head and decided against it.

"Not a date. Not a man. Not a break in the plan."

With that, she walked back into the den to find him on the couch, holding Lady Bug on his lap, the popcorn bowl in front of him. Had anything ever been so...attractive?

"I didn't give her any," he assured her, misreading her look.

"That's okay. She can have a kernel or two."

"Awesome." He opened his fist and let Lady Bug wolf a small bite. "Good girl," he added, petting her head.

Seriously? Did he have to be perfect? That wasn't making this easier. Fun, but not easy.

"You were right." Travis and Chloe spoke in perfect unison.

They turned to each other as the iconic fire escape scene ended and Vivian and Edward got their well-deserved happy ending.

"I was?" she asked.

"You were. You thought I was right?" He ran his hand over Lady Bug's back. The little dog had not moved from his lap since the opening credits.

"I could see that it wasn't her prostitute-ness that made her so sympathetic," she conceded.

"But I don't think it would have been quite the same," he countered, sliding into a sweet smile. "The down-on-her-luck shoplifter who gets lucky doesn't have the same ring as the 'hooker with a heart of gold.'"

She sighed, curling up under the unicorn blanket in the recliner. "That was a good choice for a movie," she said. "I don't think I've watched that since I was really young with one of my sisters."

"You were into it," he said. "Big props for not picking up your phone even though it buzzed through the whole movie."

She looked for her cell on the end table between her chair and the sofa, spying it next to the empty popcorn bowl. "I never even heard it, to be honest."

He inched the phone closer. "Here you go."

She picked it up and forced herself to look at the screen, a little unwilling to be dragged out of the bygone era of sweet romantic movies and the incredibly attractive man who'd just watched one with her.

"Oh." She recoiled, blinking at the screen and the many, many, many texts from Kenzie, most of which said, YOU WENT VIRAL in screaming capital letters. "Oh, my."

"Everything okay?" he asked.

"Yeah, I..." She let out a surprised laugh as she started skimming the screenshots of likes, shares, duets, and comments on the TikTok video. "I didn't expect this."

The phone buzzed with a call from Kenzie.

"Gimme a sec," she said. "It's my niece and I have to—"

"No worries." He pushed up. "Sorry, little pup. Gotta hit the bathroom."

She smiled at him and touched the phone as he walked out, Lady Bug not two feet behind her new obsession. "Kenzie?"

"I've been texting you but we just got out of the movie. Oh my *gawd*, Chloe. This is huge. People loved that makeup video! They like Georgia and they *loved* you!"

She let out a little laugh as she skimmed more of the comments in Kenzie's screenshots, zeroing in on one.

Forget the actress, who's the cute reporter?

A reporter? She wasn't a...well, wait a second, she thought. No need to get strangled by Imposter Syndrome.

She was the reporter and even on the part of the segment she thought was lead-in and throwaway, she'd asked smart questions, let the answers dictate the next question, and helped deliver real information to the viewer.

Okay, maybe it was how an actress applied eye shadow, but that was still reporting.

"I have almost two hundred new followers, Chloe," Kenzie said. "And it's all due to you. We better start your own profile and load up all these videos. You'll be a star in no time."

"Okay, I will, but..." But she didn't want to be a star. She wanted to be a reporter. Wasn't there a difference?

"But what?" Kenzie asked as Travis walked back into the room, now holding Lady Bug.

"But I have to go," she said. "Great work, Kenz. What about the actual interview?"

"That goes up tomorrow," Kenzie said. "And we have to make more content. Gotta run!"

Chloe hung up and looked at Travis, feeling the smile pull. "You have yourself a friend, I see."

"She tried to walk me to the door," he said. "Think she wants me to leave?"

"I think she wants to hit the grass." Chloe pushed out of the recliner and angled her head toward the back door. "I'll take her out."

"I'll come with you."

She pushed open one of the French doors to the patio and backyard, the summer evening air warm and welcoming after the air-conditioned house.

"Here you go, Lady...Gaga."

"Bug," she corrected on a laugh. "She's named after the little red creature that brings good luck, a lady bug."

"Gotcha. So what were all the calls about? Everything okay in the Wingate family?" he asked as they stepped onto the grass and Lady Bug took off for a run around the fenced-in yard, sniffing at the bushes and the scent of basil and tomatoes that seemed to emanate from the little greenhouse.

"You know I'm doing those videos about the movie? On TikTok?" She'd talked about it the other night when Travis had been here for dinner. "Well, one of them went kind of viral...ish. Nothing major, but..." She shrugged. "It's cool."

"Oh, so now you're like one of those influencers."

"That's not what I want," she said, as much to herself as to him. "But it proves I was right all along. I could have been a television reporter."

He glanced at her, making a face. "You doubted that? What's stopping you?"

"You have an hour?" she asked with a groan. "A week? A year?"

"I'd say yes to all three but then you'd remind me you're on some kind of man break and I can't have the next hour, week, or year." He leaned into her. "But please let me know when the time's up and I can make my move."

She smiled up at him, a little dizzy at the honesty and the way his long eyelashes cast a shadow over his cheeks in the soft vineyard lights that Gabe had hung all over the backyard.

Tamping down a flirtatious response, she took a mental step backwards to answer the first question.

"I gave up the dream," she said simply. "I did the work, got the degree, had the internships, but then...I met Hunter Landry and..."

"And ran away from him at your wedding," he finished for her. "What's stopping you now?"

"Nothing. Everything. The mountain is so high and I'm already too old, if you can believe that, and now it feels like a childhood dream."

"Sorry, kiddo, you're talking to the wrong man if you expect me to agree."

"What do you mean?"

He exhaled softly and walked to a stone bench outside of the greenhouse, dropping down on it and gesturing her closer.

Without giving it too much thought, she joined him.

"I had a professional dream that I thought was finished because I was too old and it seemed like a silly, kid thing."

"Being a firefighter?" she guessed.

"Bingo. My whole life..." He laughed and stabbed his hands into his short, chestnut hair, his gaze off in the distance now. "From the time I was..." He reached down to indicate someone who might only be a foot or two off the ground. "I wanted to be a firefighter. But I somehow snagged a full scholarship to NYU, then I got an MBA because, I don't know, because I could. I got a job at one of the top business consulting firms in Manhattan making stupid money, and then...my mom got sick."

"Oh." She hadn't been expecting that. "What happened?"

He didn't answer for a long time, still staring ahead. "My parents are divorced, and my dad is long out of the picture, and I knew someone had to take care of her during chemo and all that."

"So you did?"

He nodded. "I moved out of my city apartment and back in with her, out on Long Island, where I was raised. I commuted and mostly worked from home—and watched rom-coms," he added on a dry laugh. "Anyway, I spent that last year with her and we talked. A *lot*. She knew she was looking at the end, because the cancer was pretty aggressive, but that made her really philosophical. And she asked me to promise her that when I died, I would have no regrets with how I lived my life. That's all she wanted from me—no regrets. She used to take my hand and say, 'No regrets, coyote.'" He chuckled at the memory.

"Her nickname for you? Coyote?"

"No, it's the first line of an old song she used to listen to. Anyway, I made that promise, and I kept it."

She studied him, fascinated. "So, how does one live life with no regrets? Because, whoa, that sounds like the life I'd like."

He smiled. "Well, for one thing, one walks away from a fat paycheck and becomes the lowest man on the totem pole in a fire station."

"Why here if you lived in New York?" she asked.

"I couldn't break into the training in New York. But I

dug and dug, and found this little station in Florida willing to give me a shot as a probie. And here I am, living proof that you are never too old to follow your dreams. Anyway, what are you? Twenty-six?"

"I'm almost thirty, and in the world of TV news, I might as well be fifty. In fact, that would be better and give me some street cred. Now I'm just another blonde who thinks she can report news. Hate to say it, but we're a dime a dozen."

He eyed her. "Try being a thirty-three-year-old wanna-be firefighter with no experience, up against guys coming out of the military who were trained overseas or on aircraft carriers." He gave a dry snort. "I don't think people realize how competitive it is. And I'm sure TV news is the same."

"It is," she said. "You have to start in tiny markets—like you're doing—and claw your way to the top. I'm not sure I have what it takes."

"You know what Maggie McCall would say?"

"No regrets, coyote," she said softly as Lady Bug came bounding over. Chloe leaned over to love on the little dog. "No regrets, Bugaboo."

Lady Bug panted and wagged and slipped out of Chloe's touch to stare up at Travis like he'd hung the very moon overhead.

"Well, *she* is certainly not on a man break," he joked, bending over to pick up the dog in loving, gentle hands. Had Hunter ever held Lady Bug so tenderly? "Are you, fluff ball?" He kissed her silky head and something inside

Chloe melted. If she had a tail, it would be flipping as hard as little Lady B's.

Just then, lights from a car pulling into the driveway stole their attention and the garage door rose as Gabe and the boys got home, ending the moment and the mood.

But later that night, when Chloe scrolled through TikTok and read every single comment and watched the interview twenty times, she sure had a lot to think about.

No regrets, coyote.

She googled the words and found an old Joni Mitchell song and listened to the haunting melody, imagining Maggie McCall, sick and dying, humming along and teaching life lessons to her dear, handsome, sweet son.

So dear, so handsome, and so sweet that not giving in to his obvious interest might result in one big, fat, unimaginable *regret*.

Chapter Fourteen

Raina

"Well, this is a first," Raina said, glancing at her passenger. "Taking my sister with me to a doctor appointment."

"You can't do this one alone, Rain," Tori said. "I'm honored. Hope I'm the one you have in the delivery room, too. Or maybe we'll have the whole fam damily, as Dad likes to say."

Raina winced, hoping saying that didn't jinx her. "Let's get through today first. Then we'll worry about who's in the delivery room."

"We should all be there," Tori said. "A giggle-gaggle of Wingates. Good heavens, that man had a funny way of describing his daughters."

"He still does," Raina reminded her. "I heard him use that expression the other day."

"Really?" Tori turned at this news. "That's a good sign. Dad's getting back to normal."

"Inching his way there, I'd say, but still a little down in the dumps," Raina said as she pulled into the medical office parking lot.

"I know. Getting the part of Santa hasn't even cheered him up," Tori said. "Although it did help to catch me in a liplock with Hottypants that he seemed to like."

Raina smiled at that. "I'm really grateful to Marcus for the Santa thing. He had to call in a favor to get that."

"There haven't been any production issues, have there?" Tori asked.

"So far, so good. They're shooting at Grace's store, then Madeline's shop for a big scene. Fortunately, that's left me some time to pay attention to Wingate Properties for a while."

"And things are going well there?"

Raina nodded, then laughed softly. "Except I can't figure what to make of Dad's assistant, Blake the Fake."

Tori snorted. "Why do you call him that?"

"I don't know. He's so...weirdly pushy. He has me on some pedestal that feels strange." She shrugged. "Whatever. I can't really think about it today. It's Baby Doctor Day."

Tori reached over and put her hand on Raina's arm. "You scared? Nervous? Excited? How are you feeling?"

Raina huffed out a breath and tried to think about how to answer the question. "I'm...refusing to get too excited. I think the term is 'cautiously optimistic.' This isn't my first 'hearing the heartbeat' rodeo, you know."

"I know." She gave her hand a squeeze. "But it's the first with me at your side. Auntie Tori is lucky."

"I guess I feel really guilty about keeping Jack away, too," Raina admitted. "It's his kid. Yes, he forfeited heartbeat-hearing rights, but it's still *his* kid. He will have to have *some* rights, which I assume will be pounded out by lawyers over the next few months."

"Or years," Tori said, making Raina groan. "Have you talked to him since he found out?"

"Only the most cursory texts, only about business." Raina pulled into a parking spot, staring straight ahead, then closing her eyes as the truth hit. "I'm sure he thinks I'll lose it and the whole thing will go away."

"Or...not."

At Tori's weird tone, Raina opened her eyes and glanced at her sister, who was staring at the building. Raina followed her gaze and gasped softly at the sight of Jack sitting on a bench outside the doctor's office, looking at his phone.

"He's *here*?"

"You did say he got that call about the appointment," Tori said. "Somehow I'm not completely shocked."

Raina blinked at the sight of him, bracing for a cascade of emotions—sadness, regret, fury, maybe a little joy or hope, and, of course, the love she always felt when she saw Jack Wallace. But none of that happened.

"Nothing," she muttered as reality hit.

"What?" Tori looked at her. "What did you say?"

"I don't feel anything. For him, I mean. No bitter-sweet ache, no anger, no...nothing."

"That's impossible," Tori shot back. "You can't be married to a man for sixteen years, carrying his child, and separated after he cheated and feel...*nothing*."

Raina flicked her brows in disagreement. "Sorry. Maybe I'm numb to him."

Just then, Jack looked up, saw her car, and stood. He gave a tight, kind of guilty smile, and tucked his hands into his trouser pockets as he watched and waited.

"What are you going to do?" Tori asked.

"What do you mean?"

"Are you going to let him come to the appointment?"

"I guess I have to, right?" Raina tried to breathe, but her whole chest felt tight. "Like I said, he is the father."

Tori grunted and reached for her door handle, then stopped as Jack started walking toward the car. "Should I wait here? So you can talk privately to him."

"No. Come along and we'll all get the news together."

"What news?" Tori asked.

"There's either a heartbeat or there isn't, Tor. Last time I did this, there wasn't. Of course, I'd been bleeding for hours, so I already knew what the doctor was going to tell me."

She didn't wait to hear Tori's response, but pushed open her door, stood and looked at Jack, still waiting for one of those deep emotions to hit. But maybe she'd protected herself so thoroughly from any pain, disappointment, or hope today that she was incapable of feeling a thing.

"I hope you don't mind, Raina," he said as he walked toward the car. "I couldn't help myself. I had to come."

She nodded. "It's fine."

"I mean, I didn't want you to be here alone."

"I said it's fine, Jack." She slammed the door maybe a little harder than she had to, more affected by the gentleness in his voice than anything. "I'm not alone."

Tori's door opened and she climbed out. "Jack," she said simply.

"Hey, Tori."

For a moment, the two of them looked at each other, the awkward silence broken only by the sound of a car driving by.

"Come on," Raina said. "My appointment is in one minute."

"They're running late," Jack told them. "I checked."

Irritation punched, but Raina squeezed the fob on her keys to lock her door and tucked them into her purse, grateful that Jack didn't try to hug or kiss her. Not that she expected him to, but she loathed hypocrisy.

A minute later, all three of them entered the office and Raina checked in, then sat with them in the small waiting room.

Jack propped his elbows on his knees and looked straight ahead, silent.

Tori picked up a magazine and thumbed through it, turning the pages with poorly-disguised disgust.

And Raina looked down at the floor and tried to breathe. She didn't care that Jack was here, really. She didn't care how uncomfortable this was or that she was probably facing a lifetime of moments like this. All she cared about was the sound of that heartbeat and whatever they'd see on the ultrasound.

"Regina Wingate?"

A little taken aback by the use of a first name she rarely heard, Raina stood and held a palm out to both of them. "I'm going to talk to the doctor alone first."

"Aren't you going to hear the heartbeat?" Jack asked, his brows raised with interest and concern.

"If I do, you can come in for the ultrasound."

Tori reached for Raina's hand, giving it a squeeze. "I'm here for you, hon."

She nodded and followed the nurse, going through the motions of doing her vitals, weight, and the questions. Then she got shuffled to another room, changed into a gown, and waited about ten more minutes until Dr. Milwood breezed in with a clipboard and a wide smile on her face.

"Hello, Raina," she said, reaching out a hand.

"Dr. Milwood." She only realized how damp her palms were when she shook the cool, dry, steady one of the other woman. "Sorry." She wiped it on the gown. "I'm more nervous than I realized."

"Don't be. You've reached ten weeks, which is a milestone. Your baby is no longer an embryo, but a fetus. How do you feel?"

"Guarded," she admitted. "I made it to ten weeks once before, as you know."

She nodded and glanced at the chart. "Nearly twelve, you said." She looked up, her dark eyes warm with hope and sympathy. "There's no reason to be worried, but let's do this exam and get to that ultrasound."

"Can I hear the heartbeat now?"

"Not with this stethoscope, not yet. Let's use the Doppler in the ultrasound room. Are you alone today?" she asked, gently guiding Raina to her back.

"Um, no. My sister and my, uh, husband are here."

The words caught in her throat, but not because of what she was saying. Because it suddenly all felt so familiar. The cool leather of the exam table against her skin. The fluorescent lights beaming from the drop ceiling. The antiseptic smell, the doctor's warm hand, the hope and desire and inevitable disappointment that gripped her whole body.

Could she even bear to go through losing another baby? It hurt so much the last time, which had been the worst. And sad and frustrating agony and grief that she never, ever wanted to endure again. She'd felt hollow and empty and robbed each time, but the last one? That was—

"All right, everything looks good," Dr. Milwood said, easing her up into a sitting position. "Let's get to the fun part. Emily will walk you into the ultrasound room and get your family to join you."

She blinked, suddenly unsure. Did she want Jack in that room? Did she want to look into the eyes of a man who openly admitted he was in love with another woman? Did she want his hand to touch hers when they saw the baby...the hand that touched Lisa Godfrey probably as recently as this morning?

She swallowed as bile rose in her throat.

"Yes, of course," she said, as much to the doctor as to herself. "He has a right to be there."

Dr. Milwood's eyes flickered at that, but she was too cool to ask what Raina meant.

"Then are you ready to get your first look at your baby?" she asked instead.

"So ready."

THE ROOM WAS small and crowded with the ultrasound tech, Dr. Milwood, Tori, Jack, and Raina on yet another exam table.

"Heartbeat first," the doctor said as she slipped on latex gloves and positioned Raina for privacy from the others.

Raina swallowed and winced at the feel of the cold device, amazed that it could pick up any heartbeat other than her own slamming against her ribs.

"It just takes..." Dr. Milwood closed her eyes and moved the monitor. "A few seconds to...there we go."

A slurpy, soft thump echoed through the machine. One, two, three, four.

"And there you go, Mom," the doctor said, meeting Raina's gaze with a huge smile.

"Really?"

Behind her, Tori let out a little whimper.

"That's it?" Jack asked. "That's the heartbeat? Is it loud enough?"

"It's...very strong," the doctor said with a chuckle.

"Is it okay?" Raina asked, not even trying to hide the worry in her voice.

"All good. Let's take a look, Emily," she instructed the tech.

Taking a slow, steadying breath, Raina braced for the gel and intrusion of the ultrasound wand. It was warm,

Emily was gentle, but none of that calmed her as the screen was angled toward Raina.

Déjà vu hit so hard, it took her breath away. All she could remember was the last time, and the time before.

After having one miscarriage, she never looked at the screen for the next two. She'd stared at the tech instead of the screen, looking for that flash of sadness, and she'd known she'd lost the baby.

Could she bear it again? No. She might not be able to take that ache.

Still, she watched Emily's expression, taking in her intense blue eyes and creamy skin. She had a gentle touch and hummed softly as she worked, and a sweet smile that pulled as she looked at the screen.

"There's your baby, Raina. Moving little arms and legs."

"What?" Jack came closer. "He's moving?"

"He or she," Emily said on a laugh. "And before you ask, we cannot tell yet. But your little one is..." She tapped a few keys on the machine next to her, moving the wand. "About an inch and a half long."

"Really?" Finally Raina looked at the screen, seeing nothing but a grayscale blob that most certainly did seem to be moving.

"She or he," Emily corrected again with a chuckle, "is growing nicely. The yolk sac is kind of hiding things there, but the umbilical cord looks strong, everything looks normal and perfect." She shifted her gaze from the screen to Raina. "You're carrying a healthy baby, Ms. Wingate."

"Oh." Tori let out another whimper. "That's so good."

Raina looked up over her shoulder, instantly meeting Jack's gaze. And that's when she...felt. *All* the things.

His tears ripped her heart out. His smile kicked her gut in. His eyes, locked on her, were so full of wonder and love she almost cried out.

"Rain." He came around the table, next to her, taking her hand. "Do you see that?"

She stared at him and suddenly she knew that the only thing that mattered on this Earth was the inch-and-a-half-long fetus—no longer an embryo—that she was keeping alive in her womb.

Nothing. Not Jack or his affair or her life or Wingate Properties or anything. The only thing that mattered was this baby.

"I do see...her. Or him." She let her fingers close around his hand.

"It's...amazing," he whispered. "I'm blown away."

She nodded, not trusting her voice to say anything.

"Thank you for letting me see that," he added. "I'll let you go now, but..." He looked at the screen. "Thank you."

Emily looked up from her computer, a little confusion in her eyes. "If you wait, I'll print out some pictures for you."

"No," he said without hesitation. "I...I...just wanted to see...this. I shouldn't be here." He gave her hand a squeeze. "Take care and I'll call you."

With that, he left the room, and Tori instantly came to her other side.

"I'm here, Rain," she whispered. "I'm right here."

And she stayed next to Raina through the remainder of the appointment, while she made the next one, and until they were back in the car alone.

"You feel better now?" Tori asked.

Raina took a second to think, to pull her feelings together, to make priorities and figure everything out.

"What's best for the baby," Raina finally whispered.

"What do you mean?"

"That's all I can do. That's my whole life. My whole reason for breathing and moving and eating and sleeping. This baby. Tori." She grabbed her sister's hand. "I have to do what's best for this baby."

"And you will."

She blinked at her, words she'd tried to tamp down still bubbling up. "Aren't two parents best?" she asked on a ragged whisper.

"Oh, Rain. You're thinking about going back with him, aren't you?"

She hadn't realized it, at least not until she touched his hand. "I don't know," she confessed. "I want to do what's best for this baby. That's all."

Tori exhaled and nodded. "I understand. You will put the child first, from this day forward. That never changes."

Raina dropped her head back and closed her eyes. "It dictates every decision, doesn't it?"

"Every one," Tori agreed.

"Maybe I should..." *Give him another chance.* But she couldn't even bear to give voice to that thought.

"Maybe I should go home and rest," she finished. "I'm wiped out."

"As you should be," Tori said. "Are you going to tell the family now, Rain? Jack knows."

She sighed. "I want to wait a little while longer, Tori. I want to...be sure."

"I get that."

They drove home in silence, but it wasn't quiet in Raina's head. She had one thought, over and over, loud and clear.

What's best for the baby?

Chapter Fifteen

Tori

S he's going to forgive him. She's going to get back with him. She's going to get hurt again, and hard.

Tori's gut was on fire with the certainty that Raina—especially pregnant Raina—was going to make a huge mistake. But it wasn't Tori's place to tell her that. Just because Tori's experience was that the cheating leopard husband would never change his spots didn't mean that the same thing was true for Raina and Jack.

Except...something told her it was.

She'd never really adored Jack Wallace, as a person or as a brother-in-law, so it was no surprise she was on Team Raina, and Raina alone. He was always the outsider who pulled Raina away. Not only physically, but emotionally. When she was with him, she was distant from the family. But now, with a baby—

A call flashed on the dashboard screen, pulling her thoughts to the present. And not just any call, but one she longed for—her son.

"Finnie! How's it going, honey? How's life out in left

field?" she teased, using one of their favorite inside jokes. "Are you having a blast on your adventure in an RV?"

The silence on the other end lasted long enough for Tori's heart to sink. "Finn?"

"Mom." His voice was rough, gruff, and low. But then again, he was thirteen, and that voice could be any pitch on any day.

"What's wrong?" she asked, already sensing this was serious.

"Mom, I...I can't do this. I can't." That wasn't hormones that cracked his voice. That was pain and a sob that nearly ripped her heart out.

"What's the matter? Why? Tell me everything, Finn. I'm here for you."

Again, there was a long silence. "I have to...hang on, Mom. I don't want anyone to hear me."

She could hear what sounded like movement—a breeze over the phone, footsteps, his breathing—then finally a long groan.

"Mom, I hate this trip. I hate everything. My headaches are back."

"Oh, no, Finn. Did you get hit or anything?" She believed—and his doctor agreed—that the recurring headaches were due to stress, but she also knew that he had a bone-deep fear of that baseball coming right at his head, a fear that was a source of so many arguments with Trey.

You can't own the ball if you're scared of it, Finn!

No doubt the kid was getting that lecture every minute of every day.

"No, no. I haven't been hit. But the headaches are so bad, Mom. I can't see straight."

"Maybe you need glasses?" Even as she said it, she knew that wasn't the problem. He'd had his vision tested a few months ago.

Finn sighed, sounding a million miles away and broken.

"Maybe you shouldn't play."

"Mom," he said, slathering the word with a pound of emotion and teen disdain.

Tori eyed her surroundings and spotted a gas station, pulling in so she could concentrate on her son's problems.

"I have to play," he said. "Dad's the coach! How would it look if his own kid is on the bench?"

"Like he cares about you and your headaches. Does he even know about them?"

"No. I don't want to tell him."

"Why not?"

He was quiet for a long moment, then, "I think there's something wrong with me."

"What do you mean?" she asked, working hard to keep any panic from her voice at the fact that her baby was...somewhere...far away and hurting. "Please be specific so I can help you, Finn."

"Okay, but don't freak out."

She rolled her eyes at the words every mother loved. "Tell me."

"I want to throw up all the time, and every time I get in that bunkbed? It's like a coffin, Mom. That's all I can think of. I think I'm gonna die and I can't breathe and my head hurts and I want to scream."

"Oh, Finn. I told you that you've always had this reaction to small spaces. It's claustrophobia and lots of people have it."

"Do you think it's giving me the headaches?"

"Maybe." She itched to call Justin. "I'm going to talk to Grandpa's neurologist. He might know."

"Okay. You're sure that's not serious? Like I'm messed up for life?"

"It's a very common thing, a fear of small places. And you should tell your dad so you can get air and maybe sleep in a better bunk."

He sighed noisily. "I don't want to tell him, Mom. I don't want to be a wuss. Chris is fine, you know? He's a beast and he'd make me feel like such a loser if he knew."

She squeezed her eyes shut and thought about the other boy who was on the trip, a fellow baseball player named Chris Devine. He was a one of those thirteen-going-on-eighteen teenagers who mocked anything that wasn't cool or manly.

"You have to talk to Dad, Finn. You have to tell him you're in pain and can't play. I'll tell him—"

"No, no, please. He'd kill me."

"For having headaches? Don't be ridiculous."

"I don't want him to know. I don't want to be a big, fat disappointment. He's kind of a big deal in this league, you know. Since he was in the Red Sox organization."

"As a failed Minor League player," Tori shot back. "Don't let his ego get in your way, Finn."

"Mom, this isn't about you and Dad fighting. I don't want him to be embarrassed by his own kid. So I'm playing, but not well. And it hurts. My head hurts."

"All day, all the time?" She was already lining up questions to share with Justin.

"Mostly at night, but once one starts, I can barely see and I want to throw up."

That sounded like a migraine to her, but what could be causing it? And why would Trey expect him to play with a debilitating headache?

"Where are you?" she asked.

"I don't know. Somewhere in North Carolina, I think. We're camping in these totally gross and buggy woods tonight and then going to the next tournament, which is at a university north of Atlanta, but..." He moaned. "I'm hoping I can make it through. Unless..."

"Unless what?"

"You tell Dad you want me to come home," he said. "Can you make something up?"

"No," she said simply. "I'm not going to lie. But he has to know what you're going through, and he has to figure out a solution. Have you had any flashes of weird light in your eyes? Eaten anything strange?"

She tried to remember all the questions his pediatrician had asked last year when he had the headaches, and they'd even done a CT scan. Then the headaches went away as mysteriously as they'd started. Well, when baseball season ended.

"No, just the usual, you know. Nothing weird. A lot

of s'mores, since there's a campfire every night and Heidi loves to make them."

She exhaled, sorry the headaches were ruining his summer but worried they were a sign of something serious. "You can't spend the next—what?—four weeks like this."

"Man, that's like an eternity."

"Oh, Finn. All you have to do is quit these tournaments and all of you go home. Better yet, maybe Dad would let you come here and stay for the summer." Just saying the idea out loud made her heart hurt for how much she wanted that.

"I wish," he muttered. "Plus, Dad's committed as the coach. He can't quit. And I can't stand the way he looks at me when my butt's on the bench. Like I'm the biggest loser in his life."

Anger wormed through her, but she tempered her reaction. "You're not a loser, Finn. On the bench or off."

"Well, I feel like one."

Tori hated that. "I can talk to Dad, but I can't lie to him, Finn."

"No, no. I just needed to talk to you. Gimme a couple more days," he said. "Maybe the headaches will go away."

"Can you sleep outside?" she suggested. "If you're at a campsite? Maybe someone has a sleeping bag? At least you wouldn't feel trapped in the camper."

"It's an RV, Mom. And if I was outside, a bear could eat me." He snorted. "Then maybe Dad would let me sit out a game."

She sighed, knowing full well the dynamic at play.

Trey wanted to relive his glory days through Finn and Finn wanted...to play video games and not baseball.

"Sorry for being a downer, Mom. Are you and Kenzie having fun?"

She honestly didn't want to tell him how much. "Yes, it's good."

"Those TikToks she's making are nuts. Aunt Chloe is, like, so good. She's blowing up."

She smiled through unexpected tears. "I wish you were here, Finnie."

"Me, too, Mom."

"I could tell your—"

"I'm okay. I'm better," he said. "I needed to talk. I'm fine."

She didn't believe a word of that, but appreciated that he was trying so hard. "Are you sure you don't want me to talk to Dad?"

"Not yet. I'll holler if I really do think I'm going to die."

"Not funny," she said. "Don't wait until you're dying. Make him take you to a doctor."

"We're in the middle of nowhere."

"Well, wherever you are," she said. "I can be there in a day."

"I know. Love you, Mom."

The rare affection from a thirteen-year-old really touched. "I love you, too, Finn."

After they hung up, she sat for a few minutes, her whole body aching. He was right about Trey, of course. Finn's father would be angry, disappointed, belittling, and scoff at the idea that his son was weak enough to need a doctor for "a little headache." She could hear him, and she despised the sound of his voice in her head.

But it wasn't Trey's voice haunting her. It was Finn's —her baby, her boy. He needed her and she was down here having a summer romance. Did that make her the worst mother in the world?

No, but it made her heart hurt.

Fortunately, she knew exactly where to get help.

Tori waited in the reception area of Fernandina Beach Neurological Partners for exactly one minute before Justin came out of his office, a look of concern on his face.

For one brief second, she allowed herself to appreciate Dr. Hottypants when he wasn't in scrubs or his sailing outfit of cargo shorts and a T-shirt. For office hours, he wore a crisp white shirt, black dress pants, and a narrow, understated blue and white tie that made him look sophisticated and sexy and gorgeous.

"Tori." He reached for both her hands as she stood and pulled her close. "Is everything okay?"

"Yes. No. Maybe. Finn has a problem and it was too much to text and you were on a call, so I thought I'd wait. Do you have a minute? I'm sorry to barge—"

"No, don't apologize. Come to my office." He put a hand on her back and ushered her toward the door. "I don't have an appointment for almost a half hour. I was doing paperwork when I got off the call." He eyed her. "You look upset."

"I am," she admitted, stepping into a sun-washed corner office with a huge oak desk, a wall of certifications and diplomas, and a comfy loveseat under the window where he took her to sit down. "Nice digs, doc."

"Welcome to my home away from boat. That sofa pulls out in case of super inclement weather and I need a place to sleep."

"I never think of you anywhere but on a boat or wandering around the hospital."

He chuckled. "Wandering around? Do I look like I'm lost or something?"

"No, you look important. Which..." She gestured to the medical school diploma from the University of Pittsburgh. *Summa cum laude*, no less. "You obviously are."

"Only to the patient in front of me, which is you at the moment. Or Finn, did you say? What's going on?"

He was so kind and caring, she almost melted into his arms, wanting to be held and reassured that her son was fine. "Headaches. Bad, blinding headaches."

He winced. "Was he hit with a ball?"

"No, and that's his greatest fear. But this isn't the first time. Last year, he had horrible migraines, off and on. We took him to the pediatrician, who did a CT scan, found nothing, and then it mysteriously disappeared. Could it be stress? Claustrophobia? He hates that closed-in RV."

He considered that, then slowly shook his head. "Possibly, but stress headaches don't usually have the migraine-type symptoms. It almost sounds like a food allergy to me."

"Just as long as it's not a brain tumor."

"That would most likely have shown up on a scan," he reassured her. "Do you need a referral? I can get him into a neurologist in any city. Where are they?"

"I don't even know. Some campsite in the mountains of North Carolina, then I think they're going to..." She thought about the schedule Trey had sent her. "I think it's the University of North Georgia."

He nodded, then stood to go to his desk. "I can find a neurologist in Atlanta or at that school. I actually know a guy with a—"

"I need to go there." The minute the words were out, she realized how much she ached to get to Finn.

"You want to drive up to him? Take him to a doctor yourself?"

"Yes. I have to." She could practically feel herself pushing up from the sofa, ready to roll. "Kenzie will be okay here and Miguel can run the café for a few days. My dad's fine. I've got to hold that kid and...and..." Her voice grew thick.

"You have to be his mother."

"Yes." She blinked at him, not surprised tears were blurring her vision. "I have to go and it's probably a six-hour drive. More. And I'm not sure where they'll be but I can call Trey and—"

Before she finished, he was next to her, taking her hands. "Let me take you, Tori."

"No, no, you can't—"

"Oh, I can. With one call, I can clear my calendar, get one of my partners to cover my patients for a few days, and go with you to see Finn myself. And keep you company. And drive, because you're upset. And—"

She stopped him with a kiss, pulling him close and needing nothing as much as contact and a way to show him how much she appreciated him.

"And that..." He finished his sentence against her lips and slowly drew back. "When do you want to leave?"

She searched his face, quiet for a moment, lost and happy and already feeling a thousand times better than when she walked in here.

"I don't want to leave," she whispered.

"I thought you said—"

"I mean...Amelia Island. In August. When we have to say goodbye." She bit her lip and realized she was probably saying too much, but couldn't stop herself. "I only wanted to have a little summer fling with Dr. Hottypants and now you're...you're..." She shook her head and laughed. "I guess you can't help being perfect."

He smiled at her, then smoothed her hair off her face. "You know, in my line of work, you see...things."

"Brain tumors and such," she supplied.

He conceded that with a tip of his head. "You see things that remind you that life can be very, very short. Fleeting. And all you can do is make the best of the time you're given."

"And we've been given this summer."

He leaned in, kissing her again. "So let's make it count. Now, you get your stuff together, get an address where Finn will be tonight or tomorrow, whenever you want to leave. I can be on the road by six tonight, or wait and leave in the morning. You figure out the logistics, and I'll get us there and will take a good look at your boy, I promise."

She wrapped her arms around him and let her head rest on his impossibly wonderful shoulder.

Yes, she'd make the best of this summer with him but, good heavens, it was going to hurt to say goodbye.

Chapter Sixteen

Grace

They were shooting the Christmas movie all day at the bookstore, so Grace got Nikki Lou dressed and out the door for her "play-care" school way too early that morning.

Her little girl was so disinterested in, well, anything that she wouldn't even pick at her breakfast.

"Want to stop at the café and get a pastry, Nik?" she asked as they rounded the back of the bookstore to her van.

She muttered a, "No, fank you," and shuffled along like she was sleepwalking.

"Guess what?" Grace kept her voice high and upbeat. "When I pick you up today, we can go to the park, then get ice cream, and go to see Auntie Rose and your cousins tonight. I'm not working all day. Isn't that fun?"

She didn't respond, but climbed into her car seat with no excitement.

"I know Avery and Alyson can't wait to see you and you can take Aunt Chloe's dog for a walk again. You liked that, right?"

Nikki looked straight ahead, silent.

"Did you hear me, Nik? You can walk Lady Bug?"

Still nothing, making Grace's heart drop. With a sigh, she buckled up the car seat and walked slowly around to the driver's side, swallowing hard as she thought about the autism checklist she'd forced herself to read after her conversation with Rose.

Do you sometimes wonder if your child is having a hard time hearing?

As she climbed in, she turned and looked at Nikki, gasping at the tears that rolled down her cheeks. "Nikki Lou! What's the matter, honey?"

"I don't want to."

"Walk the dog?"

"Go to school." The lip protruded and quivered. "I hate school."

"Oh, baby. What do you hate about it?"

"Kids."

Does your child show no interest in playing with other children?

"But you like the kids, Nik. Once you start playing with them, you have fun."

"I don't want to go."

Oh, boy. Here it goes. Instantly, Grace thought about all she'd scheduled to do this morning, all the errands she wanted to run, all the plans that would be derailed, including coffee with Isaiah, which she'd been looking forward to.

What was the right thing to do? Give in or force Nikki Lou into a situation she didn't want?

Giving it some time, Grace took the long way to school, pulling into an almost empty lot, with only one other car. As she parked, Miss Betsy climbed out of the other car and headed toward the door.

"Mommy, please!"

Just as Grace was about to throw it in reverse and leave, the teacher turned, spotted them and waved. Now what?

Nikki Lou's crying went up an octave, loud enough that the teacher might have heard it. Grace watched her pause, lower her keys, and walk closer to them.

Moving slowly, Grace unlatched her seatbelt and opened the door, stepping out and closing the door on Nikki Lou's tantrum.

"We're having an issue," she said with an apologetic laugh. "Too early for us."

The teacher came closer, lowering sunglasses as she did, her gaze direct on Grace. "Can I talk to her?"

"I don't think that's going to help," Grace admitted, glancing over her shoulder as the screams got louder. "She'll be fine as soon as I pull out. Does that make her spoiled?"

Betsy reached her, quiet for a moment, not reacting to the crying from the van. "You need to know," she said softly.

"If she's spoiled?"

Betsy tipped her head, looking much more like a caring friend than a preschool teacher. "The test is easy, Grace. It doesn't take long and she'll think she's having fun. They'll likely give you results and a diagnosis on the spot, or recommend another specialist."

But what if she didn't want to hear the results or see specialist after specialist? "And then what?" Grace asked. "What changes?"

"Everything and nothing," Betsy said. "You will become a student, learn all you can, and adjust how you handle her in every situation. You will have a new kind of anxiety, but, over time, you will be a better mother and Nikki Lou will be a happier little girl."

"But what about...her whole life?" Her voice cracked and Betsy reached for her hand.

"You will equip her to handle life," she said. "You'll help her with the best nutrition and habits and tools. She's so young, she'll be a candidate for an early intervention prog—"

"Stop," Grace said, fighting a sob. "You're writing her off already—"

"No, I'm *not*," Betsy insisted. "There's nothing wrong with having an autistic child, Grace. It's a challenge, no doubt about it, but what kid isn't? The better prepared you are, the better both your lives will be."

Grace stared at her, hearing nothing but her slamming pulse and Nikki's high-pitched screams.

"I'm going to take her..." Not home, she remembered. "With me today."

"All right. But if you change your mind, there are two fantastic autism therapists right here in Fernandina Beach. Oh, and the North Florida Autism Care Center, which is about forty-five minutes away in Jacksonville.

All excellent. They'll meet with you first, then evaluate Nikki Lou. They can help you, Grace."

For a few seconds, Grace stared at her, with only one thought.

Nick, Nick, Nick. *Why did you leave me to handle this alone?*

"Okay," she managed, her voice thick. "I appreciate it, Betsy. I do. I'm scared."

"I know you are." She closed the space and gave Grace a gentle hug. "But you don't have to be. Knowledge is power and strength, and nothing will shake your love for that little girl."

She nodded, hugged back, then climbed into the van.

"Let's go see Isaiah," she said over Nikki's wails.

Instantly, the crying stopped. And that gave Grace hope. If she could turn it on and off so fast, then nothing was wrong with her.

"Zayuh."

"Yep. Zayuh." They both needed his comfort and kindness right now.

There's nothing wrong with having an autistic child, Grace.

Betsy's words echoed louder than the cries that had filled this van, and Grace hung on to the words all the way to Wingate House.

WITH ONE LOOK at Grace when she walked into the inn, Isaiah must have sensed she was falling apart. He didn't question the arrival of both of them or the fact that Grace was a few hours earlier than she'd promised, walking in right when the inn guests were expecting their spectacular breakfasts.

He swooped them off to the empty library, got Nikki settled at a coffee table with coloring books, then returned with her favorite waffles and coffee for Grace, all with minimum fuss and questions.

"Relax and color and eat and breathe," he said. "I'll come back when the breakfast rush is over."

While Nikki Lou followed those orders, Grace pulled out her phone and dove deeper into the subject that had her heart cracking. She found the names of the local autism therapists, and read more about the ways the "disorder" manifested itself. She read case studies about autistic children and adults, and eventually found a "Moms of Spectrum Kids" forum that she couldn't bring herself to join.

"What are you doing here?"

Grace looked up at the sharp voice, turning her phone over at the sight of Doreen Parrish. "The dining room was busy and Isaiah made Nikki Lou breakfast."

Doreen's gaze flitted over to Nikki, who was too fixated on her coloring book to look up.

"This isn't a daycare center, you know."

Why did this woman have to be so utterly nasty? What was her problem? What caused that ugly side to always come out?

"I know that, Doreen," she said. "But no one's in here right now and Nikki is well-behaved."

Once again, she looked at the little girl, her expression softening ever so slightly.

"How is he?" she asked, the question making Grace draw back and wonder who she meant. Then she realized it was Dad, and that Doreen frequently spoke in non sequiturs, following a logic that only she understood.

"He's doing better every..." Her voice trailed off as she looked at the other woman, words and phrases from all the articles she'd read popping into her head.

Distant. Disjointed conversations. Stilted social interaction. Seeming blunt or rude. Preferring to be alone. Despises change and may stay in a non-challenging job for decades.

Good heavens. Was Doreen on the spectrum and they'd missed it all these years? Had they called her "Dor-mean" out of sheer ignorance and lack of sympathy?

Shame rolled over her as she stared at the other woman, a million questions rising.

But before she could ask any of them, Doreen turned and walked out without a goodbye because...of course. It made so much sense.

"Mommy. Look."

She practically folded on the floor next to Nikki Lou, wrapping her arms around her the way she wanted to wrap them around Doreen. Tears threatened as she hugged her daughter, all of the new knowledge and old fear and no small amount of shame pouring out of her. It wasn't her fault. It wasn't anyone's—

"I'm finally free."

She looked up when Isaiah walked in, not surprised when he stopped dead in his tracks.

"Grace!" Instantly, he was down on the floor next to them, his big arms enclosing both of them in a hug. "What's happening here?"

"Oh, nothing, just..." She laughed at her tears, wiping her face. "We're just very emotional today."

His dark eyes searched her face. "Anything I can help with?"

"Maybe."

"I can take a walk. There's a park around the corner for playing...and talking."

"Can you leave? Will Doreen..."

He held up a hand. "I got Doe covered. Come on. There's a slide and swings and a view of the water. You know the park?"

"I do," she said, pushing up. "And I love this idea."

A few minutes later, they were sitting side by side at a blissfully empty park where Nikki climbed and slid down a plastic slide about fifteen times in a row. Beyond the playground, the sun shone on the Amelia River, sparkling with warmth and hope.

"What has you so emotional, Amazing Grace?"

She smiled at him, as soothed by his presence as Nikki Lou seemed to be. "Can I ask you a question, Isaiah?'"

"Of course."

"Do you think Doreen is...on the spectrum?"

He gave a soft snort. "Aren't we all?"

"Actually, no," she said. "It's a disorder, and everything I've read makes me think that maybe she is, but we've overlooked it."

"I don't like that word, disorder," he said.

"I admit it sounds slightly un-PC, but that's the term they use. Whoever *they* are," she added with a soft laugh.

"I don't like the word because nothing in God's world is out of order. If it is created by Him, then it is perfect."

"If that's true," she said, "you'd have to have a very generous definition of perfection."

"Everything God does is perfect," he repeated softly. "Perfect for His plan. If His plan was to have Doreen Parrish have certain mental or emotional characteristics, that's what He gave her."

She let her lids shutter, not wanting to get into a theological discussion with him. He was obviously a believer and she was...a big fat doubter who had a dead husband and now a child with a possible disorder to prove that not everything God did was perfect. Not by a long shot.

"Regardless of the semantics, do you think I'm right?" she asked.

"I suppose. It doesn't change anything, but if you need an explanation for her quirky personality? Go with the spectrum, but I refuse to call it a disorder."

She took a breath. "And do you think Nikki Lou is... like that?"

To his credit, he didn't scoff at the question but sat very still, looking at Nikki as she danced around the slide. "I think she is a beautiful little girl made in the image of God."

Grace tamped down her frustration. "I'm serious, Isaiah."

"So am I," he countered, then his expression softened. "What I'm saying is you don't have to be scared."

"I'm terrified," she admitted in a strangled voice. "I know I have to have her tested and I'm so, so..." Tears rose and instantly he reached for her hand.

"Don't be afraid."

"How can I not be?" she asked, vaguely aware that she clung to his big hand because it was so warm and comforting.

"Because you have to trust the Lord."

"I don't!" she fired back. "I'm sorry. I don't have that kind of faith and the Lord isn't...let's just say I've been let down in this life."

"He doesn't promise that you won't have troubles," Isaiah said. "On the contrary. But He does promise that He will carry you through anything and give you the strength to handle, and even praise Him, for whatever happens."

She exhaled slowly, then shook her head. "I don't understand how He can do that, but I sure wish you were right."

"I am. And here's how He does it. At the moment when you need Him the very most, He will be there."

"Where is He now?" she asked in a taut voice. "Where was God when Nick was killed or something got mis-wired in my daughter's head?"

Isaiah barely blinked, but rubbed his thumb over her

knuckles, soothing her. "He's here, I promise you. And He's going to help you through me. I can feel it."

"What do you mean?" she asked.

He inched closer. "Would you like me to go with you? I can stay and pray and help you."

She stared at him, stunned and touched. "Thank you, Isaiah. I appreciate it more than you can imagine, but if—when—I go, I'll probably bring a sister or three."

He smiled at that. "Absolutely. But please let me know when you go, because these knees will hit the ground for you."

"What will you pray for? That she's not...that she doesn't...that—"

"I'll pray for peace. Yours and hers. Regardless of what His will is, I want you to be at peace with the process."

She sighed, realizing how much she longed for that peace.

"Thank you," she said simply. "I will happily accept those prayers."

He smiled as Nikki Lou ran over, a sheen of sweat on her happy face.

Nothing was wrong—or out of order—with this child, Grace thought. Nothing at all. Maybe all she did need was faith. And the kindness of a friend like Isaiah.

Chapter Seventeen

Raina

With the cast and crew of the movie hunkered down and filming for the week and Tori off with Dr. Hottypants to take care of Finn, Raina headed into Dad's office, determined to take care of several pending Wingate Properties projects.

Walking up the stairs to the office, she took a deep inhale, loving the morning scent of coffee and...woods? Something musky. Something that smelled like...Blake Youngblood's cologne.

"Good morning, Raina," he greeted her brightly from her old desk where he worked not too far from Dad's office door. "How are you on this fine June morning?"

She mustered up a smile, tamping down the thought that his officious personality was exactly like his cologne—a bit much but not entirely unpleasant.

"Doing great, Blake. And you?"

"Please. Never been better." He pushed up, gathering some papers. "I got a new listing for the firm, one hour ago I finished an online class for my Florida Realtor's license, and yesterday, we got the amended offer on the Bodarts' ranch house. Got all those weird stippies taken out, just like you suggested."

Stippies. She stared at him and he at least had the self-awareness to laugh.

"Stipulations and contingency clauses," he said with a sigh of resignation. "If you must be so official, Raina Wingate-Wallace."

"Only Wingate," she said.

"Isn't it hyphenated? I could have sworn I saw that somewhere."

"I've never been consistent and didn't legally change it," she said as she walked into her office. "I was loathe to part with Wingate, and now..."

Now she was glad she hadn't. What would the baby's last name be, she wondered as she took a seat behind the desk and looked up, not surprised that Blake waited intently for her to finish.

"Now I'll use Wingate." She looked down at her desk, searching for something that could change the subject.

"I do not blame you," he said in a tone that made her look up. "I mean, in this town? Why would you want to be anything else?"

She smiled—and this time it was genuine, because how could you not kind of laugh at this overeager little goofball?

"So true, Blake. Why don't you leave all the docs with me and I'll go over them?"

He placed the pile on her desk. "Would you like

coffee? I know, I know. You switched to decaf, and I ordered more so you don't run out."

And another smile because he was goofy...and efficient. "Yes, thank you."

A few minutes later she had the documents spread over Dad's desk, noticing quite a few excellent changes on the amended offer, all made by Blake. Maybe she'd been too hard on the kid. He meant well, and he did do good work.

Maybe she needed to pay more attention to this slightly annoying but valuable staff member. Her father hardly talked about work at all anymore, and he seemed to forget he even hired Blake, but the young man had only been on staff a few weeks when Dad had his stroke.

When he brought her coffee, she complimented him on the changes that benefited their client, and then gestured to the guest chair, inviting him to sit down.

"How did you find your way to Wingate Properties in the first place, Blake?"

He seemed a little surprised at her sudden interest, but settled in across from her. "Well, I'm a 'work for the best' kind of guy, so when I came to town, it wasn't hard to figure out who had the best real estate business on this island."

"And how did you meet my father?"

"Uh, in the interview. That was the first time I ever met him."

"How did you get the interview, then? Did you know one of the agents or..."

She could have sworn he paled ever so slightly. "I, uh, you know. Just in town."

Was he evading the answer? "You met someone in town?" she pressed, sensing he didn't like the subject, which only made her more curious.

"Yeah. I heard about the opening when Rachel left. I actually met her at an open house for a Wingate listing where I was snooping around. We got chatting, and she told me she was moving out of town for her husband's job and that there would be an opening here. I swooped in like an eagle on a mission."

"Rachel." She frowned, knowing that was Dad's former assistant. "I'm not sure I ever met her."

"No, no, probably not. She wasn't here that long." He stood and reached for the paper on the top. "You put all the initials on here, right? Then we're good to go."

Why was he suddenly in a rush to end this conversation? He always took any excuse to linger in this office.

"No, no. Stay. We've hardly had a chance to talk because I've been so swamped with that movie." She tapped the stack of papers. "You did a great job on these amendments."

"Thanks. I just finished studying the contracts section of the licensing test, so it was top of mind."

"You finished it an hour ago and made these changes?" she asked on a laugh.

"Well, it's not my first contract class. I had a license in another state, but it isn't reciprocal with Florida."

"Ohhh." She leaned back and searched his face, a

little surprised and embarrassed. "Gosh, Blake. I'm so sorry I didn't know that."

"Nothing to be sorry about, Raina."

Actually, there was. She hadn't bothered to take a minute to learn about his background.

"You've been so preoccupied with your dad's health and the deal with the movie company and all," he added, nicely letting her off the hook. "I didn't expect you to focus on one more cog in your oh-so-important wheel."

Was he being facetious? She could never tell with him.

"Not that important," she corrected him. "And I have been preoccupied." Mostly with her broken marriage and shocking pregnancy. Still, that wasn't an excuse for being dismissive of someone trying so hard. "And you're clearly a critical cog in this, the Wingate wheel."

"Thanks. And no worries." He took the top contract and tipped his head to the door. "I'll get this scanned and sent over to the other agent and you can get on with the rest of them. Let me know when you're done," he added as he walked toward the door.

"What state?"

He stopped but didn't turn. "Excuse me?"

"Where did you get your license?"

"Well, I spent the last few years in Chicago, which is a really competitive market. Nothing like this."

"Oh, yes, I know. I have a really good friend who owns a flourishing agency there. John Rodgers? Rodgers and Sons? Do you know them?"

"Actually, no, I don't. Oh, I hear my phone. That's probably the agent looking for this amendment."

He blew out and left her staring at a pile of papers, frowning. There was no way someone in Chicago didn't know Rodgers and Sons Real Estate. They did everything —commercial, residential, new builds, renos. They'd done a reality TV show about "selling the Windy City" not a year ago.

How could he not know them? And if his "I go for the best" claim was true, how could he not have tried to get a job with them?

She tried to concentrate on the next contract, but something was bugging her. Why did she feel like he wasn't being honest? Because he was Blake the Fake, a slick salesman's phony personality or...was he actually lying about something?

She grabbed her phone, hit the search engine, and typed in "reciprocal real estate license Florida" in the bar, immediately seeing ten states that shared reciprocity. Ten states she could practice in tomorrow with no testing or relicensing, and Illinois was third on that list.

Why would he lie?

Before she confronted him, she turned to her father's computer and clicked into his files, which were starting to feel as familiar to her as this chair, this office, and the view across Wingate Way.

She zipped through the labels, going straight to Employees. She scanned the contents, looking for Blake Youngblood, which she found instantly. Inside, there was an employee contract, and a tax form and...that was it.

No resume, no letters of recommendation, no head-hunter's pitch, nothing.

Did Rachel recommend him for the job, or did he orchestrate being in the right place at the right time? And why was he lying about the reciprocity for his license?

"Blake?" she called.

"Coming, Raina."

She took a minute to consider how best to handle this, but then decided there was only one way—the way Rex would manage a situation like this. With total and complete honesty.

"Yep?" he asked, all fresh-faced in her doorway.

"Illinois has reciprocity with Florida. You don't need to retest to get a license here, just apply."

This time, he definitely paled. "Oh, yeah, well, that's not where I got my license, but where I lived before here."

"Why lie?"

"It's, um, a little embarrassing is all."

"The truth or the reason you're lying?"

He looked down, then back up. "Both. My license is from Iowa and I'm a cow-town farm boy, which really hurts my image, you know?"

"Iowa?" She sat up a little straighter, the word snapping her to attention. "You're from Iowa?"

"Yeah. And I tried to make it in Chicago, but got my butt whupped by big city guys and gals. So, if you must know the truth, I decided to start here where I thought I could be a bigger fish in a smaller pond. I really zeroed in on your father, wanting him as a mentor, because..." He let out a huge sigh and took a few steps into the office. "I read an article about you in *Realtor Magazine* and I got a little starstruck."

She stared at him for a moment, unsure if he was telling the truth or not. "Me?"

"I'm embarrassed, Raina," he added as he held her gaze and probably saw the doubt in her eyes. "I feel like some kind of stalker, which I swear I'm not. I mean, I had no idea Rex would get sick or that I'd actually meet you."

"Iowa," she whispered, letting the word settle right on her heart as she pictured the Iowa City Credit Union website, a place on the internet she'd been to many times looking for...five hundred thousand missing dollars.

All her blood went cold at the thought.

Had Blake taken the money? And Dad accepted that? *Why?* Somehow she managed not to react, not to throw out the question, not to let him know anything.

"You have nothing to be embarrassed about," she said in a remarkably cool voice. "I'm flattered, of course, and impressed by your resourcefulness and determination to get ahead."

He visibly relaxed. "Thanks, Raina. I really do want to impress you."

"Well, you've certainly left an impression." She gave him a tight smile, all the warmth she'd felt earlier gone as she pushed the papers away. "And I have an errand to run now, so I'll finish these later."

She had to talk to Dad. She had to figure out this... this Iowa connection.

When Raina arrived at the beach house, Dad was in the middle of PT, so she slipped upstairs and found Susannah working at the desk in the kitchen.

"Hey, Suze."

She turned, surprised to see Raina. "I didn't know you'd be here for lunch, honey."

"No, no, I'm not. I kind of had a work question for Dad, but I'll wait until he's done with PT. How is he today?"

"Oh, you know."

Raina settled on a bar stool and peered over the counter at her mother. "Did Tori come by and say goodbye?"

"She did, with her doctor, which I thought was so nice. He wanted to check in on Dad, too."

"Any medical changes?" Raina asked.

"Not physical," Susannah said.

Raina nodded, knowing exactly what she meant. "Tori told me she thinks he's still struggling with..."

Susannah held her hand up. "The D word. Please don't say it. I don't want to believe it, and if I do, I think it has to be temporary." She added a tight smile and came around the counter. "Do I sound like your ever-optimistic twin sister?"

"A little. Also like my always-keeping-up-appearances mother."

Her whole expression softened, and her bright blue eyes suddenly looked a little moist with tears. "You're such a dear, Raina. All of you girls are." She put a hand on Raina's cheek. "You never call me your stepmother."

"Sometimes, when you're not around. Preceded by 'wicked.'" She added a teasing wink. "But why bother? You're my mother in every imaginable way."

"Am I?" She searched Raina's face intently.

"Of course," Raina said on a surprised laugh. "Why would you even say that?"

"Because you're not telling me something," Susannah said, making Raina instinctively inch back. "Am I right?"

Once again, she wondered about the old wives' tale that said you could tell if a woman is pregnant by looking into her eyes.

She opened her mouth to respond to Susannah's question, her body suddenly aching to share her news, but before she said a word, the physical therapist called up the stairs.

"We're all done, Mrs. Wingate. Rex is wiped out but he gets an A for the day. See you tomorrow!"

"Goodbye!" Susannah called, keeping her questioning gaze on Raina. "Want to go see him now?"

"I want..." *To tell my parents the truth*, Raina thought. But she nodded, her mind scrambled. Was it too soon? Would she jinx it? Would they be broken if she lost another baby? Would they be shocked, considering the state of her marriage? "Yeah, I want to talk to him."

"Go on down and I'll be there in a minute."

Her heart inexplicably heavy, Raina headed down the stairs to find her father in his recliner, sipping a bottle of water, his chest rising and falling with the exertion of his physical therapy.

"Hey, Dad."

"Raina." He turned to her and she waited for his expression to brighten the way it did when he saw any of his girls, but he just looked at her. Through her, even. His dark eyes seemed rimmed with...sadness. There was no other way to describe it.

She came closer and planted a kiss on his white hair, then dropped into the chair across from him. "How was physical torture?" she joked.

He didn't even smile, barely lifting a shoulder. "Same."

"It's a long row to hoe, as they say. Well, I suppose as a farmer would say," she added, still trying to find some levity. "I don't know any of those personally."

His eyes flashed like her humor was offensive to him, then his face returned to the dim shadow of his former self.

"Dad, what's wrong?" she asked, not even tempering her voice or the question.

"I'm tired," he said gruffly. "I played ping-pong with a virtual-reality helmet on my head and walked around this room without a walker seventeen times, tapping out before I could get to twenty. You'd be in a lousy mood, too."

"Is that all?"

"Raina!" The exclamation was so "old" Dad, so pre-stroke Dad, that her heart lifted. Yes, he had a quick temper but he was just as fast to forgive and forget.

"I'm serious, Dad. You seem so disconnected and down in the dumps lately. You can't get mad at any of us for worrying that you're...different."

He let his eyes shutter and close completely. "What did you want, Raina?"

"To make you happy again," she said softly. "I thought the movie and getting all that money—"

"Don't." He barked the word, reminding her that she could talk about anything but that money. Well, that rule had to be broken, because she had to know if there was a connection between his assistant—*from Iowa*—and that money.

But she had to be careful not to upset him. Yes, he was out of the "danger zone," according to his neurologist, but she didn't want to be the one to push him back there. Especially with Justin on the road with Tori. Bad time for another seizure.

"So, I had an interesting conversation with Blake, your assistant."

"Mmm." He took a sip of water. "Something wrong?"

"No, no. I was surprised to find out he already had a real estate license from another state. Did you know that?"

He frowned. "Not sure I did, but he did say he was going to get his Florida license soon and I don't doubt he will. He's eager and hungry." He smiled that sweet, crooked smile. "Reminded me of you back in your early days."

"Yeah, I get that," she said. "Still, he seems like, I don't know, an interesting hire for you."

"He's ambitious. Nothing wrong with that. You, of all people, should respect that, Raina."

She inhaled slowly. She had to know if he realized the connection between Blake from Iowa and the emptied account...*also from Iowa.*

"He's...all up in your business," she said.

"Where he's supposed to be. What is your point? I'm tired. I'm sick of being sick. I'm downright miserable."

Just then, Susannah walked in and Raina closed her eyes. "Sorry. I'm not helping his mood."

"What could?" her father countered. "My existence is...useless."

"Oh, Rex," Susannah said, coming right up to her husband and wrapping both arms around his shoulders. "How can you say that? You are loved by so many."

He leaned into her and sighed, quiet for a long time.

As they sat in silence, Raina looked from one to the other, from the face of her father, who'd never looked this lost in his life, to her mother, who'd never looked more desperate to make her man happy.

Her heart ached for how much she wanted to help them both.

Suddenly, a bolt of realization shot through her. What was she trying to do by stirring this Iowa pot? Dad had made his feelings clear—whatever happened to that money, he knew and didn't care. So what if there was a connection to Blake? It didn't bother Dad; why should it bother her?

She wasn't here to cause trouble! She was here to solve his problems and make him happy.

And Raina knew exactly how to do that. *Exactly*.

"Well, then," she said, opening up the side compartment of her purse where she kept the printout that she got at the doctor's office. "I have a little something here that will lift your spirits."

Susannah looked sharply at her.

"And, yes, Suze, before you ask, I *have* been keeping something from you. From everyone but Tori, who was with me when I found out."

"Found out what?" her mother asked.

Very slowly, she withdrew the ultrasound paper and opened it, showing the surprisingly clear black and white image. "I'm coming up on eleven weeks," she said softly. "If I make it to twelve, I've officially broken my own record."

Susannah fell right to her knees and hit the floor between Dad and Raina, her whole face as lit up as a Christmas tree. "Raina!" she whispered in awe, reaching for the paper.

Through teary eyes, Raina looked at her father, who, for the first time in months, looked exactly like Rex Wingate at his happiest. His brows lifted, his smile cut all the way across his face, his cheeks deepened with color.

"A baby?" he managed to say.

"I know, probably not the best time in my life, forty-three and separated from my cheating husband, but..." She felt a smile pull, genuine and wide. "It's still a dream come true."

"Oh, look at this baby!" Susannah cooed.

"Come on, Suze," Raina said on a laugh. "Even you

can't make out the actual fetus there, which is, I'm happy to inform you, the size of a juicy little strawberry at eleven weeks."

"I see...perfection. Rex, look." She shoved the paper in front of him. "Perfection."

But tears were pouring down his face and all he could do was let them fall. "Raina, honey." He reached his good hand out to her and she immediately jumped up to kneel in front of him.

"Don't cry, Dad. Please."

"It's good to cry," he said in a husky voice. "I need to cry. I like to cry sometimes." He laughed a little, then gave in to a sob and wrapped his arm around her head and pulled her close.

Susannah slid over and joined them. "I'm so happy for you, Raina."

"Well, let's not count our proverbial chickens until I can actually hatch one. And I'm not ready to tell everyone yet. I want to get through the next few weeks. Only Tori knows. And Jack."

"Oh, honey, what did he say?" Susannah asked. "He probably wants to reconcile now."

"I don't know, Suze," she said. "I'm not there yet. I'm taking things one day at a time."

Her mother nodded and Dad added some pressure to his touch. "I hope you don't do something stupid, Rain," he said.

"Cheating is cheating," Susannah added. "And a baby doesn't mean you have to forgive him."

"Oh, I have to forgive him at some point," she said,

glancing down at the image again. "But right now, all I want to do is make sure my little strawberry survives."

"Then take it easy!" her mother chided.

She looked up at her father, who finally, finally had the old spark in his eyes.

Smiling, she dropped her head on his lap, satisfied with her decision. Her job was to ease his troubles, not make them worse. She wanted to give him joy, not grief. No more mentions of money, Iowa, Blake, or anything except things that made him happy.

"I love you, Dad," she whispered.

And she never meant it more.

Chapter Eighteen

Tori

The only "address" Tori could get from Finn was the location of the tournament, in a massive complex that was part of the University of North Georgia. He had a game in the afternoon, so Tori told him to expect a surprise guest on the sidelines. She didn't want him to freak out when he saw her.

"You ready?" Justin turned to her after he parked his car in an extremely crowded lot outside the complex, seven hours after he'd picked her up at the beach bungalow and insisted on spending a few minutes with Rex before they left.

"I am, but..." She let out a sigh and reached for his hand. "I'm not sure how Finn will react. Or Trey, for that matter."

"If you prefer, you don't even have to tell anyone I'm a doctor. I can do a pretty crafty patient interview without someone knowing it. It's your call."

She nodded, appreciating that. "I'm not sure."

"What will throw Finn more?" he asked. "The fact

that you brought a doctor four hundred and fifty miles for a house call, or that you have a boyfriend?"

"A...boyfriend?"

He lifted a shoulder. "Got a better handle? And if you say Hottypants, I'm going to triple charge you for this visit."

She laughed, still letting the word "boyfriend" slide around her chest and settle on her heart. "I don't know about throwing Finn, but you do...send *me* somewhere."

He leaned in. "Over the moon?"

"You are a little otherworldly." Laughing, she met him and gave him a light kiss. "I don't want to lie, so I'll tell them I brought the neurologist."

"The one who has his arm around you and kisses you whenever he gets the urge? Which is frequent."

"Yep." She drew back, a little surprised that this man could give her butterflies with such ease. At forty-five! She didn't even know it was possible. "Rex Wingate says honesty over everything."

"Smart man, that Rex." He reached for the door and threw one more wink at her. "And I like 'boyfriend.' Makes me feel young again."

She was still smiling at that while they walked through the enormous sports complex, which was unlike any venue where Finn had ever played. No wonder the kid was getting headaches—this level of competition was stressful and he was only thirteen.

It took a few minutes, but they finally found the field and game where his team, the Concord Cougars, were on the field in the seventh inning.

"That's the last one in AAU ball," Tori told Justin.

"We missed the whole game?" he asked.

"Oh, don't worry. There will be another, unless this is an elimination tournament and they lose." She got on her tiptoes to look at the field, seeing the familiar black and gold of her son's travel team uniforms.

"There he is," she said, pointing toward the narrow-shouldered kid out in left field. "My Finnie, number nine."

"I thought it might be you."

Tori whipped around at the familiar voice of her ex-husband, looking up at Trey's unsmiling face.

"The surprise guest," he added. "Finn told me to expect one."

"Well, this is the furthest south you go," she said, happy she knew that little fact. "So we thought we'd make the drive and watch him play."

Trey's blue-gray gaze shifted to Justin, a question in his eyes.

"Trey Hathaway, this is Dr. Justin Verona."

Justin extended his hand. "Trey, it's a pleasure."

As he shook Justin's hand, the crack of a bat had them all turning as the crowd cheered and Tori's eyes went straight to left, where she saw Finn staring up, his mitt cupped around his fist, and even from here she could see he wasn't sure he could catch the ball.

"Can of corn, Finnie!" Trey hollered so loud she felt her eardrums vibrate.

And the ball hit the grass a foot from Finnie with a

deafening, "No!" from the crowd and a grunt of sheer disgust from Trey.

"Oh, baby," Tori whispered as she watched him scramble to scoop up the ball and throw a hard shot at first, where the batter slid with ease to the base and the guy on second scored to thunderous applause.

"Baby my ass," Trey muttered, shooting her a look. "That's why he plays that way, Tori. Because you treat him like he's three, not thirteen. It was a tie game until that play."

She felt her eyes slip shut behind her sunglasses, and Justin's fingers closed around her hand as Trey turned back to the field, clapping and screaming at the field.

"You'll get it next time, Finn!" He pointed to the stands. "Heidi's right up there in the third row, if you want to join her. I'll be in the dugout."

"Okay," she said, not sure she really wanted to sit with Heidi-Ho.

"Let's go now!" Trey yelled back at the field, walking away. "Look alive out there, boys! Alive!"

As his voice faded away, Tori sighed, a little embarrassed at her always loud ex-husband, who seemed especially jarring when compared to cool, calm, collected Dr. Verona.

"Do you want to sit with her?" she asked. "Because we don't have to."

"I definitely want to sit with her. I can learn a lot about Finn's health from a casual chat. Unless you'd rather not."

"It's fine," she agreed, turning to look at the field one more time.

The next batter hit into a double play—which had Trey screaming more—and they walked to the bleachers as the other team took the field.

"I'm always happy when he's not out there," Tori confided as they walked. "Of course, he may have to bat, which is a pressure all by itself, but at least he's not out there praying his way through each pitch."

Justin frowned at her. "Why is he in this sport? And at this level, which I imagine, even if they are thirteen, is pretty fierce. Most travel teams are, if I recall from my son's soccer days."

"Take three guesses and the first two don't count," she said dryly. "Dad pressure."

"That alone could give the kid headaches," he said.

She peeked into the dugout as they passed and caught sight of Finn with his head hanging, his hands on both temples, then he rubbed under his eyes.

"He must have one now," she whispered.

"In the front, near his sinuses," Justin noted. "That's good."

"Why?"

"Because it's more likely hormonal or an allergic reaction."

"So not a brain tumor."

He squeezed her hand. "It's not a brain tumor, Mom," he assured her.

"Do you know that for a fact?"

"No, but that would be very unusual and his pain would be way worse."

Holding that thought, they climbed the bleacher steps and spotted an attractive brunette waving to them.

"Tori! Trey texted me that you came. We have room here."

Tori smiled at Heidi, who she'd met a few times, and Marcie and David Devine, their traveling companions.

They slid down the row, did a quick round of introductions, making some small talk about the game and getting the score.

"Finnie should be up in this inning," Heidi said excitedly.

"Oh, good," Tori said with false enthusiasm. Tori wasn't sure what she hated more—that he had to bat or that Heidi called him "Finnie." He wasn't *her* son.

"But Chris is up next," Marcie announced, already standing for her kid. "He'll tie it back up and then we'll advance. You watch!"

"So what do you do, Justin?" Heidi asked between pitches.

"I'm a neurologist," he said.

"He's taking care of my dad," Tori added.

"Oh, yeah." Heidi nodded. "How is he?"

The question sounded like an afterthought, but it didn't get answered, because a cheer rose when Chris hit a long line drive for a double, bringing everyone to their feet with some particularly raucous cheering from Marcie and David.

Poor Finn. He hated what he called "the Loud Family" —his name for families who had to make their presence known. Were Wingates loud? Finn had never had an issue with them. They weren't loud—they were *fun*.

When they sat back down, Heidi leaned over to look at Justin. "A neurologist? Maybe you can help us figure out what's causing Finn's headaches."

Tori inched back, surprised by the statement and sorry she'd had an unkind thought about Heidi. At least she cared.

"I'd like to," he said.

Before they could talk again, the next batter sacrificed an out and moved Chris to third. After that, a boy was out on a blooper to first and then...

"Oh, God," Tori muttered.

It was Finn, with two outs and Chris Devine on third, ready to score the tying run. If Finn struck out, the game was over.

Why did Trey put him in a position like that?

All around them, the parents were on their feet, so Tori and Justin joined in. Once again, he put a hand on her back, comforting and understanding that this stressed her out.

Finn adjusted his batting helmet and walked to the plate, trying for a swagger she knew he didn't have.

They screamed his name from the stands, no doubt thinking it encouraged him, but Tori saw the impercep- tible drop in his shoulders. He reached under his helmet again and rubbed his head.

Tori looked up at Justin and made a sad face.

"'Sokay," he whispered, totally understanding.

But it wasn't okay, not for her Finnie with his headache and desire to make everyone happy—especially his dad. He wasn't a clutch guy. He wasn't a clean-up hitter. He wasn't a dang *baseball* player.

The first ball whizzed by him so fast, Tori wasn't sure he actually saw it.

"Not your pitch, Finn!" Trey yelled from the dugout. "Get the next one, buddy!"

Finn pounded the clay with his cleats, tapped the bat twice—for luck, she knew—and got into his stance, swinging a few times.

Whoosh. Strike two.

Tori whimpered softly and leaned into Justin, all of Finn's nerves and fears and headache ricocheting through her body with pure motherly empathy. The screaming faded away—even Trey's booming voice—the parents and players disappeared, and she stared at her son, who she loved so much it hurt.

Come on, baby. Just connect. Just connect. Please, God, give him an easy pitch.

No such luck. The third strike was right down the middle, and even in the chaos of one team's disappointment and another one's joy, she could hear Trey chewing out their son as he walked off the field.

"No wonder the kid has headaches," Justin muttered.

Tori looked up at him with a mix of affection and embarrassment. Affection won as she squeezed his hand and got on her toes to kiss his cheek.

"What was that for?" he asked with a smile.

"'Cause...I like you."

"Then we're on the same page, Vicky."

She shot him a look for the name and joined the others leaving the bleachers to go give pep talks to their kids. Except for Trey, who was still letting Finn have it for his game-losing strikeout.

As they joined the crowd milling about, Trey finally let Finn go pack his bag and help with cleanup, then sauntered over to where Tori and Justin stood with Heidi.

"Justin's a neurologist," Heidi announced before anyone had a chance to say a word.

Instantly, Trey's eyes narrowed. "Yeah?"

"He's working with my father," Tori said.

"Oh, I thought you two were..."

"We are," Justin said coolly. "But I understand Finn's been having some headaches, so—"

"We don't need a doctor to figure it out," Trey cut him off. "Kid has raging hormones at thirteen, doesn't sleep enough, and could eat his way through a supermarket and still be hungry. Don't need a neuroscientist to figure out why he gets a little pain once in a while. Thanks anyway."

Tori stared at Trey, trying to give him the benefit of the doubt—all those things were true about Finn—but why was he so clueless and rude?

"I think it's more serious," Heidi said and shot an apologetic look to Tori. "The boys like to play things down."

Tori nodded, mentally noting that she would say

good things about "Heidi-Ho" to Kenzie, because this woman at least had a heart where Trey had none.

"He mentioned those headaches to me," Tori said. "I'd love Justin to talk to him for a few minutes and maybe get an idea of what's going on."

Trey glared at her. "You seriously brought a brain doctor all the way up here 'cause Finn said he had a headache?" He practically choked the question. "Man, you have got to stop babying him, Tori. He's fine."

"Actually, coming here was my idea," Justin said, putting a protective arm around Tori. "I want to meet my girlfriend's son, and if I can help in any way with his headaches, even if only for your peace of mind, Trey, I'm happy to do that."

Trey looked a little confounded, but the strong and kind response shut him up...and made Tori lean into Justin ever so slightly in gratitude. He responded with a silent squeeze of solidarity, a subtle gesture that somehow meant the world right then.

Trey shook his head. "I gotta give the pep talk to my team." He walked away, leaving them with a beat of awkward silence.

"Can I ask you how bad his headaches are, Heidi?" Justin asked.

She inhaled slowly, pulling back her dark hair while her golden-brown eyes shifted from Tori to Justin. "Honestly? I think they're bad. I get migraines, so I know the symptoms. He threw up the other day from the pain."

"And Trey is dismissing that?" Tori asked.

She looked guilty. "Finn asked me not to tell him."

Tori studied the other woman, torn between a bout of jealousy that Heidi and Finn had secrets together and a pang of gratitude that he had someone on this journey who at least listened to him.

"Thanks," she said, when she realized the gratitude far outweighed the jealousy. "Then I want him to see a doctor."

"I'll talk to him," Justin assured her. "Someone might have to run Dad interference, but I will talk to him."

Tori nodded her thanks.

"Does he seem stuffy?" Justin asked. "It's not allergy season, but this is a new geography."

"No," Heidi said. "He doesn't even sneeze. He just... eats." She laughed softly and glanced at Tori. "He's definitely going through a growth spurt."

The scales tipped a little toward jealousy, but Tori nodded.

"Has he been introduced to a new food? A change in his normal diet?" Justin continued.

"His diet consists of eating everything not nailed down," she said on a laugh. "So maybe."

"Has he ever had food allergies?" He directed this question to Tori.

"Not that I've been aware of. He doesn't tolerate sugar well, but what kid does? He's never really liked sweets, so I didn't make a big deal out of it."

"Really?" Heidi seemed surprised. "Because the only thing he loves about the whole RV experience is s'mores around the campfire before bed. But once he's in the RV, he's quiet. He's not a fan of the small space."

Again, Tori was thankful this woman was on top of her son's issues on the trip. Because Trey certainly wasn't.

"You know what?" Justin whispered to her, pulling her from the group of parents and players around them. "I'd like to talk to him alone for a few minutes. Tell him why I'm here and get him to answer some questions. Without you or—more importantly, if I'm being honest—his father. He'll be more open."

"Mom!"

Tori whipped around to see Finn bounding toward her, arms outstretched.

Her heart soared as he threw his arms around her and squeezed, giving a soul-satisfying hug that she felt right down to her toes. Holding him close, she inhaled the familiar smell of grass and sweat and her sweet little boy.

After they hugged and laughed and glossed over his game-losing error and strikeout, she gestured for Justin to come closer and introduced them.

"Hey, hi." Finn took the hand that Justin offered. "Sorry. I'm kinda sweaty."

"With good reason," Justin said. "That's quite a field you were playing on. Must have felt like the MLB."

"Felt like something," Finn said with a self-deprecating laugh.

"I'd love a tour of this place," Justin said. "Before your dad gets done. Can you walk me around?"

Finn's eyes flickered with a little surprise, but Tori nodded. "Go, honey. Talk to Justin. He's a headache specialist."

Just then, Trey came over and Finn's eyes widened to

deer-in-the-headlights status, but Heidi swooped in and took Trey's arm, and walked him away with some chatter no one else heard.

Major, major points for Heidi.

"Let's go," Finn said.

Justin and Finn walked off, talking. Something slipped in her chest, something she couldn't define or grab hold of. She wanted them to be together. She wanted Justin to appreciate Finn for the awesome kid he was...and for Finn to recognize greatness in Justin.

Why did it matter?

Because she was falling for him, and the harder she fell, the more she wanted the people she loved to fall a little, too.

THEY CAME BACK LAUGHING, which Tori thought was a good sign, and the five of them enjoyed a surprisingly upbeat meal together, considering Tori and Trey weren't ever that comfortable around each other.

But Finn seemed happy to have Tori there, and Heidi was a conversation pro, keeping things easy and light.

Until after dessert, when Finn suddenly grew quiet.

When Trey and Heidi both got up to go to the bathroom, Finn leaned across the table and looked at Tori.

"It's starting again. Right here." He tapped his temple.

"I thought they were usually at night."

"They are. After that campfire when I know I have to get into the coffin they call a bed."

Justin looked down at the remains of chocolate mousse pie in front of Finn. "At the campfire, you have s'mores?"

"Every night."

"When did you start eating so many sweets?" Tori asked. "I never even remember you having dessert."

"I'm always hungry, Mom. I can't get enough."

"Chocolate," Justin said, and they both looked at him. "Do you normally eat it?"

"Only on Halloween and I—"

"Always get a headache!" Tori exclaimed. "Like clockwork, every year. I figured it was the sugar."

He blinked and looked at Justin. "It's chocolate?"

"Super common," Justin said. "So common I would have thought you'd notice it by now."

"I don't eat it much, like my mom says."

"And it could simply be a certain type of cocoa mix, or a combination," Justin said, pointing to the plate. "That has a graham cracker crust, like a s'more. They both contain tyramine and phenylethylamine, which is a neurotransmitter with stimulating effects on certain parts of the brain. You might be able to eat chocolate in small doses, but mix it with something that has the same ingredient that's reacting to your chemistry and you're—"

Finn put his head down and pressed his hands on his face, sucking in a noisy moan. "It hurts," he murmured. "How am I going to play the next game?"

"There's another game?" Tori asked in disbelief.

"The Losers Tourney. Playing for third."

"You're not playing that," she said. "You're not playing with a headache."

He looked miserable. "Dad wants me to get right back on the horse and all. He'd never let me—"

"What's wrong?" Trey came back to the table, staring at Finn. "If you are going to wimp out with another—"

"It hurts, Dad."

"Oh, please." Trey shot into the booth next to him. "No other kid on this team has an issue but you." He practically spat the last word.

"Trey!" Tori breathed his name. "You can't make him play with a splitting headache."

He shot her a withering look. "If it were up to you, he'd be in a bubble playing video games."

"Dad, I don't think I can—"

"It's not up to you," Trey shot back.

"It's up to me."

All of them stared at Justin as he brought the conversation to a halt with that, and made Trey snort.

"Don't barge into this family, buddy, and throw your degree around. He's my son and I know what's good for him."

"I'm speaking as a neurologist who spent some time understanding his symptoms. He is having an allergic, chemical reaction in his brain. With rest, a dark room, and a lot of water, he'll get through it. Exertion, sweat, and, God forbid, a ball to the head, could make him sicker or give him a seizure. You can't risk that."

Trey glared across the table at Justin. "Do *not* blow in here and tell me what to do with my son."

"He's my son, too," Tori ground out. "And he cannot play the next game."

"I don't want to play, Dad," Finn muttered, pressing his hands to his head. "It hurts too much."

"Oh, Finnie." Tori reached for him. "Let's go find somewhere quiet and dark and I'll get you wa—"

"Leave, Tori," Trey demanded. "Just get in the car and go back to wherever you were and take your quack doctor and leave. I can handle Finn."

"Dad, please," Finn practically cried. "Let me go. Just let me go."

Trey didn't move, but his face reddened as he blocked Finn's escape from the booth. "Finley Hathaway, if you don't play the next game, we're done for the summer. I'll stay with the team and you can figure it out."

Tori bit her lip, giving Finn the chance to defend himself or make a decision that she knew was very, very difficult for him. He stared at the pie remnants and didn't move. Trey set his jaw in his most obstinate expression, and God knew he had dozens of those.

"Finn," Justin said softly. "Look at me."

After a second, he did.

"Look left and look right without moving your head."

Again, he followed the order, but only as Trey huffed in disgust.

"Where in your head is the pain?"

"Here." He swiped up his cheekbones to his temples.

"It's in his head all right," Trey said. "He's trying to get out of playing."

"What's going on?" Heidi came up to the table, looking from one person to the next. "Finn, are you okay?"

"He's not," Tori said.

"He's faking it," Trey spoke right over her, adding to the extreme tension of the moment.

Justin held his finger up to Finn's face. "Follow this as I move it."

"Stop it!" Trey demanded, loud enough for people around them to turn and look. "You win, Finn. You don't want to play, don't. You don't want to be on this trip, leave. You want to run home with Mommy like a big fat baby, goodbye."

Tori seethed as Trey shot out of the booth and bolted by Heidi, who stood almost as dumbstruck as the rest of them.

Then Finn dropped his head and visibly worked not to cry.

"Finn," Tori said, reaching to take his hand. "This is your call. Home to Boston? I'll get you there. Back to Amelia Island with me? I'll take you now. Stay here and work it out with Dad? That's fine, too. But it's all up to you."

He finally lifted his head and gave her a teary-eyed look.

Heidi held out her hand. "I'll let you guys have privacy to talk, and I'll find Trey."

As she walked away, Finn blew out a breath it

seemed like he'd been holding since...well, since Trey came back from the bathroom.

"What would you like to do?" Tori asked gently.

He shifted his gaze to Justin. "What were you doing with your finger and my eyes? Is everything okay?"

"I wasn't doing anything but buying some time and giving you a way out of the next game if you choose to take it."

He gave a dry laugh. "Nice. It worked. Can I play?"

Justin lifted his brows. "Can you? Yes. Should you? No."

Finn stared at him, then sighed, shaking his head. "I want to go with you. I wanna see my cousins and everyone on Amelia Island. Kenzie's killing me with every text, it sounds like so much fun. Is that going to cause World War Three?"

"We've already been through that war," Tori said, gathering her purse and wits. "He's had you for weeks, and I can take you for a few now. And I'm sorry, Finn, that you have to go through this."

He gave a slow smile and nodded. "Thanks. And thanks for coming all the way up here, Mom. And..." His eyes widened. "Are you the guy Kenzie told me they call—"

Justin held his hand up. "Don't rat me out, buddy. I'm on your side."

The three of them laughed, and Tori was certain it was the first time Finn had relaxed since he left Boston.

"Let's go get your stuff and say your goodbyes, Finn," she said.

Two hours later, the three of them were back in Justin's car, headed south. In the back seat, Finn was conked out, mouth open, snoring contentedly.

"Six *more* hours in the car?" Tori reached over and took his hand. "Surely you had a better way to spend this day."

"Nothing better," he said softly.

"Please, don't make me resurrect the name Saint Hottypants that my sisters hung on you."

He threw her a grin. "I've missed it, Tori."

"The name? Driving?"

"Being a parent. I liked those days of family trips with the kids, but they're over now. I miss them. My kids are grown and..." He shook his head. "I liked being a father, so I should thank you for this family day."

"Well, we're hardly a model family. My ex is a brute, as you saw. My son is a wreck. And I'm..."

"You are an incredible mother, something I also saw." He took her hand. "We did the right thing today, and you have to feel good about that."

"What I feel good about," she whispered as they threaded their fingers. "Is you."

He smiled and gave her hand a squeeze. "Same."

She let her head fall back and closed her eyes with a sigh.

Chapter Nineteen

Chloe

"I can't believe they're on their way back and they have Finn," Kenzie said as she gathered up the large serving dish of onion rings that Miguel had slid across the food pass. "Mom's going to be exhausted."

"Which is why we've got to hold down the fort for the cast and crew tonight." Chloe peeked out through the kitchen door into the dining area of the restaurant, gauging how busy they'd be after tonight's shoot.

Chloe was used to working at the café at night now, which was much more fun than breakfast and lunch. There were no menus, no orders, no paying customers. They were only open to the movie cast and crew, who came in and out, used tables for meetings, and ate from a buffet that Tori had created to feed thirty or forty people over the course of several hours.

"And the boss is here," she murmured as the front door opened and Marcus Ferrari walked in.

Kenzie came up behind her. "My mom?"

"No," Chloe laughed. "The other boss. I know he

gets VIP treatment. I'll go make sure he can have his favorite table."

"I'll make his half-caf coffee," Kenzie offered.

"And I'll whip up a bacon-egg-and-cheese—not Swiss —on an everything bagel," Miguel offered.

"Look at us, a bunch of pros," Chloe joked as she stepped out of the kitchen to greet their most important client—the one paying for all this. "Hey, Marcus."

"Chloe! Just who I wanted to see."

She inched back. "Me? It's Raina who solves your problems. Unless your problem is hunger, then Miguel is already working on your favorite sandwich and Kenzie's cutting the caffeine in half."

He chuckled. "Love this place. And my favorite table is clean."

"Life is good, huh?" She gestured toward it. "Water or anything else?"

"You," he said, pointing to the table. "Sit with me and let me change your life."

"Excuse me?" she asked on a laugh.

"You heard me. Just don't bring your sidekick and her camera. I want to talk honestly with you."

Curious, she followed him to the two-top and perched on the opposite chair, quiet while he settled in, glanced at his phone, then put his elbows on the table to stare at her.

"You know who Abigail Ferrari is?"

"Um...your wife? Your sister? Your mother? The lady who invented the sports car?"

"I'm surprised you don't know her name," he said. "You do such in-depth research."

"And I'm surprised you noticed, Marcus. Thanks. Who is she?"

"She is my sister, you're right. She's also in show business, like me, but in a different way." He waited a beat, then inched closer. "She's a news segment producer for *A-List Access.* I assume you're familiar with the show?"

"Sure." Chloe nodded, not wanting to admit she didn't watch it very often because she preferred "real" news, but she wasn't above the occasional celebrity gossipfest.

"Well, it seems you've caught her attention."

She blinked in surprise. "Really?"

"She's been watching your little TikTok videos."

"She has?" Chloe knew lots of people had seen them, especially the one with the actress that went kind of viral, but...someone with the title of news segment producer at a nationally syndicated TV show?

"Yep. And she likes you."

Chloe stared at him, not sure what to make of this. "I'm...flattered."

"Well, what you need to be...wait, wait. Let me back up and ask you something. May I?"

"Anything," she said. "And if you want to confirm that I am the actual runaway bride you've heard about, the answer is yes. That was me, tearing out of the church, veil, dress, and bouquet, but no husband, in hand. Wait. I think I tossed the bouquet on the way out. It's a blur, honestly."

Brows went up behind his rimless glasses. "I'd heard there was one of those, but I thought it was small-town folklore," he joked, making her laugh.

Just then, Kenzie came over with a steaming cup of coffee and his favorite sandwich.

"Oh, thank you, Kenzie," he said, smiling up at her. "Can you spare your star reporter for a few more minutes?"

She assured him she could, but Chloe's heart flipped. Had he called her a star reporter?

When he turned back to her, Chloe sat a little straighter, more curious than ever at what his sister, the *news segment producer*, had to say.

"All right, we can stop this train before it starts with one simple question," Marcus said. "How glued are you to this town?"

"How...glued am I? Well, I moved back here recently. I've been in Jacksonville and several other markets—er, places—before that."

"Markets." He grinned and lifted the gooey sandwich. "As I suspected. You know your business, don't you? Must run in the family, like Raina, who is a low-key shark."

"Not sure if it's so low-key," she cracked. "Can you be more specific about what you're asking, and why?"

"My sister is looking for a fresh, unknown name for her segments and she wants to interview you. You don't need to forward samples of your work, because she likes what she's seen on TikTok and wants the same thing."

"Oh...wow. That's..." She literally couldn't find the words.

He shrugged as if he knew the news left her speechless. "Anyway, she liked your reporting, so she asked me to see if you were available. Are you?"

She tipped her head smiling, channeling Julia Roberts's best pal from *Pretty Woman*. "'What? And leave all this?'" She gestured around the café, and made him laugh.

"See? You got the goods, Chloe. And apparently Abby's looking for a combination of man-on-the-street and silly acts and showing off that gorgeous face of yours, but it is a job in television." He took a bite and chewed, wiping his mouth as a little mayo escaped. "Sorry."

She wasn't sure if he was apologizing for the chin dribble or the fact that a producer was interested in her... "silly acts" and "gorgeous face."

"'Sokay," she said, regardless of what he was apologizing for. "What do you mean, 'interview.' For a job? A permanent position? Where?"

"Oh, in Los Angeles, of course."

She let out a soft whimper. "Los Angeles?"

"Which is why I asked how attached you are to this place." He swallowed and wiped his mouth again. "You seem destined for bigger things, Chloe. The camera loves you, if you want to act."

"I don't," she said quickly. "I, um, have a master's degree in journalism, and I..." She let out a breath. "I've always wanted to be an on-air reporter."

He shrugged and added a smug smile. "You're welcome."

"Well, I don't know. Los Angeles? That's a big market."

"*A-List Access* is a nationally syndicated show with millions of viewers around the world. This isn't about markets, this is about exposure," he said. "Abby thinks you've got something special and wants to interview you. That's it. No guarantees, no salary discussions from me. She wants to see if you're as good in person as you are on the tiny screen in her hand."

She leaned back and tried to process what he was saying, but her head was thrumming with the news. "I kind of can't believe this."

He swallowed his next bite, washing it down with coffee. "This is how it happens, Chloe. Not by knocking on doors at TV stations and showing them your work and letting some slimeball news guy drool over you with promises of more air time if you'll just get a little bit closer."

She shuddered. "It's like you were there."

"Please. I've been around a long time. But this is how people get breaks." He jutted his head toward the crewmembers talking a few tables away. "Every one of them knew somebody who knew somebody who got them this gig. You couldn't have walked into Abby's office and even qualified for an interview."

"No kidding.'"

"And if the subject matter of your TikTok videos hadn't been my TV movie? She'd have never seen you.

This is how Hollywood and any entertainment industry works. Even news, which is entertainment now."

He was right, and she knew it clear down to her bones. It was the biggest frustration with the industry—who you knew was more important that what you knew. And this moment? Clear proof of that.

"So, should I tell her you'll fly out for an interview? Next week? Tomorrow? When are you able to sneak away from this café?"

"I...I...can go anytime," she said slowly, the words sort of taking on a life of their own. Because...why would she say no? This was a dream come true. "And thank you, Marcus."

"Hey, you did the work that got her attention." He pushed his phone across the table. "Put your number in there and expect a call from my wise-cracking sister, Abby. You'll love her."

She typed in her number with one thought: she loved her own wise-cracking sisters...but something told her she was going to end up in Los Angeles, one way or another.

WHEN CHLOE HEARD the front door of the café open with yet another straggler from the crew, she let out a long, frustrated sigh. Miguel and Kenzie were gone, and all she had left to do was lock up and get home to a hot bath and a whole lot of research about Abigail Ferrari and *A-List Access.*

She stepped out of the kitchen, ready to break the news that almost all the food was gone, but—

"Oh. Hello." She couldn't help but smile at the sight of the tall, handsome firefighter standing near the hostess stand. "I certainly wasn't expecting you, Probie McCall."

A slow, way-too-sexy smile pulled. "I saw the light and thought I'd check on you. But..." He pointed to the door and glanced around the dim and empty dining area. "You should lock up when you're not serving customers."

A protector. She liked that.

"I was about to." She took a few steps closer, suddenly a little fluttery inside as she wiped her hands on the apron she wore. "Most of the catering is put away, but I can scare something up if you're hungry."

"I'm not." He laughed and shook his head. "Actually, that's a lie. I just finished a long shift and I'm famished. But you don't have to feed me. How about we go somewhere that's open? Salty Pelican? Or a taco at the Mexican place?"

"I'm..." *On a man hiatus. And need to do research. Also exhausted.* But none of those words came out. In fact, they wouldn't even form. "Almost done," she said instead, untying the apron. "If you don't mind my work clothes."

He gestured to the standard-issue blue T-shirt. "Same. I'd love to grab a bite with you."

Grabbing a bite. Wearing work clothes. This wasn't a date...was it?

At the moment, Chloe didn't care. She had floated through the night and would love nothing more than talking to someone about the opportunity that might have landed in her lap.

They went to the Salty Pelican and she waited until they were settled into a table outside in the warm evening air, the chatter of tourists walking along the river and the sweet scent of jasmine trees in the air. They each had a cold beer in front of them, so when they shared a casual toast, she leaned in and held his glinting green gaze.

"You are never going to believe what happened tonight," she said without even taking a drink. "The most unexpected and amazing and exciting thing."

"A charming firefighter-in-training swooped into your café and took you out for dinner?"

She laughed, but her smile wavered a little when she realized that this *was* a date, at least to him.

"Almost as unexpected," she volleyed back. "It seems I have attracted the eye of an entertainment news producer, who happens to be the sister of the guy who is the head honcho on the movie, and I have been offered an interview for an on-air position on *A-List Access*."

His jaw dropped, suitably blown away. "Wow. You mean I'm out with, like, a TV star?"

Yep, a date to him. She let it go and waved off the compliment. "At the moment, I'm a not-quite-employed waitress at the Riverfront Café and not much more. But..." She bit her lip. "This is pretty huge."

"I'll say." He studied her, his gaze intense. "Where's the job?"

She made a face. "In a faraway land called Los Angeles."

"*Oof.*" The reaction was all she needed to know. He liked her. And if she spent too much time with him, she'd like him right back. One man derailing her career was enough in this lifetime.

"How will your family feel about that?" he asked.

She shrugged. "No one would stop me." Finally, she took a sip of her beer, eyeing him over the bottle. "I almost went there with my ex anyway."

"Oh, he's there? In L.A.?"

"He might be, if he got the job he wanted." And that reminded her that no one from his plastic surgery practice ever contacted her for dirt on their break-up. "But don't worry, it's a big city. I never plan to see him again."

"Why would I worry?"

She smiled and took another quick sip.

"Well, congrats, Chloe. National television is a big deal and you've earned it."

"It's only an interview, and all I've really done is make some lame TikTok videos, but..." She let out a soft moan. "It would be kind of a dream."

"Then you know what I say."

She smiled. "'No regrets, coyote.'"

He pointed at her. "Bingo. And you should talk to Gabe about it if you want another perspective. You might be surprised what he says."

"Gabe?" She frowned. "He'll tell me to stay."

"Maybe not. He and I had a long talk about when a person walks away from it all and follows their dreams. I think he has a few regrets, but you didn't hear that from me."

"Regrets? My brother-in-law? What would he...oh... yeah..." She snapped her fingers, going way back in time. "Medical school?"

He nodded. "He wishes he'd stuck it out when Zach was born."

Chloe had been a freshman in high school when Rose had gotten pregnant with their first child, and Gabe had a few years under his belt at UNF's Brooks College of Health, studying to be an internist. The cost and time and massive commitment had been enough for him to decide to drop out and become an EMT and firefighter instead.

"That's funny, because he never mentions it. Even those times I brought Hunter to family events, Gabe didn't say a thing about when he wanted to be a doctor, which was his childhood dream, if I recall correctly."

"Well, he mentioned it to me. Maybe it was a moment of weakness, because he was ticked at a situation at the station, or maybe we were deep in a philosophical discussion, but he'd be one to tell you to follow those dreams, girl." He leaned in to add, "Although I don't love the idea of meeting someone as awesome as you, then... saying goodbye."

She rooted around for a quippy reply, something that would remind him that they'd spent little more than a few hours together. But anything she said would sound flippant and disrespectful, and he deserved more than that.

"And I'm sure you'll meet lots of awesome people as you become part of this community, Travis."

"Maybe, but you set the bar pretty darn high."

She angled her head and exhaled. "You knew from the moment we ran into each other—literally—that I am not dating now. I just got out of a really complicated and messy situation and I...I..."

He put a light hand over hers. "You don't have to explain, Chloe. I honestly can't imagine how tough it must have been not to just...go through with it. You were right there, at the altar, and making that choice couldn't have been easy."

"It wasn't. I joke about being a runaway bride, but I'm not proud of it. I hurt Hunter and I shook up my family and I put everyone through a very difficult situation because I didn't take a stand sooner." She felt her shoulders sink with relief. "It's actually good to admit it and not try to be funny. It was an awful moment in my life, and not one I'd wish on my worst enemy."

He nodded, sipped his drink, and then leaned in. "What was the turning point?" he asked. "When did you know for sure you weren't going to marry him?"

"When my dad showed up on a walker, taking some of the first steps I'd seen him take since he had a stroke."

"He talked you out of it?"

"Oh, no. I'd talked with him that morning and confessed I was having cold feet. Icy, frozen feet, to be honest."

He smiled at that, and leaned back when the server came with a platter of lemon pepper wings that looked almost as good as they smelled.

Once they were alone again, he inched closer, putting

his paper napkin on his lap. "Didn't your father tell you then you should call it, and save the whole scene in the church?"

"He told me to follow my heart and do exactly what felt right."

"Good father." He picked up a wing.

"I bet your father would have said the same thing."

He gave her a dubious look. "If he hadn't up and left my mother when I was seven, maybe. Doubtful, though."

"Oh." She remembered the dad he said was not in the picture. "I'm sorry. That must have been rough."

He shrugged. "Sometimes it's better when a parent leaves. In our case, it was. But your family? Well, I don't know all the Wingates yet, but from what I see?"

"You see Rose and Gabe, the happiest couple on Earth."

"They do seem solid," he agreed. "Exactly what I'm looking for."

She drew back at the unexpected candor.

"What?" He laughed. "I watch rom-coms for fun. What did you think I wanted out of life? A happy ending, of course. Don't we all?"

"I guess. I mean...you're so certain. Not many men are like that."

"I know what I want, like I did when I quit my gig and took up firefighting."

"And you want a wife, two kids, and a picket fence?"

He looked at her for a long time. "Yes to the wife. Kids? Three would be better, and fences are optional."

She thought about that, plucking at her wing then taking a bite, letting the peppery taste heat her mouth.

"I'm sure you'll find that," she said after swallowing. "You're great-looking, kind, and honest." She studied him for a moment. "You'll be swooped up in no time."

"I'm also very picky," he said.

"Yeah?" She lifted her brows, intrigued. "What's your dream woman?"

For a long time he didn't answer, but looked at her with enough intention that her whole body warmed and this time it wasn't the pepper seasoning.

"She's smart, caring, beautiful, talented, funny, and" —he reached over the table and touched her upper lip— "has a little sauce on her mouth."

Her heart flipped at the smooth move and she covered with a laugh and a dab of her napkin.

"And you?" he said. "Are you still too close to your last breakup, or do you have a nice high bar I could dream about climbing?"

"Good heavens, you're an astonishingly good flirt, Travis."

"Not flirting," he countered. "And what do I have to lose? You're flying off to Los Angeles to become rich and famous, and I'm gonna be riding around in the rig looking at houses behind picket fences and wishing I was in one with you."

She shook her head. "Like I said, astonishingly good."

He leaned over the table. "For the record, I'm not flirting, I'm being straight with you. I've got a massive crush and it's not going away until you do."

She had to laugh. "Why are you doing this?"

He lifted a shoulder. "You said it. I'm honest. I know what I want and I go for it."

"And...you want me?" she barely whispered the words.

"From the minute I met you, but..." He wiped his mouth again, then his hand hovered over the wings as he chose his next one. "But like the song says, you can't always get what you want."

She closed her eyes, the music and lyrics playing in her head.

...You get what you need.

"I thought you said the song lyrics were, 'No regrets, coyote.'"

"Oh, I'm gonna have regrets."

"You are?"

"I'm going to regret I didn't meet you sooner, sweep you off your feet, and finish it off at the altar, with no one running anywhere."

She stared at him, her heart crawling up to her throat to take permanent residence there.

"But I would regret...not following my dreams," she managed to whisper.

"I get that, Chloe. I really do."

And she'd regret leaving this man who, by the time she got back for the next Wingate family Christmas party, would have everything he wanted, including that wife and picket fence.

She had to admit, that would be one lucky lady.

Chapter Twenty

Grace

When the day came to test Nikki Lou, Grace asked Rose to come with her. She couldn't bring herself to make some big announcement to the family about the appointment she had with a pediatric psychologist. She would, when she knew.

But she knew she couldn't do this all alone, and even though Isaiah had offered, she wanted a sister in the passenger seat of her minivan.

In the back, Nikki Lou had no idea this was unusual, and no idea she was headed into an office to be tested for developmental disorders. According to the doctor Grace had already met with once, Nikki would draw, answer questions, and play some simple games that would feel like fun to her.

But as they pulled into the parking lot and saw brightly colored letters and a playground at the side of the building, Nikki's eyes grew wide. "Are kids here?"

"Nope. Just a nice lady who has blocks and coloring books and all kinds of toys for you to play with," Grace told her.

"Oh, play. You play, Aunt Rosie?"

Rose smiled. "Your mom and I are going to wait while you play, baby girl," she said and when Nikki Lou looked sad, she added, "Then we'll take a spin on that swing set when you're all done."

A few minutes later, they walked into a welcoming reception area, and Grace filled out the final forms but Nikki seemed...uncertain. Loathing new situations, she didn't say anything, but got as close as possible, her little fingers digging into Grace's thighs.

Oh, no. Here comes the scene, Grace thought as they waited, her whole body tensing when a young woman came out of the back door, smiling at them and holding a stuffed animal.

"Hello, Nikki Lou," she said, coming closer to Grace. "We're very excited to play with you." She lifted her hands, showing Nikki a cow. "This is Moo-moo." She leaned closer and made a mooing sound. "You know what she said?"

Nikki shook her head, gripping Grace for dear life.

"She said she wants to play with you." She jiggled the cow and mooed again. "Did you hear that? She's got a baby doll in the back. Do you play with baby dolls?"

Very slowly, Nikki nodded and relaxed a bit.

"Okay, let's go. Let's meet Moo-moo's favorite doll. Want to?" Her voice rose enough to lure Nikki closer, but then she realized what was going on and she looked up at Grace.

"Come, Mommy."

"Only cows and kids," the woman said. "And baby dolls."

Her lip protruded with a quiver and Grace inhaled, ready to start her litany of excuses, but Moo-moo made another funny sound and coaxed Nikki Lou closer.

"Go with Mr. Cow," Grace said.

Nikki Lou looked up. "It's a girl."

Grace laughed softly, fighting the urge to say, "See how smart she is?" but smiled instead. "Yep, cow, Nik. That'd be a girl."

"Let's go, Nikki Lou," the woman made the cow say in a deep cow voice. "It'll be fun."

Grace gave her the gentlest nudge and that seemed like all she needed to go along, walking through the back door and disappearing.

Only then did Grace collapse into a chair and let out a breath of relief and agony and worry and hope.

"Hey." Rose sat next to her, wrapping an arm around her shoulders. "You want to take a walk or sit here and wait? I saw a bench in the sun outside, if you prefer. Whatever you want, sweetie."

She stared ahead, not sure how to answer that. What did she want? For life to be simple. For her husband to still be alive. For her daughter to be in her classroom, making paper flowers. And she wanted...Wingates. Suddenly, she wanted them more than anything.

"Yes," she finally said. "And can you call in the troops?"

Rose smiled. "I already did."

AN HOUR OR SO LATER, Grace sat across from Dr. Amanda Alberino, a lovely woman with smooth auburn hair and elegant bone structure, trying to absorb every word that was spoken.

But some of them were hard to digest. "Level One Autism Spectrum Disorder? What is that?"

"Years ago, I might have used the term Asperger's Syndrome. Have you heard of it?"

Grace nodded. "It's...milder?"

She shrugged. "It's easier to manage from a support standpoint."

"And that's what Nikki Lou has?"

"Possibly," she said slowly. "But Nikki's case is special, because I believe she also has extraordinary intelligence, which is also frequently present with ASD, along with occasional 'islands of genius' or what you might have heard called 'savant' skills."

Grace nodded, vaguely recalling reading about that.

"I simply don't know yet," Dr. Alberino said. "The entire issue of young savants isn't quite as well researched as we'd like. She might have merely a very high IQ, or...more."

"Like she's specially gifted?"

"It usually means she could develop a very specific area of expertise that would make itself known to you organically as she gets older. Math, art, music —something."

"Oh." Grace leaned back, thinking of all Nikki Lou's

favorite pastimes. She loved coloring, but was no artist. Music? Possibly. "She does love our piano."

"That's good and you should encourage her to play, but..." The doctor tilted her head. "I can't sugarcoat this, Grace. Your daughter is facing some serious challenges, as are you. She will always struggle with socialization, and some of the most basic people skills will never be second nature to her."

A picture of old "Dor-mean" flashed into Grace's head, giving her a shot of guilt and fear. She didn't want Nikki to be a cranky old woman, or even a nasty young one.

"What can I do?"

"Many, many things," the other woman said. "If you are willing to put in the time and effort, you can take advantage of your daughter's sweet nature, coaxing that personality out of her, surrounding her with friends, family, and an active life. Can you do that?"

Grace smiled. "There is no shortage of family," she said. "She's adored by many cousins, and I'm one of seven girls."

"Wow, that's a gift to her. And you."

"I know it is," Grace admitted. "And what can I—we —do for her?"

"First and foremost, I'd like to have her examined by two colleagues who specialize in testing in this area. They'll help me determine the level of Nikki Lou's ASD. One is in Jacksonville, the other in Orlando. After I get their assessments, I will put together a long-term plan for her education and behavioral therapy. We don't know enough to do that yet, but we will."

"Okay." Grace let out a long sigh. "I guess that wasn't what I was hoping to hear, but it's a start."

Amanda leaned forward and smiled. "She's a doll, Grace. With love, time, and patience, you will raise a beautiful young lady."

Grace searched her face. "Will she have a normal life?"

"I guess it depends on your definition of normal," she said, which sounded surprisingly like something Isaiah would say. "She will have a wonderful life. Will it have unique challenges? Some thrilling highs and some brutal lows? Yes, yes, and yes."

"Will she..." Grace swallowed. "Fall in love?"

"With some very lucky man," Amanda said. "But you have a long way to go before that. Are you up for it?"

"Completely," Grace answered without a second's hesitation. "I mean, with your help."

"I'm already thinking of...well, don't let me get ahead of myself. Thank you for the vote of confidence. I would be thrilled to work with Nikki for many years in the future. But first, meet with the two other doctors, let us strategize a plan, and then we'll start her..."

"Treatment?" Grace finished.

"Her life," Amanda corrected with a smile.

And something about that gave Grace a much-needed injection of hope.

After setting up the two appointments, Grace finally

left the office and stepped out to an empty reception area, looking for Rose and Nikki.

"They've gone outside," the woman behind the desk said. "We have a small playground in the back. You can go through that other door."

Following the instructions, Grace pushed open a side exit and immediately heard laughter. She rounded the corner to a play area, not at all surprised to see Tori at the bottom of a slide, shouting up to Kenzie and Finn at the top. Nikki was on a swing, being pushed by Chloe and Rose, while Madeline and Raina watched the whole thing unfold.

Family, friends, and an active life. Well, they were sure getting a head start.

"Mommy!" Nikki squealed as her swing shot up. "I'm going higher!"

Everyone turned and called out her name, coming closer to a stunned and still Grace.

Before she knew what was happening, they were all descending on her, and she was wrapped in loving arms, comforted by all the right words, and laughing at the fact that not one of them could stay away.

They only parted when Nikki Lou came running over, holding Rose's hand, her cheeks flushed, her hair wild, her eyes on fire with her inner joy.

"I went high!" she announced as Grace scooped her up.

She twirled her around, squeezing the tiny body with everything she had. The faces she loved blurred in

Grace's vision, nothing but a collage of love and sister-hood, concern and caring.

As she held Grace, another face came into view, showing up around the corner.

"Isaiah," she whispered.

"Zayah!" Nikki hollered, bending backwards to see him.

"Couldn't stay away," he admitted as he sauntered forward, ruffling Nikki's hair. "You know I love a good playground, Nik."

Lowering Nikki to the ground, Grace held his gaze, feeling a smile pull as her little girl scampered away with Kenzie and Finn. For a moment, the rest of her family seemed to disappear around the edges of her vision, and she felt drawn to this strong, steady man who silently seemed to offer her...something. Another chance? A foundation? A friendship she didn't know she needed?

Something wonderful and impossible to ignore.

"So," Isaiah said as he took one step closer. "You look pretty happy."

"I am," she confessed, surprised at that.

"You got good news? Nikki Lou is..."

"She's perfect," Grace said. "Exactly..."

"As God made her," he finished.

"Yes." She let out a little laugh.

She saw his broad shoulders drop with a sigh. "That's good."

Stepping back, she tore her gaze from his face to the others, looking from one sister to the next.

"Which is not to say that I—that we—don't have some

challenges ahead," she added. "But..." She settled her attention on Isaiah. "Someone told me that everything happens for a reason, and that there's a...plan. And whatever that plan is, we'll be fine, because we have each other and this family and that is all we need."

They cooed their encouraging responses, hugging her and wiping tears, while Grace could feel her whole world shift ever so slightly on the axis that held it in place. But, for the first time in many months, maybe years, she wasn't scared. And she surely wasn't alone, even though Nick wasn't here.

She had Nikki Lou, the world's greatest daughter, and all the Wingates, the world's greatest family. And she even had Isaiah, the most unexpected new light in her life.

So she had everything she needed.

Chapter Twenty-one

Raina

Raina's last showing for the day ended at well past eight, but the good news was that her clients had made an offer for a small townhouse right in the same complex where Madeline lived off Centre Street.

As tempting as it was to knock on her oldest sister's door after the couple left, she decided it was more important to present the offer to the seller and get the deal done. And since it was a beautiful June night and she hadn't exercised all day, she opted to walk the short distance to her office at Wingate Properties.

As she inhaled the brackish scent from the river and turned onto Wingate Way, she put her hand on her stomach as if to hold her baby even closer. With the all-important week twelve starting the next day, she felt ready to break the news soon. Her little fruit had grown from a cucumber seed to a strawberry and would soon be the size of a small lime.

That made her smile and quicken her step until she reached the gate at Wingate Properties, and peered up at the building that took up so much of this block.

Why was there a light on upstairs?

Was Blake still at work? Why? And what was he doing...other than helping himself to Dad's money?

Spurred by the low-grade anger that thought incited, she pushed open the wrought-iron gate and marched in, baby forgotten for the moment. She'd kept her vow not to bring up the subject with Dad again. Her pregnancy had given him a much-needed lift and even a cursory mention of the missing money, or Blake, could send him into a black mood.

She'd accepted that her father had his reasons for not explaining what happened to the money, especially now that the movie deal essentially replaced it all. And she'd promised herself to let the subject of who, why, and how drop. With Dad, anyway.

But Raina wanted answers for herself. She had to know.

A little ashamed but still determined, she slipped off her heels when she unlocked the front door so her footsteps wouldn't echo over the marble on the first floor. No reason to lose the element of surprise when she confronted him.

Silently, she took the stairs two at a time and stopped at the top, noticing Blake's desk was empty and the light in her—well, Dad's—office was on. She heard a deep sigh, then he cleared his throat.

"I don't see it that way, Mom."

She froze, caught off-guard. She certainly didn't expect him to be talking to his mother, whom he'd never mentioned at all. Never mentioned his family in any way. Never mentioned that he was from *Iowa* until pressed.

She stayed well out of sight and listened, clinging to the fact that this was her family's office, he was an employee, and, like it or not, she suspected his involvement with the inexplicable loss of half a million bucks. She had every right to eavesdrop.

"Please, Mom, please listen to me." His plea included a pathetic break in his voice, followed by a long pause. "I know. I know you do. I get that. He's your husband. But *I'm* your son."

Poor kid! No matter what she might suspect him of doing, that sounded...bad.

"Yeah, well, that's not happening," he said. "I'm staying here. This is where I belong."

Except...why did he belong here? He had no one here and had plucked the place off the pages of a Realtor magazine, as he explained it. Heck, he'd probably stalked her father, found his weakness, and siphoned the money for—

"Oh...oh, really?" His voice rose and Raina couldn't help inching closer, driven by curiosity. "He paid it off? Completely? Well...good for him."

Whoever he was talking about, he didn't sound genuinely happy. And that gave her enough shame to step back and open her mouth to announce her presence when she heard him say, "Well, I guess million-dollar miracles do happen, Mom. Or half-million, anyway."

She almost choked. Did he say *half-million*? Bingo!

She had him. That was as close to an admission as she was going to get.

"All right, goodbye. I'll...be in touch, I guess."

She didn't give herself a minute to think, to feel sorry —sorrier—for him, but marched in on her bare feet and stared at him.

"Raina!" A little color drained from his face. "Oh my good gracious, you scared me."

"Blake," she said, crossing her arms. "If I told you that Wingate Properties is missing half a million dollars, what would you say?"

"What?" Now *all* the color left him.

"Please." She could feel her blood pressure spike as she worked to stay calm...and suddenly realized she was alone in a building at night with a veritable stranger who could be a thief. Taking a breath to deescalate things, she came closer and leaned on the guest chair in front of the desk—where he looked mighty comfortable sitting— maintaining her position of strength by standing.

"Please...what?"

She squeezed her eyes shut. "Look, I'm not stupid and I've combed the files and I've talked to my dad and I know...a lot." She sure didn't know everything, but strongly suspected this man did.

"Raina, what are you talking about?" He sounded genuinely perplexed, but no doubt he'd spent time perfecting that act.

"I'm talking about someone who emptied a bank account during the time that my father was utterly incapacitated."

He shook his head, pushing up, which put her on alert. He was a little bigger, stronger, and an unknown.

"And you're blaming me? Based on what evidence? Does Rex think I took money from him?" His voice rose with disbelief.

"No. Apparently he knew all about it and is fine with it. I'm not quite so easily appeased, and I want answers."

For a long time, he stared at her, his jaw slack, genuine confusion on his features. "What exactly are your questions, Raina?"

"Why did you take it and why doesn't my father care?"

"I...I...I didn't," he said softly.

"Did he give it to you?"

"I don't know what you're talking about, I swear." He started to come around the desk, but she held her hand up.

"Just stop. Don't move. Except your mouth. Move that and tell me...your story."

"My..." He shook his head and backed up a step, falling into the chair. "You want to know my story? Like how I'm here and why?"

"Yes." She almost sat down but something kept her standing, holding on to the back of the chair.

"I grew up on a farm in Iowa, the gay outcast son."

She frowned at the admission, because that wasn't the story she meant. Why did he come *here*? Why work for Rex? Why read about her in a magazine? It felt intrusive, and she didn't care about his personal life.

"I was the fourth or fifth generation of farmers who

worked the land with their hands and drove tractors and fixed...things. I was a little afraid of tractors, to be honest."

She stifled a groan of frustration, unwilling to dismiss his truth, but not getting the truth *she* wanted.

"So I stayed firmly and deeply in the closet while I pursued a career of...not farming. I helped a neighbor sell her house after her husband died, and she knew someone in real estate and I started doing part-time work at the office in town."

"Blake, I—"

He held up his hand. "I got a license, I did okay, but when I came out and told my parents, my father—not the nicest man—flipped out. He told me to leave and go as far away as possible and never come back. He disowned me. Do you have any idea how that feels, Raina?"

She shook her head. "No, I don't."

"Of course not. Well, I made it to Chicago and that's why I legally changed my last name, since the one I had didn't mean anything anymore. That's why I have the problem with the real estate license. It's in the name Young."

"Young?"

"That's the name I was born with. Blake Young, but I changed it to Youngblood."

"Because your family...disowned you?" That was beyond harsh, and she still wasn't entirely sure she believed that. Was this a con? Is that how he got half a million dollars from Dad?

"Yes, and because...blood is important."

What the heck was he talking about? "Please tell me the truth, Blake!" As she shouted the words, a sharp pain shot through her stomach, making her gasp in surprise.

"I am telling you the truth."

"Explain how it is that someone shows up from Iowa..." She grit her teeth through the words when another pain stabbed her, making her put her hand on her stomach.

"Are you okay?"

She shook her head, not willing to let a cramp derail her when she was so close to what she needed to know. "You showed up at the very same time that someone cleaned out a weird account in an *Iowa* credit union! I do not believe in coincidences, Blake."

"Iowa...City Credit Union?" Very slowly, he stood, turning ghost white with a sheen of perspiration on his upper lip.

Absently, she wiped her own, which was also damp. Was it hot in here? Because she suddenly felt light-headed. "Yes, that's the name of the institution. Does it mean anything to you?" she asked.

"Um...maybe." He looked worse than she felt. "Oh my God, maybe. How could he..."

"Blake, can you—"

He let out a moan and swore under his breath. "I never...I didn't think...oh, man. *That's* where the money came from. Corn sales? As if."

"What are you talking about?" she demanded.

"I didn't take any money, Raina. I did not. But I know

who did and I know why." He shot out from behind the desk and blew by her, through the door.

"Blake!" She whipped around and as she did, her legs buckled a little. She grunted as a low, searing fire shot through her belly, blinding her for a second.

What was going on?

But she already knew. Without thinking, she pushed her hand lower on her belly, letting out a soft whimper of abject misery. Another one? Was this it? The pain, the dizziness and then...the end. Again? *Why?* Why couldn't she keep a baby?

She cried out at the next agonizing pain, dropping to her knees. She opened her mouth to call for help, but all she could hear was the sound of footsteps, heavy and fast, going in the wrong direction—downstairs.

"Blake!" Her voice was weak from the shock and pain. "Blake?"

Nothing but silence.

He was leaving her? She pushed up, somehow standing to look for her bag and get her phone, remembering she'd put it down with her shoes. About a million miles away at the top of the stairs.

She needed help. She needed—

"Oh!" Doubling over in pain, she hung on to the chair to keep from faceplanting on the ground, lowering herself to the floor again.

She had to get to her phone. Rex didn't even have a landline in here. The only other phone in this office was downstairs on the first floor unless...

No, of course, Blake had taken his phone with him.

"Come on, Raina. You can do this." Clenching her jaw, she tried to crawl to the door, but as she did, she felt the all-too-familiar warmth of blood between her legs. "No! No! *No!*"

She banged on the floor in frustration and fury and disappointment.

"Not my lime," she murmured through tears. "Not my little lime."

She sobbed hard, digging for the strength to get up and get help. But what difference would it make? They'd do the ultrasound, make a sad face, deliver the news, wheel her in for a D&C, wish her better luck next time.

But she was forty-three, about to be divorced, and there would be no next time. None at all.

"Raina! I have it! I have the proof you need. Remember the day you came in here and asked if I knew of a contract cancellation?"

She shot her head up at the voice, echoing along with heavy footsteps on the stairs. And suddenly he was in the doorway, face bright red and covered in...tears?

"Well, I found one a few weeks ago and—" He waved a packet of paper, then froze at the sight of her. "Oh my God, Raina!"

"Help me, please, Blake. Help me. Get me to a doctor, because I'm losing my baby."

He dropped right down to the ground next to her, papers fluttering all around. "Oh, no, you are not. Not on my watch. Nothing is gonna happen to my little buzzin' cousin."

She barely heard the words, her head so light she felt

like she might truly black out.

"Can you walk?"

"I can, but..." She tried to get up but felt more blood release and dropped her head back with a sob. "I can't believe this is happening again."

He cradled her, surprisingly gentle. "I'll call 911. Hang on. Can you hang on?"

"Yes, yes. Please." Closing her eyes, she rolled into a ball, vaguely aware of his voice giving the address and explaining the situation. "Uh, just a second. Raina? How many weeks?"

"Twelve weeks tomorrow," she said as tears poured. "Almost a lime." Her lime. Her sweet baby lime.

Blake looked a little confused but relayed the information, a tender hand on her cheek. "Yes, yes, I'll stay on the line. Just send help."

She shuddered at the touch she desperately needed, her mind drifting off and back. What caused this? The missing money? Stress? Trying to get the truth out of Blake Youngblood?

"They're on the way, Raina," he said gently. "Hang in there. Does it hurt?"

She stared up at him, taking in his somewhat baby-faced features and dark brown eyes that looked familiar but she couldn't place them. There was something strange and still sweet about him, something...

"Did you take the money, Blake?"

He huffed out a breath. "Really, Raina? Now? No, I did not take it. I swear on...on your baby."

"Then who?"

"There's no name on those papers but..." His voice trailed off and he muttered something she didn't hear as a wave of dizziness and pain washed over her and she closed her eyes.

She tried to open her eyes, but it was such an effort. What did he say? "Blake...*who?*"

Her eyes closed. She could feel him getting up.

"Blake?"

He straightened over her, on his knees but still feeling far away as he looked down at her.

"I made a huge mistake, Raina." He spoke so softly, she could barely hear him. "I thought I deserved...things. People of my own, a family, a place I could call home. I was wrong."

"Who took the money?" She ground out the question through gritted teeth.

"It's all right there." He gestured toward the papers spread all over the floor. "Five hundred thousand. No one *took* it, Raina. Rex gave it away, but not to me. To my father, Bradley Young."

Who was Bradley Young?

Her eyes fluttered again and when she opened them, she saw him walking across the open office area toward the stairs.

"Where are you going?" she called, panicked at being left alone.

"Unlocking the door for the EMTs!"

She watched him disappear again, trying to catch her breath, trying—and *failing*—to understand one word of what he'd said.

Rex gave it away...to Blake's father? Why?

She wanted to know. What did he mean—a place, a family, a home? What did that have to do with the money? And...*where did he go?*

"Blake!" she tried to call, but the pain had stolen her voice. "Blake, please come back!"

She kept her gaze locked on the doorway, willing him to reappear, counting seconds, then minutes, and finally she heard the siren.

While she waited, she turned on the floor, curling up. Her hand landed on one of the fallen papers and she crinkled it in her fist as another wave of pain rolled through her stomach.

When it passed, she lifted the paper and stared at the words blurred in front of her. They were...familiar. So familiar.

With a grunt, she forced herself to focus on the page, which had nothing but one handwritten line, with the words in capital letters.

ALL DEBTS ERASED BY RW

A distant memory floated in her brain. Burned pages. A contract that her father had been destroying when he had a stroke. One page left untouched and all it said was...

ALL DEBTS ERASED BY RW.

All *what* debts erased by Rex? And why? And who? And how did Blake know?

But as she stared, something became very clear. The word *BY* was in a different script. It was written by another person.

It wasn't the word *by* at all. It was initials! Bradley Young. All debts erased and it was *initialed* by Bradley Young and Rex Wingate. But who—

The door banged.

"Raina! Raina!" Gabe's voice echoed from downstairs, followed by the clunking sound of EMTs, far too many for one nearly middle-aged woman who probably shouldn't have gotten pregnant in the first place.

Suddenly, they charged in, her brother-in-law in the lead.

On a miserable sigh, she closed her eyes and let her tears fall as they tended to her, asked questions, took vitals, and lifted her onto a stretcher. As they reached the bottom of the stairs, she looked left and right.

"Where's Blake?" she asked Gabe.

"Who? No one's here."

"The guy who called 911."

"No one's here, Raina. Relax, hon. We're going to get you help and that's all that matters. Pregnant, huh?" He smiled at her. "I've never known you to keep a secret from Rose."

"It's not a secret anymore. And it's not...a baby anymore."

"You don't know that," he whispered, putting a hand on her arm.

Rose always said Gabe walked in the light, and where he went, good things happened. She hoped her sister was right, because all Raina wanted in the whole world was to hold on to this precious little lime.

Chapter Twenty-two

Tori

"Do you hate it down there?" Tori grinned at Finn when he came up from below deck on Justin's sailboat. "It's a pretty tight space."

Finn laughed—an easy, familiar chuckle that she heard more and more every day now—and shook his head, his dark blond hair blowing in the breeze that snapped the sail. They were on their way back to the wharf after a two-hour sail up and down the Amelia River, just Tori, the kids, and Justin.

Night had fallen, but between the moon and the lights along the shore and the beam on the front—er, bow —of the boat, it was easy to see where they were going.

"Not sure I could sleep down there, but it wasn't so bad. And this?" Finn gestured toward the water. "It beats sweatin' my you know whats off in left field praying the next guy hits to right."

"Ew. Why is he so gross?" Kenzie muttered, but even her usual griping about all things Finn couldn't hide her joy at having her brother here.

"Seriously," Tori agreed.

"Totally get that," Justin chimed. "Especially when you're way out for a strong hitter and the sun's low. You can't see to save your life."

"Exactly!" Finn looked at him with true respect, and not for the first time. She wasn't exactly surprised, but it did warm Tori's heart to see these two guys get along so well. "Why doesn't my dad get that?"

Tori opened her mouth, but Justin leaned forward to say, "He wants you to live your life to the fullest, Finn. Maybe that means pushing you a little."

And, of course, Saint Hottypants was defending Finn's father. He was simply going to have to stop being so perfect.

"Or pushing me a lot," Finn said, dropping down on the bench next to Tori. "Just because he played college ball and made it to the minor leagues doesn't mean I'll ever do that."

Kenzie snorted. "Pretty sure you aren't headed for The Show, Finn-Finn," she said, using an old childhood nickname.

"Which is fine with me," he muttered.

Tori put an arm around him. "You try to make both your parents happy, Finnie, and I love you for that."

He slid her a look. "I'd rather cook, Mom. You know I'm more comfortable in the kitchen than the dugout. And when I tell Dad that, he shoots through the roof."

"Then while you're here, we'll put you next to Miguel at the Riverfront Café. You can probably teach him a thing or two."

His whole face lit up. "Cool! I can cook in a real restaurant."

"You can't wait tables, though, until you're sixteen," Kenzie reminded him, tucking deeper into Tori's jacket, borrowed because it was chilly out on the open water. "By the way, you owe me a birthday present since you missed mine. But could we get videos of you cooking? That would rock. Something like..." She tapped her phone and grunted in frustration. "Why is there no service out here?"

"That's the beauty of it, Kenzie," Justin told her. "Give it a few minutes. I get internet when we're a little closer to Amelia Island."

"Put your phone down, dingbat," Finn said to her, giving her shoulder a jab. "Let's go look for dolphins."

"Oooh, good content!"

"In the dark?"

Laughing, the two of them scrambled up to the bow, leaning over the railing, joking around the way kids should all summer long.

Tori stood and joined Justin, sliding an arm around his waist. "Thanks for being so great with both of them."

"It's so easy, Tori. They're awesome kids."

Smiling at that, she let her head fall on his shoulder and inhaled the salty night air, utterly and completely content. Everything about this summer was a dream.

He let out a long exhale that dropped his broad shoulders, making Tori wonder if he was thinking the same thing.

"What is it?" she asked.

"I, uh, like your kids. Both of them."

She laughed softly. "Well, that's good."

"And I like your family, as you know."

"They're quite likeable," she agreed.

"And, man, Tori." He turned her toward him, lowering his face to steal the lightest kiss. And then one more, not so light. "I really, really like you."

Her heart lifted and fell like the hull of the boat over whitewater. Not just because of the admission—it was lovely, but she knew he liked her. It was the tone of his voice. The sadness in it.

"And that's good, too, I think," she whispered with a doubtful chuckle. "But why do you sound a little defeated by that?"

"Not defeated, no." He shook his head and looked back at the horizon. "It's just...I don't know how to describe it."

"Finally!" Kenzie cried out. "We have a signal."

Ignoring her, Tori tightened her grip on Justin. "Try," she said. "Try to describe it."

"Okay." He nodded, thinking. "What's the word for when you think something's going to be fleeting and not all that important, but then it turns out that it's actually *everything* and you really want more and more of it, and won't be completely happy if you don't get it?"

She stared at him, her whole body humming as she processed what he was saying, which was pretty confusing for a great communicator like Justin. What was he saying? That he felt that way about *her*? That "it" was "them" and that made him completely happy?

"I'm not sure there *is* a word for that," she said softly, chills that had nothing to do with the air rising all over her arms.

"Oh, I know the word," Justin said. "I know it."

She looked up at him, waiting.

"It's a scary word," he whispered on a laugh. "Thrown around a lot, but still foundational and life-changing."

Did he mean...

"I think the word is love, Tori."

"Mom! Mom!" Kenzie screamed, whirling around and stumbling closer, waving her phone.

Really? Now? Kenzie wanted to make some dumb video now when he—

"Aunt Raina is in the ER!"

"No!" She grabbed the phone and blinked at the screen, her soaring heart plummeting to Earth as she read the text. "Oh, my God. She's losing her baby."

Instantly, Justin dove into action.

"Finn! Help me lower the sails. Kenzie, you're steering when we go to motor. Tori...get my phone. I want to see who's at the hospital. What's her doctor's name?"

The next few minutes went by in a blur as they moved like a well-oiled machine to get the sailboat under motor. During it all, Justin worked the phone, talked to the attending physician at the hospital, and pulled some strings to call Raina's ob/gyn, Dr. Milwood, at home.

Tori watched it all unfold, splitting her attention between group texts and the movement on the boat, aware of her kids following every order like little sailors in training, and Justin—competent, caring, wonderful Justin, who not seconds ago used the word...

Love.

She pushed it all away to think about Raina as the lights of the wharf beckoned them home. Poor, poor, darling Raina. This was not fair!

They docked in record time, gathered their things, and tore to his car in the lot as a group.

"I didn't know Aunt Raina was pregnant," Kenzie said as they ran.

"No one does," Tori said. "Well, no one did. They all do now."

"She's kind of old, isn't she?"

"Old*er*," Tori said. "But..."

"But isn't she going to divorce Uncle Jack?"

"That won't stop her. Nothing stops Raina Wingate." Except she couldn't keep a baby.

Tori's heart cracked at the thought of what Raina must be going through. And alone! Gabe told Rose that the first responders got called to Wingate Properties, and Raina had been on the floor in the doorway of Dad's office.

Justin drove like a beast, zipping through a few yellow—pink?—lights, silent and intent on his mission. At the medical center, the same one where they'd met, he dropped Tori and Kenzie off at the door.

"We'll meet you in there," he called out before she closed the door.

"He's a good guy, Mom," Kenzie murmured as they rushed toward the doors.

"The best," Tori agreed.

"You gonna let him go?"

Tori almost tripped. "Now? You want to know that now?"

"I'm curious. Finn and I were talking about it when we saw you kiss. We like him. We like Amelia Island. We..."

"Honey, please. My sister is having a miscarriage. My boyfriend just said the L word. And my ex-husband has me prisoner in New England. Not now."

She charged into the waiting room, instantly spotting Madeline and Susannah.

"*The L word*?" Kenzie choked, but Tori ignored it, wrapping her arms around Madeline and then their mother.

"Her ob/gyn is here," Madeline said. "She already went back there."

Rose came rushing in, followed by Grace and, instantly, it was déjà vu all over again as they huddled to hug and talk and wait for news. Weren't they just here for Dad?

When Justin and Finn came in, Finn joined them but Justin went straight to the desk.

"He's a badass, Mom," Finn said, then flinched at her look. "Sorry. But you know he is."

"He's..." She looked past her son at Justin, who was leaning over and talking to the nurse at the reception desk. A moment later, he came over, his navy blue gaze locked on Tori. "I can take one of you back," he said. "Susannah?"

Her heart folded at the offer to take her mother, which was so kind and respectful. But Susannah sighed and looked around. "Please, Justin. Can we all go?"

He thought about it for a millisecond and lifted one broad shoulder. "I do have a little weight around here. Finn and Kenzie, why don't you two wait out here while I take the ladies back?"

Yep, a badass.

They nodded and the others were up in a flash. A moment later, they all followed Justin through the double doors, down the hall, and into the triage area.

"They took her for an ultrasound," a nurse announced, then her eyes flickered over the group.

"Special case," Justin said.

"Of course, Dr. Verona." She gave a nod of concession. "Down the hall in Imaging B."

Tori bit back a smile, grateful that all the nurses had a bit of a crush on ol' Dr. Hottypants.

The door to the imaging room popped open as they arrived and another nurse came out, giving them a glimpse of the room inside, with Raina facing away on the table in a hospital gown.

"Do you hear that?" Dr. Milwood's question floated out. "Raina, listen."

Susannah gasped softly as they all stopped like a pack in the doorway. "Listen? That means—"

"There's a heartbeat," Justin confirmed, holding the door open, looking over Madeline's head at the visible screen.

They all froze and listened to the *thump-whoomf-thump...thump-whoomf-thump*.

Tori put her hand to her mouth to stifle a cry of joy, momentarily wondering if that was her own heart hammering...or her yet-unborn niece or nephew?

Thump-whoomf-thump.

"Oh!" Raina cried. "The heartbeat!"

"Strong and hearty," Dr. Milwood said. "And...and...um, Raina."

"What? What's wrong?"

"Not a thing, but brace yourself."

"For what?"

Dr. Milwood and the tech exchanged a look, both of them smiling.

"Look at the screen and see what Inez found," the doctor said.

Tori looked up at Justin, who gave her a wry, sly smile, obviously able to decipher the blurry screen better than she could.

"You see that, Raina? Or should I say...do you see *them*?"

Tori gasped, but so did Raina. Dr. Milwood and the tech chuckled. Every one of them reacted with moans, cries, and gasps.

"I'm having *twins*?" Raina exclaimed.

The doctor good-naturedly gestured them all into the tiny room. "Enter, fam. This is happy news."

From the bed, Raina turned and reached out a hand, which Rose took, with the rest of them close behind.

"You're all here? Tori? Suze? Grace? Rosebud." She

sobbed a little as she brought Rose's hand to her lips. "Did you hear? Did you hear what she said? Twins!"

"How is that possible?" Tori asked. "She had an ultrasound two weeks ago."

"Oh, it happens in these early weeks," Dr. Milwood said. "That little one must have been parked in the nooks and crannies of Raina's uterus, waiting to make a surprise appearance."

"Just like you, Raina," Rose reminded her.

"Are they okay?" Raina asked. "Even with the bleeding? Are they both okay?"

"Perfect. Both hearts are beating and growing and someday will be very sorry they caused a little bleeding. But nothing to be worried about, Raina. Spotting and cramping are perfectly normal, even as strong as you had, especially with two babies. More and we'll rest you, but for now, you're good."

They all came closer to ooh and aah and hug and cry, which they did for a long, long time.

When they finally left the room, Justin snagged Tori and pulled her off to a quiet, empty hall.

"Wow," she said, wiping a tear. "That was emotional."

"Good. Then you're all softened up for a little more...emotion."

She looked up at him, her heart hammering—and not only from the joy of the last few minutes.

"Just to clarify what I said on the boat..." he whispered softly, making her heart rate soar yet again. "I said *love*."

"Oh, wow." She sighed into his arms. "I'm sorry that was interrupted. Timing is everything."

"Oh, yes, it is, Victoria Wingate." He placed a finger under her chin and lifted her face to his. "Timing is everything. And you know what? *This* is our time."

"Yes. Our summer."

"Not merely this summer, but this...season. This *life*."

She nearly swayed. "What are you saying?"

"I'm saying I love you and I will do whatever is necessary to stay in your life. Move to Boston, beg your ex, win over your kids. Heck, I'll finally buy a house and we can split our time between here and there."

"Oh, Justin." She pressed her fingers to her lips. "I don't know what to say."

"Say you feel the same way."

She eased into him. "I do."

"Good. Then my next goal is to hear you say those same two words in front of your whole family and mine."

I do.

Was he—

She didn't finish the thought, because he pulled her into him and kissed her, stealing her breath and common sense. Right at that moment, she didn't know what to think except that she loved him. And nothing else mattered.

Chapter Twenty-three

Chloe

"Quick! Gimme that helmet!" Chloe reached out to Travis, who leaned against a bank of lockers in the Fernandina Beach fire station, his arms crossed, a permanent expression of amusement on his face.

"Give it back if there's a call out," he said, handing her a black helmet with *McCall* taped in white letters on the front.

"Promise." She angled it on her head and spun around to face Kenzie's camera, but as she did, she spotted her mother coming closer. "Oh, hang on, Kenz. Mom's here."

Susannah Wingate looked happier than she had for a long time. These days, the angst in her blue eyes seemed to dissipate and her smile was wide and genuine.

"Nice hat," her mother teased, tapping the helmet. "Are you two recording?"

"We were going to do a quick interview with Travis, but not if the set is ready and I can do my little Santa skit."

"It is, and Santa Rex has done one run through of his lines and he's a natural." Susannah laughed. "We may have created an acting monster. And I'm here on instructions from Marcus that you can come and record now for three minutes—and no more."

"Let's go." Chloe reached for Kenzie to drag her along, but before she got three steps, Travis snagged her arm.

"Hey, helmet head. I need that back. I'm on duty."

Laughing, she leaned forward and let him lift it off her.

"It did look pretty stinkin' cute on you, though," he added, putting it on his own head.

"Not as stinkin' cute as it looks on you, probie," she countered, the two of them holding that electric eye contact one or two heartbeats past the friend zone that she was so desperately trying to stay in with this man.

Because if things went well at her interview tomorrow, she'd be in the *California* zone and three thousand miles away from this guy who was threatening to wreck her man hiatus with one kiss. They hadn't had one yet, but—

"Come *on*." This time, Kenzie grabbed her. "We got three minutes. Let's use them!"

Chloe hesitated for a second. Stepping away from Travis wasn't easy—and this was twenty feet in the next room. How hard would it be three time zones apart?

For a job in television? *Easy peasy*.

The main living area of the fire station didn't look anything like Chloe remembered from her trips here to visit her brother-in-law. The oversized space had been completely transformed, with Christmas decorations everywhere, a lot of actors dressed as firefighters, multiple cameras, lights, and the constant hum of low-grade chaos that Chloe now realized was part of every TV movie set.

Grips moved thick cables, cameramen and lighting guys bantered and hollered, the costume team hustled around with clothes draped over their arms, and at the center of it all, Dad sat in full Santa wardrobe—including a giant white beard and precious gold-rimmed glasses— patiently having his nose powdered.

Way off to the side, a few real firefighters looked on, along with all the Wingates, who'd been allowed to stay on the set.

There was some controlled chaos there with Rose's girls dancing about excitedly in red velvet dresses, ready for their roles as extras in line. Nikki Lou didn't want to "play Christmas," but she sat perched on Grace's hip, next to Isaiah.

"Let's talk to Grandpa," Kenzie said, nudging Chloe toward the middle.

"Ho ho ho, Daddio," Chloe said as she got closer.

He turned to her and beamed, the biggest, brightest— and straightest—smile she'd seen from him since the stroke.

"Someone is happy," she said, giving him a kiss when the makeup person stepped away.

He studied her for a minute, then narrowed his dark eyes. "I'd be happier if you didn't take that job."

His voice and words were about perfect now. Only

someone who knew him his whole life would notice that he spoke with the slightest halting cadence, always taking a split second to form his words right. If that was the worst aftereffect of a stroke, then they were, indeed, blessed.

"I only have an interview," she said, crouching down next to his Santa chair, forgetting Kenzie and the video for a moment. "But if I get the job..."

He reached out his good, right hand and grazed his knuckles along her cheek. "You and Sadie. Always off and not close to home. What's better than home?"

She nuzzled her cheek into his hand affectionately. "I'm here in spirit, Dad. And you are surrounded by a..." She glanced to the group off to the side. "A giggle-gaggle of Wingate women." Then she inched closer to whisper, "With two more on the way, courtesy of Raina. I'm feeling girls, aren't you?"

"What else is there?" He chuckled and even with the beard and glasses, she could see his expression soften. "Glorious news, isn't it? I mean, it sure beats moving to Los Angeles."

"Dad, stop." She made a sad face. "I gotta do what I gotta do. You understand that, don't you?"

He gave a slow and serious nod. "I was the one who encouraged you to do the last big thing, remember?"

"You encouraged me to follow my heart. Problem was, that meant going in the other direction down that aisle."

"A moment I'll never forget." He chuckled. "You do

love drama, don't you? Always running away, my little Chloe."

She crinkled her nose, not liking that. "Dad, I'm running *toward* something. A new job, and my dream career. Last time I was running from someone. Now, are you ready to do that little skit we practiced?"

"Yeah, yeah, but..." He sighed again and leaned in. "Can I give you one piece of Santa advice, Chloe Wingate?"

She laughed softly. "Anything."

He managed to get both hands on her cheeks, although his left one was trembling a bit and didn't have the strength of the right. "Sometimes when you go running off to follow your great big giant dreams, you find out that everything you really wanted was right in your backyard."

She laughed. "You better give credit to *The Wizard of Oz* for that. Not Santa."

"The wizard of Amelia Island," he said with a shrug. "And you should listen to me. Running away isn't always the answer. What I'm saying is sometimes your heart leads you home."

That very heart dropped down to the floor so fast she heard the thud. "Dad—"

"Listen to me, Chloe." He glanced at the family, then looked deep into her eyes. "Home is where you find what you're looking for."

She stared at him for a moment, her jaw loose, trying to remember his agenda was to surround himself with family. And that wasn't her agenda, not at twenty-nine, not when she was looking at a major, national, enviable job.

"You are certainly not making this any easier, Dad."

"It's not my business to make your lives easier. I'm trying to make your life better."

"It would be better if I get a job like that."

He lifted his snow-colored brows over the Santa specs. "Really? This is what you want to do? Go off to Los Angeles and get in the television rat race, try to be some kind of famous person or important...reporter."

"That's not exactly—"

"Take it from this old man, child. Running after fame and fortune? That's not happiness. That's not fulfillment. That's not what you will wish you'd done when you're on your deathbed. Take it from a man who was *on* his deathbed not so long ago. What matters in this world is family, love, and home. Period. End of story."

"Time's up!" a woman hollered and clapped, rushing toward Chloe. "Say your goodbye to Santa, miss. We are ready to roll!"

"Oh, no! We didn't get the skit for Kenzie's TikTok."

Dad flipped his hand toward her. "Skit, schmit. This was more important."

She stood slowly, her gaze still on her father, her whole body humming.

"Thanks, Dad," she whispered, then stepped away, backing right into the unexpectedly strong chest of Travis McCall. "Oh, sorry."

"No apologies. Did you get what you needed from Santa?"

"What I needed? Yeah. What I wanted?" She shook her head, looking around for Kenzie, who'd disappeared.

"Everyone not needed on set needs to clear now!" The order echoed through the room as a dozen or so people hustled to obey it.

Defeated and torn, she walked out with Travis, her heart hammering from the conversation with her father, who was, stroke or no stroke, the smartest man she knew.

Was that what she was? A runner? But she *hated* goodbyes. Absolutely hated them—

A screaming loud noise jolted her down to her toes, making her—and a lot of other people—gasp and react. Before she could even comprehend what was happening, Travis grabbed her hand and squeezed it.

"That's me. Bye, Chloe!" He shot off into the crowd, instantly disappearing into the huge garage while the alarm wailed and a voice over a loudspeaker barked out instructions about the call.

Chloe stood stone still, shocked and lost with her father's words and Travis's farewell echoing louder than the blaring alarm.

Suddenly, another arm was around her, this one slender and familiar.

"You get used to it," Rose whispered.

"Is it a fire?" she asked, her throat tight at the thought of him walking right into danger.

"That sounded like a possible cardiac arrest. Gabe's not on duty, but he took off anyway, since he's here. He won't work, but he's the best EMT they have," she added with pride. "Come on. The family is all going out back for some pictures when Dad gets done."

"Yeah, okay." Chloe glanced around as she walked outside to a large open field with picnic tables where the firefighting crews ate lunch and worked out on easier, quieter days.

In the middle, taking up two of the tables, were all the familiar faces she knew and loved. Madeline sat with Mom close as they talked more like girlfriends than mother and daughter. Raina was across from them, flanked by Susannah on one side and Grace on the other. Little Nikki Lou had smooshed herself against her mama.

A few feet away, Justin stood talking to Tori, the two of them watching Zach, Ethan, and Finn kick a soccer ball on the grass.

What matters in this world is family, love, and home. Period. End of story.

But other things mattered, too. Career, dreams, success, opportunities.

"There's our superstar." Tori turned and came over to her, reaching out her hand. "We're all dying to know what you were talking to Dad about."

"Me being a runner," she said glumly.

Tori frowned, concern in her eyes. "A runner?" she asked. "Like run on the beach or..."

"A person who runs," she clarified. "You know, the wedding, now the job in L.A. It's the pattern of my life. I guess I do bolt more than I stay." She lifted a shoulder. "Dad wants me to stay, of course."

"He wants everyone to stay. He'd be happiest if we

lived in a compound and had dinner with him and Mom every night." Tori added a laugh. "And some of us kind of want to."

"But not me," Chloe said softly.

Rose, still next to her, gave Chloe a hug. "You're you, Chloe," she said. "Our youngest, and, like Sadie, you are brave and adventurous. Don't let Dad's soft heart make you second-guess what you want to do with your life."

She let out a sigh, grateful for Rose's optimism.

"And..." Rose added, inching closer. "If you stick around here and fall for that adorable firefighter who's crushing so hard on you, you'd better be okay with low-grade stress and the knowledge that every time he goes to work, that goodbye might be your last."

"Gabe's not going anywhere," Chloe assured her.

"From your lips to God's ears, girl."

They let the conversation dwindle and got caught up in the spirit and jovial mood as everyone agreed that getting Rex the part of Santa was the best thing they could have done for him.

The whole time, Chloe glanced around for Kenzie, who'd disappeared.

"Is she inside getting footage of the actual scene?" Chloe asked Tori.

"I have no idea," Tori said. "Finnie! Have you seen your sister?"

He yelled back a "no" and kicked the soccer ball way past everyone else, getting a cheer from the small group watching. Then he threw up both arms and did a victory dance.

"Maybe he's been in the wrong sport all this time," Raina mused, watching him from her place at a picnic table. "I've never seen him that happy."

"He's never *been* this happy," Tori said, a bittersweet note in her voice. "We're all..." She smiled and slid a look from side to side. "Pretty dang happy right now."

"Same for me," Raina said. "Well..." She put her hand on her stomach. "For all of us."

They laughed and talked about how she felt, which was good, strong, and still in shock over the news of twins.

"Have you thought about names?" Mom asked Raina, making all of them lean in closer to hear the answer and no doubt offer some opinions.

"I haven't. And I'm sure there will be no shortage of opinions on the subject," Raina added, making them laugh.

"Does, um, Jack get an opinion?" Rose asked as the laughter died down.

Raina gave a tight smile. "We're not really talking at all these days."

"Really?" Tori asked, her voice going up as if this was news. "You're not considering a reconciliation?"

"Not for a moment," Raina said, instantly getting all of their attention. "I am staying right where I am. This is home. This is my family, and this is where I belong."

The words squeezed Chloe's heart. Raina hadn't always felt that way. She'd followed her dreams and love—

"Woo-hoo! Brace yourself, Chloe Wingate!" Kenzie's

voice rang out over the field as she ran to them, her hair flying, her face flushed. "This one is going v-i-r-a-l!"

Everyone turned as she reached the tables, breathless, phone held out. "Have you looked?" she asked Chloe.

"At what?"

"The video I just posted."

Chloe frowned. "We didn't do our skit with Dad."

"Not the skit! Your conversation! I got that whole exchange, and there is actually a 'Team Chloe' and 'Team Dad' forming. I hate to break it to you, Aunt Chloe, but the world wants you to stay and find your dreams at home."

Chloe felt her jaw drop as she took Kenzie's phone with trembling fingers. "You posted that private moment with my father?"

"Nothing is sacred with her," Tori muttered. "And if you want her to take it down, she will."

"Take it down?" Kenzie choked. "This is it. This is the moment we've been trying to get for all these weeks. Real, raw, and relatable. Please! A life lesson on what's important from Santa Claus in the middle of the summer? Grandpa Rex is a national treasure! Why would we take it down?"

"Because it was private," Tori said.

But Chloe tuned out the mother-daughter exchange as she watched the video on the phone screen, which might have been small but the message was big.

"Take it from this old man, child. Running after fame and fortune? That's not happiness. That's not fulfillment. That's not what you will wish you'd done when you're on your deathbed. Take it from a man who was *on* his deathbed not so long ago," her father said, his halting speech sounding clear and strong. "What matters in this world is family, love, and home. Period. End of story."

The Like button kept flashing...four figures and growing.

"How long has this been up?" Chloe asked.

"Not even ten minutes," Kenzie exclaimed. "Can you imagine? The response is huge! Look at the comments."

But she didn't want to look. She didn't want to know that the world agreed with her father. She didn't want to acknowledge that she shouldn't chase her dreams, she should stay right here on Amelia Island and fall in love with a firefighter and spend her life with the family who loved her.

Not Chloe Wingate! She was going to run and chase and seek and, hopefully, find whatever she was looking for.

Rose, looking at her own phone, gave a soft gasp, her eyes wide.

"Are you watching it?" Chloe asked.

Rose didn't answer, but held up her hand and put the phone to her ear. "Gabe?" She walked away, leaving them all silent and frozen, sensing from her tone and posture that something was very, very wrong.

Was it...*Travis*?

Chloe's heart climbed into her throat. How would she feel if Travis got hurt? She hardly knew him, but... there was something. *He* was something. Was she making the right decision with this job? As the questions pressed, Chloe kept her gaze on Rose, and so did the others.

Rose lowered the phone but kept her back to the rest of them. A few seconds passed and her shoulders shuddered. Was she crying?

Raina went straight to one side and Mom to the other, holding unasked questions as they all came closer. Finally, Rose turned, tears streaming from her eyes.

Chloe's heart clutched as she waited.

"Doreen had a heart attack," she whispered. "And she didn't make it. She passed away in the ambulance."

No one spoke or breathed or reacted. They all stood in stunned silence, then all let out their cries and whimpers and exclamations of disbelief at once. But Chloe put her hand over her chest, shockingly relieved that Travis was okay.

Did he matter that much to her?

She'd have to consider that later, because now, they had to gather as a family and be strong for each other. They may not have liked the woman, but she'd been in their lives forever.

Her mother seemed to stumble backwards in shock, instantly flanked by Madeline and Rose, and Justin came closer with the concerned look of a doctor.

Mom was ghost white and shaking.

"Girls," she whispered. "Let me tell your father later. Tonight. Privately." She looked up at Justin. "Right? I can tell him?"

"Gently," he said. "He's known her his whole life, right?"

She nodded. "Since they were young."

"Then very, very gently."

The excitement of the day evaporated as they all grouped together to mourn the end of an era.

And that moment of family support simply drove Rex Wingate's message deeper into Chloe's heart.

Chapter Twenty-four

Raina

They'd put off the inevitable long enough, but nearly two weeks after Doreen was buried in the Wingate family plot at St. Peter's Cemetery, the time had come to clean out the third-floor apartment at the inn. A bittersweet task that none of the Wingate women relished, but all wanted to accomplish.

Susannah had offered the living quarters to Isaiah Kincaid when he accepted the job as Wingate House's manager, but he preferred to stay in the cottage out back. That meant they could rent Doreen's apartment as a full-sized family suite, an idea that Raina knew was an excellent business decision, even though it had never been done before.

Isaiah, Gabe, Travis, and a few other firefighters had removed the dated furniture, but today it was time to sort all of Doreen's belongings, clothes, books, and personal items for donation or trash.

They split into teams, with Susannah and Madeline tackling the kitchen and overcrowded bookshelves in the living room. Rose, Raina, and Tori were in Doreen's bedroom, inhaling a scent of the sadness they all associated with her. Chloe and Grace were in the second bedroom, which seemed to be a catch-all for a woman who...caught a lot. Goodness, the place was junky and cluttered.

From the bedroom, Raina could hear the comforting sounds of chatting and laughter, a sound these old walls probably hadn't heard in fifty years.

Suze and Madeline were cooing over finds like an antique tea set hidden above the oven and a gorgeous ceramic bowl that had been signed in 1979 by a local artist, now long gone.

Chloe and Grace talked in hushed tones, but Raina knew what they were discussing. Grace had an upcoming appointment in Orlando with a new specialist for Nikki Lou, and Chloe was on pins and needles waiting for an offer from *A-List Access* after her successful interview in Los Angeles.

In this bedroom, Rose hummed lightly as she sorted the closet. Tori took the dresser, and Raina had dug into the hope chest that sat at the foot of Doreen's bed.

In deference to Doreen's passing, even Tori had kept any snark to a minimum, although she had whispered, "You take the hopeless chest," to Raina when they'd divided up the work.

"She wasn't exactly a hoarder," Raina said as she peered into the depths of the antique. "But she didn't throw much away, did she?"

"No kidding." Tori held up a small orange container.

"Airspun. I didn't even know they made this talcum anymore."

Rose tsked as she worked her way through some tangled hangers. "I think someone as lonely as Doreen probably clung to things to give her life purpose and meaning."

"She ran one of the nicest inns on Amelia Island," Raina said, lifting a sweater that had been more neatly folded than the rest. "Isn't that a purpose?"

"Would you want to live in this apartment for fifty years?" Tori asked.

Raina sighed, looking around with a Realtor's eye, seeing nothing but potential. "I suppose she wasn't in the position to make changes, but if you put white shiplap on that vaulted ceiling and painted the walls a glorious sage? The right floors and rugs, some antiques? This is a roomy place with tons of light, a water view, a lovely clientele—"

"Would you like to live here?" Susannah asked, surprising them when she came into the doorway.

"Me?" Raina looked up at her. "You kicking me out of the beach house, Suze?"

Her mother smiled. "If it were up to me, you'd stay forever. But I know you want your own place, and it looks like you're sticking around for a while."

"I floated the idea of sharing a place with Chloe, but..." She shrugged. "We all know she's getting this job in L.A."

"We don't know anything," Rose said softly, but Raina ignored her twin's optimism. Chloe was halfway to California mentally.

"Well, you could stay here if you prefer," Suze said.

"As soon as I know what the divorce settlement looks like, I'd like to buy a place," Raina said, giving voice to a thought she'd only kept to herself so far. "But if you want some help remodeling this suite into something you could charge a fortune to rent, I'd be happy to."

Suze nodded, thinking about that. "Yes, let's do that, Raina. I wanted to give this apartment a major facelift years ago when I remodeled the rest of the inn but..." She gestured vaguely. "Doreen would have none of it."

Not for the first time since she'd died, Raina wondered why Doreen had dug her heels into this job, this apartment, even this town, and never left seeking...more.

"I'm glad we didn't have to sell this place," Tori muttered as she finished one drawer, then started another.

"Sell it?" Rose practically choked. "Why on Earth would we do that?"

To replace the missing half-million dollars, Raina thought. "We never would," she said instead.

She and Tori shared a secret look, knowing the Christmas movie would be wrapping this week, and Marcus had kept his end of the bargain, filling the Wingate coffers with the exact amount that had disappeared from Dad's account.

Well, maybe *disappeared* was the wrong word, Raina thought as she leaned over the hope chest that seemed to have an endless amount of cardigans and pullovers stored for cooler weather.

Thinking about the money, of course, had her thinking about Blake Youngblood's confession the night she had to go to the ER. She could still hear his voice as he whispered something that had made no sense.

No one took the money. Rex gave it away, but not to me. To my father, Bradley Young.

The statements might never make sense, she knew. With Dad rebounding from his bout with depression, the last thing Raina wanted to do was drag him into...all that. He knew the truth, whatever it was, and he didn't want to share. He knew where the money had gone and now that it was replaced, the subject was finished.

All that mattered was his health, hers, and the babies'.

As far as Blake Youngblood? Well, she'd never seen him again after that day. She thought she'd spotted him across the street at Doreen's funeral, but her mind must have been playing tricks on her that rainy afternoon at the cemetery. The man she thought was Blake disappeared onto the busy Fernandina Beach street before she could get a good look.

He'd never come back into work, never called to see how she was. And his bank returned the last paycheck from direct deposit, announcing he'd closed the account.

"Chloe just got the call!"

At Grace's announcement, Raina looked up, forgetting her train of thought. "*A-List Access?*" she asked.

Grace nodded and came into the room, followed almost immediately by Madeline, all of them exchanging anxious looks.

"Let's give her privacy," Suze said, softly closing the door. "She might be negotiating a salary."

"I think that ship sailed," Tori said. "The salary is set, and it's not thrilling, but she'll get by."

"It's expensive in L.A.," Madeline said. "I hope she knows that."

"Oh, I can't believe she's moving there," Raina said on a groan. "I was getting so used to her being here."

"She might not take it," Rose said with brightness even she couldn't really feel. At their looks, she added, "I mean, she's been spending so much time with Travis. I thought maybe..."

Grace shook her head. "She likes him, but...TV is her dream."

"It always has been," Susannah said on a sad sigh. "Remember her as a little girl?"

"Always doing a news report at the dining room table," Madeline said on a laugh. "Dad called her Barbara Walters."

"We can't *not* be happy for her if she gets the job," Rose added.

"We *can* not be happy for *us*." Raina wished she could be a little more like her optimistic twin, but she did not want Chloe to leave.

"I hope she can handle L.A.," Tori said. "And that she doesn't run into her ex, who is working there now."

As Raina scooped up the last sweater on the pile, something sharp slid under her nail, making her gasp and jerk her hand back.

"What's wrong?" Tori asked.

"I don't know. Splinter or..." She peered in, seeing the corner of something white with curled edges. Was that a picture? She reached in to retrieve yet another piece of junk from a woman who honestly should have made better use of the trash can.

As she tried to work free whatever she'd found, she realized it wasn't lodged in the wood. Someone had taped this paper or card to the bottom of the hope chest, and quite securely. Frowning, she ran her finger along the edge.

"What the heck is this?"

Tori leaned over from her drawer and looked in. "What?"

"Is that a picture? It's taped in here pretty well." Raina kneeled and bent over, sliding a nail along yellowed tape. She managed to free the corner, peeling it up as the door opened and Chloe burst in.

"I accepted," she announced breathlessly. "You're looking at the next junior weekend entertainment correspondent for *A-List Access*."

As they squealed out their congratulations, Raina freed the paper but didn't even look at it. Instead, she stood to join the group hug and closed her eyes, doing her best—they all were—to hide her disappointment.

"The money's not bad, and the title isn't impressive, but I'll get air time," Chloe said.

"You'll be their top reporter in no time!" Tori assured her.

"She'll run the anchor desk in a matter of months," Rose added, making Chloe roll her eyes.

"I doubt that, but it's a foot in the door at a very big operation, so..." She bit her lip and looked from one to the other. "Looks like I'm off again." She made a face that would make any mere mortal look unattractive. On Chloe? Well, it was obvious why the camera loved her.

"I'm sorry, you guys." She slipped an arm around Susannah. "I know you and Dad like having me here, Mom."

"We love having you here," Susannah corrected. "But you are young and you have to find your place in the world."

"I know, I know, but...it's bittersweet." She blinked back some tears. "I love Amelia Island, but this is my big break."

"And you have to take it," Rose whispered.

"We will miss you though, Chloe," Raina added, using the picture to fan her own threatening tears. "But you're right. You have to go."

"I can't have regrets." She frowned at Raina's hand. "What is that, Rain?"

"I have no idea. I found it in the bottom of the hopeless chest." She made a cringe face. "Sorry. Blame Tori for that."

As they smiled and groaned at the bad joke, Raina looked down at a color photograph with scalloped edges and a shiny surface, the way they used to print them decades ago. She squinted at a young woman holding a tiny baby wrapped in a blanket.

"Who is this?" she asked, turning it over.

There was faded blue ink on the back, words written in script.

"Doe and baby Bradley Wingate," she read aloud.

"Bradley Wingate?" Tori asked on a choke. "Is there a Bradley we don't know about in our family?"

"And who's Doe?" Madeline asked.

"Isaiah said that's what Doreen liked to be called," Grace told them.

Their reaction to that news grew faint in Raina's ears as she read the rest of the inscription so softly they may not have heard her.

"Adopted 6/15/1968 by the Young family in Cedar Rapids." Cedar Rapids...*Iowa?* Raina stared at the names.

Bradley...Young? The echo of a name she'd first heard not so long ago reverberated in Raina's head.

"Who is that?" Rose asked, tugging at the picture. "Who is Bradley?"

As they hovered around the picture, Raina let it be taken from her trembling fingers.

Tori frowned and shook her head. "But it says Bradley Wingate. Why would Doreen..."

Her voice trailed off, as did their questions and comments when they realized the one person in the room who hadn't said a word.

Susannah stood stone still, her face bloodless.

"Mom?" Chloe asked. "Do you know about this?"

Susannah inhaled and let out a very shaky breath. "Bradley was Doreen's baby, and she gave him up for adoption to the Young family of Iowa."

"But why is his last name Wingate?" Chloe asked.

For a long, long time, they all stood in complete silence.

"Because Rex is his father," Susannah whispered, looking down instead of at their shocked faces. "He found out right before his stroke. He only told me the night Doreen died."

"Wait, what?"

"This baby is *Dad's*?"

"*Doreen's* and Dad's?"

Susannah nodded imperceptibly as their questions tumbled over her.

"Doreen never told him she'd had a baby," Susannah finally explained. "All those years, she never said a word. But apparently Bradley Young found out several months ago and...and..."

"Asked for money," Raina finished as the puzzle pieces snapped into place, remembering all the things Blake had said.

Five hundred thousand. No one took it, Raina. Rex gave it away, but not to me. To my father, Bradley Young.

"Yes," Susannah replied, nodding. "He needed money for his farm, which he was going to lose. The land had been in his family—his *adopted* family—for decades. As a last-ditch effort of desperation, he approached his biological father, Rex, and secretly begged for money. Even though he is not a nice man, he *is* Rex's son—"

A few of them gasped at the term no one had ever heard before. *Rex's son.*

"So opened an account in a credit union and gave him full access to the money, which he took," Susannah finished. "But despite that, Bradley announced he wanted nothing to do with Rex. And he never even talked to Doreen, his birth mother. Awful man, truly."

"So Dad and Doreen..." Tori made a horrified face, recoiling as she said the words. "Seriously?"

Susannah shrugged. "Rex said they had a very brief... fling? Romance? They were kids. She was a teenager working here at the inn, and Rex had come home from college one summer. She had a terrible crush on him and he..." Her voice trailed off. "He's ashamed of it, to be honest."

"Well, he was human and young," Rose said. "Dad should never feel shame."

Suze nodded and smiled at her. "But he does. Anyway, she left town that fall when he went back to college, and never told him she was pregnant. She told Rex's father, though, when she came back a few years later, destitute. She may have...threatened blackmail? We really don't know. All we know is that Rex's father gave her a job here at the inn, and promised it to her for life in exchange for not ever telling Rex he had a son."

Raina still couldn't process the words. *Rex...had a son.*

"Maybe that explains why Dad never spent a lot of time with Doreen," Tori said. "I don't think I've ever seen them exchange ten words."

Susannah nodded. "She made him very uncomfortable, but he honored the agreement and would never let her go."

"She made *everyone* uncomfortable," Tori added.

"And maybe that was why she was, well, Dor-*mean*,"

Madeline noted. "A lot of history there. And Dad married twice, which she might have seen as being passed over."

"Sadly, she wasn't the most, you know, socially-adept person," Grace said. "A hard situation for everyone."

"After Rex found out, he confronted Doreen," Susannah told them. "He demanded to know why she never told him he had a child. He was going to tell me that very day, but he had a stroke. He said the stroke was God's way of keeping him quiet, so he didn't breathe a word until she died. He knew I could never look at her the same way."

"Where is this Bradley?" Madeline asked. "Can we meet him? He's our brother!"

Susannah shook her head vehemently. "No, no. No one will see Bradley Young again, including your father. The man is..." She sniffed. "Let's just say he takes after Doreen in spirit and personality. Cold, heartless, not... like Rex. That, I'm afraid, is the end of Bradley Young."

Except it wasn't the end at all, and right then, only Raina knew that. "Did Bradley tell Dad that he had kids?" she asked, her voice tight.

"Oh, no. No kids," Susannah said.

Raina bit her lip, holding the contradictory news she knew would shock them as much as this.

"Still, we have a brother," Rose said. "And that's...something."

"We have more than that," Raina said softly.

Instantly, they all turned to her, questions in their eyes.

"Bradley had—*has*—a son."

"Oh, no, no, you're wrong" Susannah insisted. "Rex asked if there were any children and Bradley said very clearly he didn't have any."

"Because he *disowned* the one he had."

"Disowned?" several of them asked, voices rising in disbelief.

"Blake Youngblood is really Blake Young," Raina explained. "You know the assistant who saved these babies and then disappeared? He told me that night that his father is Bradley Young, and that means...Rex is his grandfather and Blake is our *nephew*."

Susannah looked like she might faint. "You can't be serious."

As they dumped a barrage of questions, Raina held up her hands, sad that she had so few answers about a man who'd worked for her. A man who'd wanted desperately to have a family and a place to belong. A man who'd referred to her baby as his "buzzin' cousin"—something she'd forgotten until this very moment.

"I suspect if Blake's father knew about Rex and Doreen, then Blake did, too," Raina said.

"But Rex has no idea!" Susannah exclaimed. "He hired his own grandson. Why wouldn't Blake tell him?"

"Blake is afraid of how people will respond to him," Raina said, glad she knew at least that much about him. "My guess is that he was waiting for the right time to reveal himself, then Dad had a stroke. And now Blake's gone." Raina pressed her fingers to her lips. "He's disappeared and I never...I never got to be his aunt."

All around, her sisters and mother looked like they felt the same deep regret.

"I'll have to tell your father," Susannah whispered. "He's going to be very—"

"Don't," Raina said. "Not yet. Let me try and find Blake first. Let me assure him he's welcome and loved, and then we can give Dad a new grandson and Blake...a new family."

"Can you do that, Raina?" Susannah asked.

Tori put her arm around Raina. "This woman can do anything."

She smiled at her sister and the rest of them as they echoed the sentiment.

"I don't know about that," she admitted. "But he saved me and..." She put her hand on her stomach. "Both his little cousins. So Aunt Raina has to save him right back."

"You know we'll help," Rose said.

"Anything you need," Grace added.

She nodded, reaching out for all of them. Raina had no idea how, but somehow, some way, she'd put this fractured family back together.

Don't miss The Bookstore on Amelia Island, Book Three in the Seven Sisters series.

With her daughter's surprising diagnosis, Grace's life becomes complicated and overwhelming. Not only does Isaiah offer unexpected support, Rose also steps in to help with a project Grace simply cannot complete. But when she does, Rose makes a discovery that has her longing for a distant past.

Chloe lands in L.A. and finds her new world is quite different from what she thought it would be, and she might have to rely on her ex to survive. Through it all, Raina searches for their nephew, who has his own reasons for hiding. In the process, she runs right into a man who could facilitate that reunion, but it could come at a high price for her to pay.

When the clouds roll over the bookstore on Amelia Island, the Wingate women learn over and over again that the bond between seven sisters is as strong as steel, as gentle as an ocean breeze, and as lasting as their family legacy.

Visit www.hopeholloway.com for release dates, covers, and sneak peeks into the series!

Love Hope Holloway's books? If you haven't read her first two series you're in for a treat! Chock full of family feels and beach Florida settings, these sagas are for lovers of riveting and inspirational sagas about sisters, secrets, romance, mothers and daughters...and the moments that make life worth living.

These series are complete, and available in e-book (also in Kindle Unlimited), paperback, and audio.

The Coconut Key Series

Set in the heart of the Florida Keys, these seven delightful novels will make you laugh out loud, wipe a happy tear, and believe in all the hope and happiness of a second chance at life.

A Secret in the Keys – Book 1
A Reunion in the Keys – Book 2
A Season in the Keys – Book 3
A Haven in the Keys – Book 4
A Return to the Keys – Book 5
A Wedding in the Keys – Book 6
A Promise in the Keys – Book 7

The Shellseeker Beach Series

Come to Shellseeker Beach and fall in love with a "found family" of unforgettable characters who face life's challenges with humor, heart, and hope.

Sanibel Dreams - Book 1
Sanibel Treasures - Book 2
Sanibel Mornings – Book 3
Sanibel Sisters – Book 4
Sanibel Tides – Book 5
Sanibel Sunsets – Book 6
Sanibel Moonlight – Book 7

About the Author

Hope Holloway is the author of charming, heartwarming women's fiction featuring unforgettable families and friends, and the emotional challenges they conquer. After more than twenty years in marketing, she launched a new career as an author of beach reads and feel-good fiction. A mother of two adult children, Hope and her husband of thirty years live in Florida. When not writing, she can be found walking the beach with her two rescue dogs, who beg her to include animals in every book. Visit her site at www.hopeholloway.com.